IN THE BLOOD

WRYTER KISELEV-ROLLING

Copyright # 1-15082875491

ISBN:
Paperback: 978-1-966968-74-0
Hard Cover: 978-1-966968-75-7

Published by:

www.owlpublishers.com

360 S Market St, San Jose, CA 95113,
United States.

Printed in the United States of America

DEDICATION

This novel is for all of the adults and young adults that don't see themselves represented in fantasy literature. This is born out of my love of creating from the thought of what if. History is full of what Ifs. So is love and so is loss.

To my family Mef, Kat, Mom and my Sisters, Best Friends Shenika, Sarah, Samantha, and Erica. Thank you all for keeping me lifted though my Masters and the writing of the novel. I love you all.

ACKNOWLEDGMENTS

Writing this book has been a complete labor of love. I wasn't always the best reader, and spelling gave me the blues at a young age, however I doubled down and learned. Moreover, I was a military kid, and moving made learning difficult. I loved writing though. It was my escape. An escape from a world that had no love for a young gay black kid. Hence the reason everything I've ever written has revolved around characters from the LGBTQIA+ and BIPOC community. Not only are these stories relatable, but young adults and adults need to see themselves in the fantastical. Life is already hard, having an imagination is like having a slice of heaven on earth.

With that being said, I've been terrified for the last two years to release this book. At the end of 2024 I decided to take a leap of faith. Taking that leap of faith, came as a result of wanting to heal past traumas regarding not being good enough, not being smart enough. I am here to acknowledge those who assisted me on my healing journey.

I would like to thank my SNHU MFA Professor Kimberly Tomsic. She gave me a level of confidence that I thought I had lost so long ago. She was more than a professor. She was a sounding board, someone I could talk to about the future, and an educational supporter. Thank you, Kim.

I would like to thank my SNHU MFA Professor Jan Watson. Believe it or not, Professor Watson is the real guiding light behind how the book was written. While I was writing, my point of view constantly shifted. Jan said to me on a long ride back home to DC from Virginia Beach, "why don't you write every chapter in the point of view of a different character." I felt like it was a great idea, but I wanted to mix it up and write from the point of view of the person who the chapter was named after. When I showed her my next chapters, she said, "this is it." Her encouragement helped me complete my thesis which birthed In the Blood. So, Thank you so much Jan.

To my friends Neek, Sarah, Samantha, Shannon, Phillip, Ashley, Izzy, Essynce, Erica, Sharee, Reese, Stanley, Brandi, Carissa, Brian, Brook, and Marque. Thank you all for keeping me encouraged. When I had pages to write and had to miss pivotal events, thank you all for showing me kindness. Healing broken pieces of me with your friendship, support, and love. I could go on and on about God's grace, but he gave me all of you and I know there is a higher power because of you.

Finally, I want to thank my family. My sisters Victoria, Veronica and Vanessa. My Mom Dee, and my nieces and nephew. Vicky, we been talking about this for years so let's get cracking sis.

Last but not least, the love of my live Mefodiy. Nothing that I put out into this world is done without going through you first. You speak life into me and my work. You bring light to all of the dark places illuminating things that may be unseen. From the moment I read you a short story you said this was my passion. You could see it in my eyes. Just like you saw that in my eyes, I see my world of imagination through yours. You are the co-author I never knew I needed, the best friend I always dreamed about, and the absolute love of my life. Thank you for always believing that my gift would make way for our dreams. I love you to the moon and back.

CHAPTER 1: MARCUS

F ire roars like a medieval dragon all around me. Blood runs from my neck and side as I lay about the marbled floor. As the smoke fills my lungs, I watch the fire dance, overhead a beautiful starry night sky. It all took me back to the accident. Hyperventilating, my head began to spin, until I felt my body go limp. I know you want to know how I ended up in this predicament. To be honest with you, I think I have to go back. Back to a time before I met a gypsy and a prince.

There have been stories told over many years about the Gods and their unquenchable thirst for the women of earth. This desire goes as far back as Adam and Eve. However, we won't be going that far back. Let's go back to a time when Gaia reigned, and creatures only known to our imagination roamed the cosmos. Gaia, or as we call her mother earth, gave birth to Pontus along with a slew of other titans. It was told through Greek Mythology that Pontus along with his brothers and sisters were defeated by Zeus. However, this is not the case. As the children of the Nephilim died off following the great flood, and their offspring which we now know as humans took over the world, Gaia realized that there was very little space for magical creatures and the humans to co-exist. One day she reached out to her mother The

1

Goddess of Light and asked for a portal to be created at the depths of the ocean. There the mythical creatures could escape to other realms where they could live in peace. The Goddess gave this gift to her daughter and stated that in order for this portal to remain open it would have to be guarded. Pontus came to Gaia with his new son-in-law Poseidon who graciously accepted the offer to protect the portal.

Over many centuries Pontus would come back to earth in the form of the ocean and find a beautiful earth woman to bed. One day in particular he found himself in the brackish waters of Lake Maracaibo and stumbled upon a young woman swimming in the nude. She was far more beautiful than anyone he had ever laid eyes on. Her skin was the deepest ebony, and her hair was black as night. He knew if she stayed in the water any longer, he was going to have to make her. As she did, so did he. The young woman went by the name of Adriana. Many knew here as the local medicine woman. She was also said to be a powerful priestess. But I knew her as my Mother. As she swam, she began to feel a warmth underneath her, and it penetrated her womb causing her to convulse in ecstasy. As the pleasure ceased, she was able to make her way back to the shore. As she looked back into the sea, she touched her stomach. The creature displayed its snakelike back as it glided back into the depths.

At the time of this incident Adriana was seeing a local teacher named Leon who she was madly in love with. Afraid that he or the townspeople would call her a witch she kept the incident to herself. Out of fear that she might become pregnant by the creature, she and Leon consummated their relationship that same night. A month had passed, and Adriana realized that she hadn't had a period, and went to the local doctor who told her she was in fact pregnant. Leon was over the moon, but terrified as his meager means wouldn't be enough to support Adriana let alone a baby. At this point he decided to enlist in the Venezuelan armed forces. While away at training Adriana would often go back to the sea skinny dipping, in the hopes that Pontus would come back to her. He did not, but Poseidon did. He too was captivated by her beauty and pregnancy only made her more desirable to him. He came to her in the form of a merman, the creature she thought was the source of her pleasure. His marlin-spiked back resembled the creature that had made love to her before. They made love in the water, and he went back to his post. Every night for several weeks Poseidon took on the form of a mortal man and came to the dwelling which she shared with Leon. She fell in love with Poseidon, and he fell in love with her also.

At her eight-month mark while swimming in the lake, Pontus returned to her, wanting to have his way with her again. He saw that she was pregnant and became enraged. He could feel the power in the child and wanted nothing of the half breed. In his anger he induced her into labor and caused a storm the likes of which the lake community had never seen. Adriana was thrashed about the water, writhing in pain. Pontus finally showed himself to her in the form of water. He laid his entire girth on her body drowning her before the lake calmed as he slid back into the depths of the sea. Nearby but unable to interfere Poseidon sent a pod of dolphins to aid her, but it wasn't enough. He delivered the baby and cut the umbilical cord with The Trident of the Seven Seas. Unbeknownst to him the power of his trident revived the child. As he placed the child upon her breast a tear of saltwater fell from his eyes. The dolphins placed her upon the banks and left her. A local fisherman found her lifeless body clinging to the crying child.

Upon his return home Leon was devastated by the news of her drowning. He resorted to alcohol and drugs, unable to cope with the fact that the love of his life was no longer alive leaving him with this child. This child that without her he wanted no parts of. Before leaving for his first post, he left the baby outside of an orphanage and asked that they take care of him. The young baby reminded him so much of Adriana he could no longer bear to have it near him. It wasn't hard to find a family that wanted to take the young child in. An American couple became his parents, and that's where my story truly begins.

CHAPTER 2: MARCUS

"Aye," I screamed as I woke up covered in a dense film of sweat. I'd had the dream again. The man from the water. The woman drowned. The baby lying across her chest. I took my shirt off and wiped my body with it laying back down looking up at the merman picture I'd drawn on my ceiling beside the skylight.

As a child of adoption, the only things I knew of my parents were their national origins and where I was born. Earl and Alicen, my adopted parents, told me about them when I was younger. My birth father is Guyanese, my birth mother is Venezuelan, and I was born on the banks of Lake Maracaibo well that's at least what I was told. They told me that my mother died in a shallow nursing pool attached to the lake after being struck by lightning and drowning. I was found on top of her with my umbilical cord cut. There I was, this tiny dark-skinned baby with a streak of white hair surrounded by a black velvet bush. From a young age, I researched where I was from and was enthralled by stories of the unknown, myths and lore, surrounding the lake and its electric properties.

My adopted mother, Alicen, and father, Earl, feared they would never have children after trying for so many years. They brought Marissa into this world two years after I was adopted, and the house was filled with love. It wasn't that they didn't love me, but Alicen wanted to experience motherhood. I just told people that she wanted to experience giving birth, which is far beyond me. Marissa was the only child they bore; with the two of us, our small family was complete.

Although, they did their best to give me an ordinary life. I knew I was very different from my mother, father, and sister. Alicen is a Caucasian American from Texas; her beautiful delicate skin matches her personality. She is an absolutely stunning woman, with green eyes, red hair, and rosy, pink full lips, but even more, she is a beautiful human being. Earl is a South African Brit from Manchester; he has powerful features, tall and stocky from his Rugby days. Dark skin, deep brown eyes, almost black, with a smile that lights up a room. He a model father if there ever was one. Then there is Marissa, my light, bright sister. Although she was raised by beautiful human beings, she is pretty sarcastic, and not the nicest person. Some might even consider her a mean girl in many circles. In school, she was known as the queen bee. Her curly spiced amber hair adorns her beautifully soft tan face. I absolutely adored her during our younger years. She always took care of me even though I was older.

For many years, I was a secluded bookworm. When Marissa joined me in high school, noticing that I had no friends other than the school librarian, she took it upon herself to make sure I became popular. She placed me in sports and drama, making me join the dance team with her. We were inseparable. We walked the halls like we owned the school, and when people wanted to get on her good side, they always knew I was the way in. Things changed during my senior year. That was when I met him, the young man who would change my young adult life.

The year was 2005, and it wasn't the thing to be gay. I masked my sexuality via my height and sports. As I assumed Luke did. Yeah Luke Miller, one of the school's most preeminent soccer players. He was being scouted by teams all over the world. But I didn't know him. I just melted every time I saw his face. There was an unspoken language between the two of us. We would see each other walking down the halls, trying to avoid eye contact. One afternoon we both missed the first evening bus. I sat on the curb reading *Their Eyes are Watching God* as a shadow blacked out the sun. As I looked up, he stood in his tank top and soccer shorts. Luke Miller, his rich honey skin, full pink lips, and chestnut brown eyes. He was a vision.

"Do you mind if I sit here?" Luke asked, as he looked down upon me.

"I don't mind at all."

"Luke," he said, as a smile came across his face.

"Marcus," I replied, trying to avoid his smile. I could feel my heart fluttering and my breathing becoming fainter. My fingertips then began to do the thing they always did when I felt anxious of nervous. It felt like a static electricity. We sat in silence for a moment before he continued.

"I know who you are," he replied, continuing to look down at me.

I didn't want to turn to face him as he sat closer next to me. I knew his smile would make me smile, and I was far too afraid of anyone finding out about my sexuality. In school, I didn't make it a big deal. I didn't date, and I am sure that people questioned the fact that I didn't date, but they would have never questioned it in the open out of fear of getting on Marissa's bad side.

"Why won't you look at me?" he asked.

"Because…I am afraid that if I do, you will peer into my soul," I replied shyly, as I read on trying my best to avoid further conversation.

"You know kids don't talk like that in real life," he mocked me. I looked into his eyes, and his smile did everything I thought it would.

"I know, but that's how I talk. I am reading this book, and I have to get into character to read."

"That's right, you are a drama kid."

It was in that moment that I felt my breath leave my body. I looked into Luke's eyes again, explored his face. Covered it with my eyes like an explorer on a journey through uncharted land. His lips thinned as his pearl-white teeth came into view and then back to his eyes.

"I am," I smiled back at him.

"Can I ask you a question?"

"Yes," I closed my book.

"Why have you been avoiding me?" he asked, as I looked down a small pebble rolled underneath my shoe on the ground, the scratching slightly distracted me.

"I don't think I've been avoiding you. I've...been keeping my distance."

"Distance? Why?"

"You already know why."

"Oh, I do?"

"Yes, you know why. There's an unspoken language between the two of us."

"Unspoken? How so?"

"Luke, you really want me to say it?"

"Yeah, I want you to say it. Clearly, you know something that I am oblivious to."

"I stay to myself. I don't date. People just think it's because I am focused on school."

"Yeah, and there is nothing wrong with that."

"I think you are like me."

"Like you?"

"Yes," I looked away.

"Marcus, are you … into me?"

I wanted to say nothing. I wanted to walk away and end the conversation, but my body wouldn't allow me to move. I honestly didn't want to move. I liked his company. He felt warm and pleasant, something like home.

"I … I know how I feel when I see you."

"How is that?"

"Let's put it like this. When I don't see you, I hoped it was because I missed you. When I do see you, it makes my day."

"Then why keep your distance?"

"Because I didn't know if you felt the same way."

"If I did, is that such a bad thing?"

"I don't know. I don't…"

"Don't want anyone to know. You don't want anyone to know that you are gay?" continued Luke.

A tear rolled down my cheek, and before I could wipe it away, his hand was on my face. His hand was warm and soft like butter melting over bread. He took his thumb down upon my lips, and I heard a scuffle from the gym. In that moment, I did the only thing my body could muster. I got up, grabbed my bag, and ran.

"Marcus!" I could hear Luke screaming behind me as he tried to catch up.

I could hear him, but my body wouldn't let me turn around. I ran to the main road and proceeded to walk home. Shortly after my sprinting ended, I heard footsteps behind me, catching up to me. His breathing was heavy, and I stopped. I didn't turn around, but heard the footsteps stop. Not turning around, I uttered his name.

"Luke?"

"Yeah?" he replied. I could tell by the way he responded that his chest was heaving to get in as much air as he could. I guess I expected him to be a better runner as a soccer player. I couldn't help that I excelled in track and field.

I turned, "Why are you following me home?"

"We hadn't finished our conversation," Luke said as he sluggishly made his way to the spot where I stood.

"What more do you want to know. I like you, and I don't…"

"You don't what?"

"I don't know if you like me too!"

"Marcus, why would I chase you down like this if I didn't like you?"

"I don't know. You could just be a really nice guy."

"I am a nice guy that likes another nice guy."

"So, what now?"

"I don't know. Let's get to know one another. Maybe I can see you later?"

"That's fine with me."

Meanwhile, a car pulled up beside us.

"Aye, Luke, come on. I told your mom I was going to bring you home," said Bryan. Bryan Walker, another soccer star, and all around pretty boy. They were on the same soccer team, and he absolutely loved Marissa. "Marcus, you need a ride too?"

"No, I'm almost home."

"Okay. Come on, Luke."

"Okay," he replied, "Which house is yours?"

"That blue one in the middle."

"Okay, I'll see you later."

He jumped into the car and sped off into the distance, I could see him in the back seat looking back at me. As I made my way through the door, I was met by Marissa.

"I thought you were riding the bus."

"I decided to walk."

"Mom, this is why you need to get Marcus a car," Marissa said as she walks into the kitchen and sits on the countertop, looking at our mother.

"Marissa, you can use the other car; you just have to ask," Mom replied. "Neither of you ever asks.

"Yeah, both of you have a license," Dad replied from the living room, watching the soccer game with his feet resting upon a pillow. "You just want us to chauffeur you around."

Tears filled my eyes as I looked at my family, smiling and laughing. I just felt so conflicted that I had this wonderful thing that I wanted to tell them, but I was too afraid. They'd never given me a reason to think they wouldn't love me regardless, but the fear just held me captive for far too long. I took off upstairs and faceplanted into my pillow.

A knock came on my door, and Mom walked in. "Hey, what's going on?"

"I don't want to talk about it, mom," I replied as she sat on the bed beside me, taking her hand through my hair.

"You know you can talk to us about anything."

"Yes, ma'am."

"Is everything okay?"

"It's not completely okay, but I don't want to talk about it right now."

"Okay, I will leave you alone. Come down when you are ready."

"I will. I just need a minute."

"Okay. I love you," she said, kissing me on the cheek.

As my door closed, I turned around and just stared at my ceiling for hours. Lost in my thoughts of Luke. As the night overtook the sky, I got out of bed, walked downstairs, and grabbed dinner. Mom and Dad watched television as if everything was okay, but not Marissa. She came over to the kitchen table and sat next to me.

"Are you okay?

"Yeah."

"You seemed really happy when you walked in, and then you got sad."

"Yeah, I wanted to tell you something that happened earlier today, but I…"

"What is it?"

"What is what?"

"What happened today?"

"I met someone."

"Luke?"

"How did you know?"

"He got my phone number from Bryan and wanted to know if he could get your number."

Marissa patted me on my back as I choked on my food, lightly giggling.

"Everything okay over there?" Dad asked.

"Yes," we responded in unison.

"Marcus," she whispered. "Do you?" I stopped her by placing my finger over her lips.

"Let's go outside and talk."

I took my plate into the kitchen, and Marissa and I walked towards the front door. As I opened it, Luke stood there, his hand balled into a fist mid-knock.

"Marcus," he said, surprised.

"Luke, what are you doing here?"

"He wanted to check on you," Marissa said as she pushed me outside the house closing the door behind me.

"I told Marissa that I wanted to check on you. I didn't want to tell her that we were supposed to meet up because I was so distracted by our conversation that I didn't get your number."

"So, you called Bryan, got her number, and asked her if you could stop by vice asking for my number?"

"I wasn't thinking. I just knew I wanted to see you again, and I assumed it would be weird if I just showed up here at your house at 7."

"Smart and cute," I blushed.

We stood in front of my dark ocean-blue house for hours, saying absolutely nothing. We just looked at one another with our backs upon the pillars on the porch. I could feel Marissa staring from the kitchen, and then Mom emerged behind her.

Luke and I walked back toward his car.

"So, we never finished our conversation." I said as we walked towards the Jeep that was parked on the street.

I know, and you aren't an easy man to find. No one has your phone number, but everyone has your sisters," he laughed.

"Yeah, Marissa is Miss popularity."

"There is nothing wrong with that. Gives you a good cover because everyone knows she is not the one to mess with." He replied, moving closer to me and hopping on the car's hood.

"So, where do we go from here?" I asked.

"I don't know. I am not completely comfortable with coming out, but I don't want you to feel like a secret. Like getting to know you is something wrong."

"I honestly don't care how people feel. We are both pretty masculine guys. I don't think people would think anything of us hanging out other than being friends," he hops down from the hood, walks to the back of the car, and opens the trunk. It's completely empty. "Have a seat. I don't like looking down on you."

I smiled because this was the first time someone made me feel seen. Like I was an equal.

"So, Luke Miller, you like me?"

"Yeah, and now that I know you like me too, I want to get to know you," he said as he turned his body, dangling one leg out of the car as the other sat underneath him towards me. He held out his hand, waiting for mine. I was already sitting Indian style as he pulled me closer, and I scooted toward him.

"I wanna take you on a date," he continued.

"I can do a date."

"Okay…," he breathed out heavily.

"You breathed out like I was going to say no."

"It's not that. I really…"

"You really what?"

"I really want to kiss you right now."

It took everything inside of me to lean into it. My heart was racing, my palms were sweating, and I could feel the beads of sweat on my forehead forming. Then it happened, I leaned into his lips, he slowly slid his tongue into my mouth. His tongue tasted like strawberry mint candy and copper. It was a sweet taste. When I opened my eyes, he was staring at me. A slight shock tickled our lips as they parted, causing us to smile as he ran his hands through my hair, cupping my face.

"You're touching my face like an old man," I looked at him smiling.

"My mom always says that I have an old soul," Luke replied as he continued to hold my face inches from his, as he pecked me once more on my lips.

Over the next couple of months, our relationship grew stronger. I introduced him to my parents. We went on that date. Because of him, things in my life felt stable. For the first time in a really long time, it felt like the piece of me that was aimlessly blowing in the wind of life was not connected to another. As our bond grew, the bond between my sister and me weakened. I didn't desire to pull away from Marissa, and it was never my intention. However, life happened. She and Bryan began dating, and she got pregnant. Luke and I graduated and moved into a loft together. Marissa never had the baby, and I wasn't there at the most volatile time for her following the abortion.

Ten years after our first kiss, we were watched as we kissed again on one of the happiest days of our life, flooded by cheers in front of our families. However, there were two noticeable absences. Marissa and Luke's parents. Prior to our marriage Luke's Mother, Father, and his twin brother Logan were killed in a home invasion. It was difficult to get to the date knowing that they wouldn't be there to celebrate us. Marissa on the other hand was just absent. She said she didn't want to go to the wedding, and I was in no headspace to talk her into it.

Her relationship with Luke was lukewarm at best. When we visited my parents, she was either drunk or high and didn't even bother to acknowledge Luke's existence. This caused tension in the family. Luke and I got to a place where we rarely visited my parents. Marissa and I would only talk if she needed money, and my parents were completely tapped out.

#2023#

Luke and I had established ourselves; he is a tenured professor, and I've just finished my master's in creative writing. We longed for little but to spend time with family. With his family gone, he soon found himself missing my family too as I wished to keep my distance from Marissa.

"Good Morning, Darling. Are you ready?"

"Babe, I'm as ready as I'm going to be. I just hope Marissa is on her best behavior."

Luke poured me a coffee, "The two of you haven't been the same since we married."

"We haven't been the same since you and I got together," I replied, trying not to become irritated thinking about it.

Luke wrapped his arm around my waist and nudged his face on my shoulder, "You are the greatest love of my life. She doesn't know what that feels like. Show her grace."

I turned around and all I could do was kiss him on the lips. "People don't talk like that," I replied.

We both smiled as he continued to hold me tight.

"Are you going to put everything in the car?"

"I already did. I knew that you were going to procrastinate, so we don't leave on time," replied Luke as he placed my shoes on the floor. "Your parents are excited about Thanksgiving, and you know how much it means to me since I've lost both parents."

Honestly, I hadn't thought about how it must feel for Luke not to have either parent around the holidays that people spent with their families. He and I always had one another. I knew it was fine with me not seeing my parents, because I had him. However, I also knew that I could always see them when I wanted to. I should have been more aware that he couldn't see his parents, which just led to him wanting to be around my family, as dysfunctional as we are. I was the one who held him and brought him back to life after the terrible event. To be completely honest, I didn't think we would make it through that time in our marriage. But we did.

"I love you, and put on your seatbelt," I said, sliding into the car and snapping mine on.

As we pull out of the driveway, Luke looks over at me, pulling his seatbelt down, "I...."

When I noticed the car speeding toward us, it was too late. Suddenly bright blue light engulfed the car, and then there was the impact. The impact sent us rolling, and I was taken back in time as we spun into the large tree adjacent to our house. Back to our first kiss. As the car rocked, I slowly opened my eyes, we were upside down, and Luke was folded on the vehicle's roof. His hands were motionless like a ragdoll. Smoke and white powder filled the car as I attempted to take off my seat belt. Once freed, I hit the ceiling of the vehicle. I could hear wheels screeching, and metal crunching as the other driver took off. I had every intention of helping Luke get free, but everything hurt, and as I reached for him, my head began to spin. I faintly heard him gasp for air as he moved his body with all of his might. Then I saw them, those eyes that changed my life. The last words I heard him utter were. "I love you." Then everything went black as I felt someone drag me from the car.

CHAPTER 3: NARRATOR

S iren's blare: flashing lights, he could feel someone open his eyes and shine a bright light into his face. He closed his eyes again. He didn't know where he is; He could only remember the accident and the "I love you" that escaped Luke's lips before everything went dark. He attempted to open his eyes again and could only see flashes of quickly moving streetlights and men in ambulatory uniforms. A tightness followed a pinch on his arm as he felt something seeping into my body. He did his best attempt to speak, yet nothing came out. He tried to touch his face, and his hand was pushed back to his side and strapped.

After about fifteen minutes of siren noise, the vehicle hit a curb and abruptly stopped. The doors flung open, and cool air touched his face and caused him to inhale. He hadn't realized that he had even holding my breath. He could feel the gurney being pulled out of the ambulance and his body placed onto a different and colder gurney. Florescent lights caused him to close his eyes tightly as he could hear medical jargon being spoken all around him. At that moment, he slightly opened his eyes, and he turned his head away from the lights above him, and he briefly saw him. Luke. Lying motionless as people scattered around him. He attempted to call out his name, but a low guttural growl came from his mouth. The shock sent him spinning, and he is again enveloped in darkness.

In his unconscious state, the doctors examined him and realized he only had a few cuts, bruises, and a mild concussion. The violent impact and the injuries sustained by Luke left the doctors puzzled. After they tended to his cuts, his is taken out of triage and placed in a room under observation.

Alicen and Earl come rushing into the hospital, "Where is our son?"

"Ma'am, can you tell me your son's name?" asked the emergency room receptionist.

"Marcus Westmore," Alicen responded as tears fell from her face, Earl tried his best to pull her back.

"Marcus Westmore-Miller," Earl corrected.

"Ma'am, Mr. Westmore-Miller has just been taken out of the triage bay; he is in a room. I can't see the room number right now.

"And Luke Westmore-Miller?" asked Earl.

"Ma'am and Sir, if you want to sit in the waiting area, I will have a doctor come in to speak with you soon."

Another nurse took a shaken, Alicen and Earl, to a nearby waiting room. They waited for what felt like an eternity. A tall Hispanic doctor walked into the room and greeted them leaning down on one knee.

"Mr. and Mrs. Westmore?"

"Yes," they replied in unison.

"An update, your son Marcus is doing just fine. We have moved him into a regular room, allowing visitation."

Alicen crumbled into Earl's arms.

"However, your son Luke is still in surgery. For a while there, it was touch and go, but he is now stable, so they are finishing the procedure to stop the bleeding on his brain."

"Bleeding?"

"Yes, sir, they were hit at a high rate of speed from what we were told by the responding officer. Luke took the brunt of the impact, and the car flipped completely over."

"My God!"

"Did they find out who did it?" Asked Earl.

"Yes, sir. I have the responding officer here with me. She can explain more. After you speak with her, the nurse will take you back to Marcus."

"Thank you, Doctor."

He nods as the young female police officer walks into the room.

"Hi, Mr. and Mrs. Westmore. My name is Sergeant Lindsey. I am the responding officer. You should be comforted by your sons having quick-thinking neighbors."

"Who was the person who hit our boys?"

"I can't give you his name, but what I can tell you," she said, pausing to open her small steno notepad, "Was that at approximately twelve-thirty, your sons were hit by an eighteen-year-old drunk driver who was on his way home from a party the night before. He was driving at about sixty miles per hour down your son's street when he t-boned their vehicle, which was pulling out of the driveway. He only got about a block before he hit another car and a light pole.

"How is he?"

"He's fine, he just had a couple of scrapes, but he'll live."

"But my son-in-law is holding on for dear life."

"Mrs. Westmore, he will be charged and will be transported by me to the county jail. I just wanted to stay here to brief you on your sons. I knew there would be a lot of questions, and I wanted to give you answers."

"We thank you," Earl said, as he held his hand toward her.

They shook hands, and she placed her hand on Alicen's shoulder as she walked away.

"Mr. and Mrs. Westmore, you can follow me," called a young male nurse.

When they make it toward Marcus's room, Alicen stops and can't be moved. "I don't wanna see my baby like that."

"Baby, come on, he's okay. They said he is in stable condition."

"I … I can't. You go in. I will stand out here for a moment."

Earl walked into the room; he was shocked his beautiful boy's face was marred with scratches and stitches. His lips were busted but healing. He stood at the foot of his bed and rubbed his feet which were covered in hospital socks.

He was quickly pulled back when he heard Alicen screaming in the hallway.

"You almost killed my son," she took off down the hallway toward Sergeant Lindsey, who has the young man in custody.

Sergeant Lindsey holds up her hands as another Sargent takes the young man down another corridor. "Mrs. Westmore. Don't do this. Your son needs you."

Earl came running down the hallway. "Alicen, they will kick us out of the hospital if you don't calm down!"

"He's the reason ..." she stopped, falling into Earl's arms. "My Baby!"

"Come see him. He is sleeping. Peacefully. Just come see him," Earl replied as they walked towards Marcus's room.

She slowly made her way through the curtains and saw her son. Snot runs down her nose, and tears fell from her eye and face. Earl grabbed tissues which he handed to her. She walked to his bedside, pulled up a chair, and sat. As she took her hand through his jet-black curly hair, she smiled at Earl.

"You know he always asked me to dye that streak of white hair in the front. He said it made him feel like Rogue from the X-MEN," she said, laughing.

"Now, he embraces his differences," Earl replied as he placed his hands upon her shoulders.

"He's a good kid."

"Nothing is going to change that baby. He is always going to be good."

A deep inhale, and it's as if he was being brought back to life. The beeping sound rings in his ears.

Marcus screamed, "Where am I?"

"Oh, baby, don't move; I'm gonna get the doctor."

"Mom?"

"Doctor," Alicen screamed, as a shadow casts over his face. "Yes, baby, we are here," she said, grabbing his hand. "Earl, he's up."

"Thank the Lord."

"Where is Luke?"

The room goes deafly silent as the doctor walks in. "Your husband's in surgery. The accident left him with a punctured lung. We have gotten that bleeding to stop. However, they are now treating him for the bleeding on his brain," replied the Doctor hesitantly.

Instantly the equipment attached to Marcus began to go haywire. The beeping sped up to a rapid rate and sparks came from the monitors.

"Disconnect the monitors," exclaimed the Doctor as he and several nurses disconnected them from Marcus.

"Marcus you have to calm down," Alicen asked in a calming voice. The moment he heard her request everything seemed to subside.

"I wanna see him," I insisted, trying to get out of bed as a shooting pain landed me on my knees."

"Marcus get back in the bed right now!"

He'd never heard his mother scream like that, and her rising voice instantly took him back to his teenage years as tears filled his eyes.

"Mom, Dad, please go be with him. I don't want him to be alone," Marcus asked, tears streaming down my face.

"Earl, please go. I got him."

"Alright, baby," he replies, kissing me on the forehead.

Hour's pass, and his vision eventually came back to him. However, the pain wasn't going away. But there was no hurt more profound than the emptiness in his chest, not knowing what was going on with Luke. Every time he closed his eyes, he saw his face. Without warning, a calm came over him. This was something that he had only felt that first time Luke kissed him. But this time it was different, the string that once connected them once again felt like it was aimlessly blowing in the wind of life. The room suddenly began to tremble, and the machines came to life as if on their own the blood pressure monitor exploded, causing Marcus and Alicen to cover their faces as two nurses came into the room shocked.

"Mom. Mom! Something is not right," he screamed as he slid up and moved over, getting out of bed shaking in pain. He grabbed the walker as Alicen attempted to assist him at his side.

"Marcus, everything is okay. Nothing is…" she stops midsentence to see his dad standing in the doorway, tears swelling up in his chestnut brown eyes.

"No. No. No. No. Noooooooo!" He crawled over to his father, who embraces him with all his strength his body could muster, this caused Marcus's body to go limp.

"They did all they could do," he whispered, placing his head atop Marcus's flowing black hair.

He once again fell into complete darkness. His world forever changed, and he don't know what he was going to do.

Days after being released from the hospital, he wasn't the same. His parents wouldn't allow him to return to the home that he and Luke shared. Everything Marissa did utterly got under his skin, and to be sincere, she was trying. However, he was grieving. He laid in bed for days. He didn't call a lawyer. He didn't call a funeral home. He didn't even take a shower. He laid there in his filth, getting up to use the restroom and returning to bed. By this point, He had grown a goatee, his face began to look sunken, and his body was deteriorating. That's when she came in like the evil queen.

"Get up!"

"Marissa, I am not in the mood for your shit today. Just leave me alone."

"Get up!" she screamed as she pulled the covers from over me that were trapping the terrible smell. "What in the hell. You smell like a trashcan that has been left in the summer heat. Get up!"

"Marissa, let me be!" He screamed out, choked by the emotions bubbling over.

"He is dead. He isn't coming back. You need to snap out of it. I say good riddance."

The words hit him like a Dynasty slap as they landed upon his ears. He jumped out of bed, grabbed her by the throat, and flung her into the wall. He held her there on her tiptoes. By the look on her face, he could tell that she was terrified. He could see the look in her eyes, a look of true sadness, but also one of anger. His mother watched from the hallway with tears streaming down her face. He let her go, and she ran out of the room, slamming her door shut.

He had no more tears left on the day of Luke's Funeral. People gave him their condolences, and he couldn't hear a thing. Everything sounded like a high pitch ringing in his ear. And when people spoke to him, he could only hear white noise, static, because he knew he needed to disassociate. Then came the Eulogy.

"Luke wouldn't have asked me to do this. But this isn't your decision, my love. For almost 17 years … you were the love of my life, my confidant, and my best friend. You were everything I dreamed of and more, from the first kiss until the last. Now that you aren't here, I can't feel it. I am completely numb, and as I stand here, I can't cry another tear. The good part is that I know you wouldn't want me to. I want to thank my mother and father for being the best surrogate parents to you. Luke, I could say way more, but it's time to lay you to rest. I can no longer have you with me, but I will have our memories forever. I love you.

As I stood there watching Luke's body get lowered into the ground, I couldn't take it anymore.

"Mom, can you take me home?"

"Marcus..."

"Mom, I need to go. I can't."

Every day he went to his grave because he wanted to be close to him, and Alicen and Earl came with him every time. However, after visiting for a week, Marissa decided she wanted to come. As he'd done every day, he went to his graveside and sat Indian style, and he talked to Luke as if he were only temporarily in the grave. It was as if he didn't want him to miss out on a day of his life.

"I miss you something, crazy man. Why did you have to leave me? I wanted you to fight harder. Harder for us, harder to be here! I just want to be close to you again. To feel you holding my hand, kissing my lips." He said taking a handful of dirt between his fingers.

"Marcus! Get up off the dirt!" screams a female voice startling him.

"Marissa, why are you like this?"

"Get up. You have to move on. Luke is not here anymore. You have to move on with life and live. You come here daily, pulling mom and dad away from anything they want to do, and you sit here for hours on end. You are being selfish, just like you both were when he was alive. He wasn't that fucking special, and you can find another guy. For God's sake, you are only 36."

He didn't feel himself getting off the ground or walking over to her.

Yet, he could feel himself as he stood inches away from her face.

"You are evil. You … are … evil. You don't know what real love is, so how in the hell are you going to tell me that I need to stop grieving the loss of my husband? Please enlighten me, you worthless little …."

Before he could complete his sentence, Marissa slapped him. She slapped him with such a force it sent him spinning which caused him to land in dirt right next to Luke's grave. He slowly got up clutching his jaw, their parents ran toward the two, and momentarily he couldn't say another word.

"You don't have to worry about me! You … don't have to worry about me!" he finally uttered as he walked away from his sister for what felt like the last time.

"Marissa," screamed Alicen.

Marcus couldn't remember the drive home. He couldn't remember pulling into the driveway. As he looked up at the house he and Luke shared, things came into focus. He turned off the ignition and walked back into the house almost zombie like.

"Hey Marcus, I'm sorry for your..." one of his neighbors screamed out from across the yard. Before his neighbor could finish, he'd walked into the house, not even acknowledging her presence.

Marcus took off his clothes and slid into his bed. As he laid in bed, he closed his eyes. After only seconds, Marcus could feel a gentle hand upon his face. As he opened his eyes, he realized that he was lying face to face with Luke.

"Heeey, Baby," Luke said, gently smiling.

Marcus's eyes swell with tears, "Hey, baby."

"Why are you crying?"

"I'm just happy to see you."

"I'm happy to see you too."

"How are things where you are?"

"What do you mean?"

"You died."

"Baby, if I've passed. Could I do this?" Luke asks, touching Marcus's face. He can feel the warmth of his touch. Then his skin turns cold. His lips turn pale blue, and a mist comes from his mouth.

"What's happening to me?"

"Baby, you aren't here anymore. You died!"

"Died? Noooooooooooo," Luke screams as the skin leaves his face.

Marcus woke up screaming, and shaken, the house was pitch black. The cool fall breeze crept into the room as the curtain billows in the wind. Then he heard it.

"Maaaarcus," a voice called to him from on the wind.

"Maaaarcus," there it was again, the voice calling out for him. He looked around trying to decipher where it was from while still in bed.

The voice calling out his name continued for some time. Marcus didn't move. Tears again filled his eyes. He didn't recognize the voice, which scared him more. He wrapped himself up in the comforter and attempted to lie back down. As he laid back in the bed, he closed his eyes and saw piercing blue and red ombre eyes staring back at him. A hand swiftly reached out toward him, and the nails elongated, which caused Marcus to jerk out of sleep again. The morning sun beat down upon his face as the doorbell rang in the distance. Not wanting to move, he sat in the bed for a moment.

Bing Bong, the doorbell rang out.

The bell continued to ring. Marcus suddenly found himself slowly getting out of bed. He made his way down the stairs and opened the door.

There stood Alicen, Earl, and Marissa with coffee and breakfast food.

"It's too early in the morning. I'm not doing this. She has to go." He said as he attempted to close the door in their faces.

CHAPTER 4. NARRATOR

T he kettle bubbled as the three of them look at Marcus as he sipped his coffee as he looked out of his bay window.

"So, you just gonna let us look at you?"

"Marissa!"

"Ma, we drove here, because he stormed off like a baby."

"After you slapped me like a weak hoe," Marcus replied through a sip.

Marissa lunged as Earl grabbed her, "The two of you have to stop this."

Marcus turns looking at his father, "I don't have to stop anything. I didn't do anything."

"Marcus!" Alicen gasps.

"Mom, I didn't ask y'all to come here. As a matter of fact, I am sure

I have something to do today, but I just can't remember."

Alicen looked at the calendar on his refrigerator as she grabbed a coffee cup. "It looks like you have an appointment at," she stopped midsentence as she noticed a woman walking toward the house looking down at her note pad.

"Who is this lady walking up to the house?" Marcus asked out loud.

"That's what I was about to say. It looks like you have an in-home interview with someone from the Romanian consulate."

"You're moving to Romania?" Earl asked.

"Can y'all wait in the living room?

"Marcus, you didn't answer me."

"Daddy, I don't know. With everything going on I forgot all about this. Let me talk to the lady first." Marcus replied

"This isn't the end of this conversation. We are going to talk about this Marcus. Do you really think this is good idea with you being in the state that you are currently in?" Earl continued

"Dad I'm grown. I am going to meet with this lady, and if the opportunity presents, we will talk more about it."

A knock on the door breaks up the conversation as Earl and Marissa grabbed coffee and Marcus answers the door.

"Hello?"

"Mr. Marcus Westmore?"

"Yes Ma'am. Marcus Westmore-Miller."

"I'm Daniela Corden. I am here to conduct your interview. You do still have time for your appointment?" She asked, noticing his family as they moved toward the living room.

Daniela was a striking woman by American standards. She was tall, statuesque, with piercing blue eyes, all tied together with a somewhat supermodel strut.

"Yes ma'am. Come on in. Would you like a cup of coffee?"

"That would be nice. Can I have it with a slice of lemon and honey?"

"That's an interesting combination," Marcus commented as he poured the coffee.

"Something that I got from my grandmother. She was Swiss. She always stated that it but the bitterness.

"Interesting of course. I have to apologize. I've had a lot going on and I feel that I'm not appropriately dressed for the interview. But if you are okay, you can start with your interview questions."

"What made you interested in the job?"

"To be completely honest my husband died two months ago. I just want something new."

"My condolences, are you sure you are up for this?"

"Yes and thank you. You may continue."

"How long would you be willing to stay with the school?"

"If offered the job, I can give a definitive 1-year commitment with another year if you all want to keep me on."

Marcus hands her the coffee. "No cream? I assumed no cream but felt that I should ask."

"No thank you."

Marcus sits across from her at the small circular dining table.

"I read your credentials, and you are more than qualified for the job. How do you work with others?"

"I'm a complete team player. I provided references from me last teaching job."

"I saw those, but in your current state, do you think that you would still be considered a team player?"

Marissa yells, "No!" from the living room.

"Please disregard. That is my sister. We were in the middle of a family meeting."

"Would you like to reschedule?"

"Absolutely not. Please continue."

"Well, those were honestly all of my questions. Now it's time for you to ask me about the job."

"If I accept the position, when would I have to be in place?"

"Well, the school year has only begun, but the teachers at the school need help so the most we would be able to put it off is about a month. Is that going to be a problem?"

"Not at all. I've gotten my affairs somewhat in order. The only things I need to do is put the house on the market and see the lawyer regarding my husband's last will and testament."

"What exactly will I be doing?"

"You will be teaching the children English. It's considered a foreign language in my country. But the monarch wants it to be included so he funds it."

"Monarch? I thought the Monarchy was disestablished in Romania."

"In our province of Savarin, the Prince still remains. He and his family are independently wealthy, and they are very philanthropic. In return they still possess the privileges of their titles."

"That's interesting. Does the monarch get a vote on if I get the job or not?"

"Believe it or not, the Prince is the only reason that I am here. The last three people that I interviewed were the school's choice. However, the school and the Prince, both want you. They feel that you are the best fit."

"So, I technically have the job."

"Technically. This was merely a formality at the request of the school."

"Okay. Accommodation and pay?" Marcus asked with an inflection in his voice.

She smiles and lightly chuckles, "There we go. I was starting to think you might be make believe."

"Oh, is asking about pay taboo?"

"No, not at all. I would have thought you were a weirdo if you didn't ask about them."

"Well, I will say this, my husband did plan so I'm not broke," Marcus replied, smiling.

"No need to discuss that. As a foreign language teacher, you will be paid 4,000 euro a month, to include room and board in a fully furnished apartment in a local bed and breakfast just minutes away from the school."

"Wait, so you are saying that I will get paid 4,000 euro and will be given a fully furnished 1 bedroom 1 bath apartment minutes away from the school?"

"Yes, that is correct. The only things you will have to pay for are your cable, and internet."

"My flight?"

"All travel is included and if you would like to move your things from here you are more than welcome. But the bed and breakfast has a queen size bed."

"Where do I sign?"

"Well, I have to go back and put my notes into the system. HR should be calling you in a week," she said standing which caused Marcus to stand also.

They shook hands. "I will be standing by my email with bated breath."

"Yeah, you even speak like an English teacher," she said chuckling as he showed her to the door.

"Have a wonderful day."

"You too Marcus."

As Marcus closed the door, he rested his back upon it, smiling from ear to ear, forgetting that Alicen, Marissa, and Earl listened to the entire meeting and were waiting on him. As he made his way into the living room, he could see the concern written across his parents' face.

"Marcus, why are you doing this?" asked Alicen as she walked toward him.

"Ma, It's a great opportunity, and I can get away. Everything here reminds me of him. I even feel like I am being haunted by his ghost."

"So, you just going to sell the house? You just paid it off."

"What's it to you Marissa?"

"I live with mom and dad, and you have a house that is paid off and you want to sell it. That doesn't sound crazy to you?"

"No what sounds crazy is the fact that you want me to give you a house. After the way you've treated me and Luke over the years."

"Marcus we are still family."

"Marissa, we aren't...you know what. If you want it, it's yours. It's not going to be free. You will pay rent, cover the utilities, and in return you can stay here. The moment you stop paying or move out, the house is going on the market."

Marcus walks up the stairs. "I want it in writing,"

"Marissa, draft it up, I will sign it and have the document notarized. I am going back upstairs and getting into the bed. I don't have the strength for whatever this is anymore. You win."

"Marcus," Earl said turning around.

Marcus continues up the stairs, "Y'all don't have to leave, but you do have to leave me alone. I didn't sleep well last night, and I am tired."

***

2 weeks had elapsed, and Marcus had accepted the job and was finalizing the last few things before it was time for him to depart the

place that he and Luke had called home.

"Mr. Westmore-Miller, I'm pleased to tell you that all of your husband's assets have now been turned over into your name," explained a young Black woman in a blue pinstriped pantsuit. She sat across a large conference room table from Marcus.

"What does that exactly mean?"

"Well, all of your deceased husbands' assets have been turned over to you. This includes your current home which the both of you owned together. A condo in Old Orchard Beach that you all rented out. In addition to a property that he was given as a part of his inheritance in Victoria British Columbia."

Well, all of your deceased husband's assets have been turned over to you. This includes your current home which the both of you owned together. A condo in Old Orchard Beach that you all rented out. In addition to a property that he was given as a part of his inheritance in Victoria, British Columbia."

"BC?"

"You didn't know about the property?"

"No, Can I see it?"

Of course, I have pictures of the house. He had no relatives, but he was still afraid someone would contest this in the will because he was a dual citizen.

She slid a folder with several 8x10 photos of a large house sitting at the edge of a beautiful crystal blue lake.

"Why didn't anyone tell me about this?"

We were instructed to honor his wishes in his will, including making sure that you got that house along with everything else.

"Luke and I didn't have secrets. I just don't understand why he wouldn't tell me about this house."

"I'm sorry. I wish I had known that you didn't know. I would have said something earlier."

"That's not your fault. I couldn't bring myself to read the Will in its entirety."

"Well, there is more."

"More?"

"Yes, a substantial amount more."

"Okay?"

"In addition to those properties, Mr. Miller also left you a substantial life insurance policy. Two to be exact."

"I knew about the one with his job, but there was another one?"

"Yes, his family had a history of heart disease, and he was concerned that he would predecease you based on that family history. So in addition to the four hundred thousand dollar policy that he had with the school, the two hundred thousand in death gratuity, and the seven hundred thousand that you were awarded in the wrongful death settlement, he had an additional policy in the amount of two point five million dollars."

Marcus's mouth stood ajar as he looked at the young lady who stared back at him as tears filled his eyes.

"That's ... that's..." Marcus can't get the words out.

"That's three point eight million dollars. Which is due to be wired into your account by close of business tomorrow."

Marcus broke down in tears as the young lady grabbed a tissue and sat beside him.

"My father and I have worked with the Miller family trust for some years, and I will tell you this Marcus, he loved you."

Marcus sobs uncontrollably.

"I know. He is still taking care of me from the grave."

"Well, if you need anything my father and I have been retained by the trust for an additional 4 years. We are your attorneys. I deal more with civil litigation. My father deals more with family law, trusts, and issues of immigration. So, if you have any questions, please don't hesitate to reach out to us."

"I do have one more question before I leave."

"Okay?"

"I am set to move to Romania for a teaching job in about a week. Will I still be able to access my money from overseas?"

"Absolutely. If you would like we can set you up a foreign bank account, but I would suggest against it."

"Why is that?"

"That's how criminals hide large sums of money from the federal government," she said with a smile. "If you are going over to teach on a work visa, you can use your credit cards like you use them here in the states, and your bank will do the euro conversion. So, you will always have access to your money."

"That is great to know. If anything happens, please let us know. Here is my card. My cell phone number is on the back."

As she hands him the card, he reads her name CeTasha Nathan.

"Oh, last thing. I was able to draft up that lease agreement for your sister. The house will remain in your name; she will pay rent directly to you. However, you know that the house, along with all of the other properties, are paid off, correct?"

"What?"

"Yeah, the Old Orchard Beach location was paid off in 2019 due to it being an Airbnb. The property in British Columbia was paid off by his grandparents through Luke's trust. Your home was paid off with the remainder of Luke's trust and the ten thousand dollars that you put down for the closing."

"This is absolutely crazy."

"Your husband was a finance guru. That's why my father loved him so much. He made sure that we were always good. One of his colleagues at the university who came highly recommended is now going to follow in his footsteps."

"That is so crazy."

"It is."

"Thank you, CeTasha" Marcus replied giving her a light hug.

As CeTasha opened the door, Marcus made his way to the elevator. Her father was sitting in his office and Marcus gave him the universal head nod and continued walking. The moment seemed like decades as the elevator door finally opened. He stepped in and stood there alone with tears swelling in his eyes again.

"Luke, I didn't deserve all of this. All I ever wanted was you."

The elevator doors open to the lobby where his mother is sitting with her purse and a cup of Starbucks coffee.

"How did it go? You're crying."

"I'm a millionaire," Marcus said sadly, shrugging and placing his face into the side of her neck. She dropped her purse and cupped the back of her son's head as if he were a baby again.

"It's gonna be okay baby. That's what men, real men do. They provide for their families well after they are gone."

He continued to sob.

"Come on, let's get out of here. You still got some packing to do, and I want to spend as much time with my baby as I can before you run off to some far-off land."

Marcus picked up her purse, not saying a word, still somewhat gasping, trying to catch his breath between sobs.

The entire ride back to the house, Marcus said nothing to his mother. He just stared out of the window. She would often take a moment at a red light to look at him or place her hand upon his, but his line of sight stayed locked upon the heavens. When they finally pulled into the driveway Earl was standing outside waiting to greet them. His mother got out of the car, and Marcus sat there for a moment.

"Is he okay?" Earl asked, concerned.

"Yes, he got some shocking news today. Our very own son is a millionaire."

"What?" Marissa said overhearing.

"Marissa that doesn't concern you."

"He's a whole damn millionaire and is going to charge me fourteen hundred dollars a month to rent? That is some straight bullshit."

Marcus stepped out of the car and walked toward the house. As he made it to the door, Marissa stood in the doorway.

"Marissa, not today. Please move."

"So, you a millionaire? And you gone still make me pay rent?"

"Absolutely. As a matter of fact, these are the documents. Please sign them and get them back to me so that my lawyer can get them over to my property manager."

He slid past Marissa, as his father brings him in for an embrace. "Are you okay?"

"I'll be fine daddy. Even better when I leave."

"Marcus don't use this new job as an excuse to run away. Everything that has happened to you over these last four months you need to feel."

Marcus looked at him, "Daddy, everything that has happened I do feel. Every morning I wake up reaching out for him, and he isn't there. Every time I make two cups of coffee because that was my job in the morning. Hell, I even think about him when I make too much food for dinner and there is no one here to eat it, but me. I can hear him call my name on the wind at night which keeps me from sleeping. I can feel his touch in my dreams. I see his face everywhere. So yes, I am feeling everything. This is not about running away from y'all or my feelings. It's about starting something new so I can figure out who I am without him."

"I'm sorry I didn't." Earl stopped himself midsentence.

"You don't have to apologize. I just don't want you and mom to think that I am running away from you all. Because I'm not, and I will send for you both as soon as I can. I just want to get there, get my bearings, and then move. I mean shit what is three point eight million dollars for if I can't show my parents the world," Marcus continued, kissing Earl on the cheek. He walked up the stairs and they could hear the door close behind him.

"Damn, three point eight million. He can pay off the rest of our house."

Alicen slaps Earl on the shoulder, "Don't you even go there."

"I mean, I'm just saying."

Marissa fumes at the bottom of the stairs as Earl and Alicen walk out into the backyard. A knock comes across Marcus's door as he is placing clothes in his suitcase.

"Come in."

"Marcus I want to talk to you about this."

"About what Marissa?"

"This contract?"

"Did you read it?"

"Yes, and fourteen hundred is a lot of money."

"You didn't read it."

"What are you talking about? I said I read it."

"Then read it again."

"Marcus now you are being an asshole."

Marcus snatches the contract out of her hand and flips to a page, "What does that say?"

"Marissa Westmore is to pay rent in the amount of one…dollar? Marcus?"

"I was mad at you yesterday, but today I wasn't. You have a lot of shit going on too, and I know that. So, I am not going to pile it on. So yes, you can live in the house. You will pay one dollar for rent, the utilities, and the electricity. That's it."

Marcus goes back to packing. Marissa slowly hugs him from behind, causing him to stop. "I'm sorry, but when you married him, I lost you. Now that he is no longer here, I feel like I am losing you for a second time."

"Marissa, I am not going anywhere. I am here. I'm sorry that I have been grieving, but I was with this man all of my young adult life. We built a life together. So, it's going to take time for me to bounce back. But I will always love you."

The two of them sat on the floor. Alicen walked in on the two of them and began to smile.

"Ma, you know you are supposed to knock," Marissa laughed.

"Look at my babies," Alicen said, as she sat with them on the floor.

***

Later that night

Marcus tossed and turned in his sleep.

"Maaaaaaaaaarrrrrrrrrrcuuuuuuuuuss," the distinctive male voice drifted into his open window upon the wind. "Maaaaaaaaaarrrrrrrrrrcuuuuuuuuuss."

A dense fog seeped into the window, surrounding Marcus's bed. A pale hand reached up from it, clinging to Marcus's bed. A figure crawled underneath the sheets with Marcus. The moment he felt a cold hand upon his leg, Marcus's eyes shot open. He screamed, pulling back the sheets. A male with no distinct facial features looked up at him. He again screamed a blood-curdling scream, which sent off soundwaves throughout the house, as his body lit up and the light overhead blew. This caused Earl to take off running toward his room with a side arm.

"MARCUS," Earl screamed over Marcus's scream.

Marcus screams with his eyes closed, rocking in the bed. Earl walks over to him, placing his side arm on the nightstand. Marcus is still screaming, as Earl shakes him, causing him to open his eyes. Marissa and Alicen come running into the room also. When they walk in, Marcus is crying into Earl's shoulder.

"What happened?" Earl asks as Alicen and Marissa sit on the edge of   the   bed.
"I don't know, it felt so real. It didn't feel like a dream."

"What was it?"

"A man with no face."

"Was it Luke?" Marissa asks.

"At this point, I don't think it's him."

"Then who was it?" Alicen asks.

"I have no idea. I just know that I have to get away from here," Marcus says with tears in his eyes.

For the first time since they found out that he was leaving, his entire family felt that it was a good idea that he leaves. They all laid down with him in his California King bed. Marcus sits up with his back upon his headboard as everyone else fell asleep around him. A figure stands in his backyard surrounded by fog.

CHAPTER 5: MARCUS

"Do you have everything?"

"Yes, Mom."

"You know, you don't have to go?"

"Yes, Dad."

As they follow me to the security checkpoint, the two hold hands. How could these two wonderful people, who gave me such a wonderful life, be feeling right now? Their oldest child is leaving the country, and they don't know when I will return. They know they can't change my mind or shield me from the pain I am still dealing with. Do they even understand that what I'm dealing with is too much to bear?

"Well, this is where I have to leave you. I love you both."

"Marcus, please reconsider. I worry about you going all the way there with no family and no support system this soon after Luke's passing."

"Mom, I already signed my contract with the school. I literally start in two days. I don't have time to sit up and think about all of that stuff. I will be okay."

"He gonna be fine, bae," said Earl as he placed his hand on her shoulder. Tears swell in the corners of her eyes.

"Now come here, give me love so that I can cry my eyes out at my terminal," I continued, with a light chuckle.

They come in for an embrace. The hug honestly felt like it would be the last I ever felt. That brought up a whole new set of emotions. Then as if Moses had parted the people himself, I saw her. Striding like a wounded animal.

"Got room for one more?"

Mom breaks down in tears as Marissa walked up.

"Always," I replied, holding out my arms toward her. She places her head on my shoulder and lightly sobs.

"I'm sorry."

I looked into her eyes and could tell that she was being genuine. "I'm sorry that we moved so far away from one another. Maybe this distance will be what we need to come back together."

"I hope so," she replied, tears rolled down her cheeks.

"Alright y'all. I gotta get out of here. Y'all have pulled all of the emotions out of me that I can spare," I said, laughing as I walked toward the security entrance. For one moment, as a bustle of people pushed by me, I thought I saw Luke standing beside them. Smiling as if letting me know I was making the right decision. His smile left me feeling warm as a tear rolled down my cheek.

As I sat in a seat waiting to board my plane, I thought about the life

I was leaving behind. Suddenly my phone began to vibrate, and I pulled it out quickly.

"Hello?"

"Hey."

"What's wrong, Marissa?"

"Nothing; you leaving this way just made me feel some type of way."

"What are you talking about?"

"You just left, and we didn't even get to repair the damage that was made."

"Marissa, we don't have to do that."

"I know, but I think it would have made me feel better."

"Again, the distance will get us back to where we used to be."

"Maybe you're right."

The speaker calls overhead, "Now Boarding United Flight to Munich."

"Bae, I gotta go. They are now boarding my flight."

"Okay, please call me when you make it to Munich."

"I will; it won't be until tomorrow."

"I love you, Marcus."

"I love you too. Speak to you soon," I folded my phone closed as I grabbed my bags and placed my headphones around my neck.

As I got onto the plane, I took my seat in first class by the window and placed my headphones over my ears. Again, my phone rings.

"Hello?"

"Hello, Mister Westmore-Miller?"

"Speaking."

"My name is Anna. I will be meeting you in Munich, and we will fly to Cluj International Airport. From there, we will take a private car to the inn that you will call home for the next year."

"Okay, my flight gets to Munich at seven forty-five."

"I am tracking that time. Well, have a nice flight, and look forward to meeting you in person tomorrow morning."

"Same here," I replied, as I hung up the phone. That was unusual to me. I've taken many flights for business, but never have I needed a guide. Anna sounded sweet though. Brits tend to have that going for them with that built-in accent.

The plane taxied and took off. As we became weightless and the city became all but a distant blur, I laid my head upon the window and fell asleep.

I don't know if it was the emotions of leaving the city, my family, or the fact that I'd been sleep deprived for over a month. I slept the entire 8-hour flight, only awakened by the feeling of the plane's tires hitting the runway. The gentleman sitting next to me looked over at me as he was shaken awake also.

"You slept the entire flight."

"I haven't slept much in the last couple of months."

"Why is that?"

"Not to get too personal, I lost my husband three months ago. I've been taking the loss a little harder than I think most people think I should have."

"That is absolutely crazy, mate. You lost a lover. There is no pain worse than that, short of a parent losing a child."

For the first time since Luke's death, no one had given me this reaction. Everyone assumed I would pick myself up by my bootstraps and jump back into life headfirst.

"I thank you for that," I replied as my eyes swelled with tears again.

"Awe, man, cry if you need to cry."

The older gentleman pulled me in and gave me a tight hug. It was warm, like the ones my dad would give me. The reassuring kind that you need after you scrape your knee as a kid.

"Do I smell good?" he asked me.

Although a strange question to ask, I completely understood why he would ask. He had given me a hug, and due to the proximity and the length of the flight, it was a reasonable question.

I laughed as a rogue tear landed on his shoulder. "You smell great, considering we were flying for more than eight hours."

We chatted small talk all the way off the plane. At the entrance of the walkway, I noticed a young blonde woman holding a sign with my name written on it. She was looking at the faces of the older people leaving the plane. As I walked toward her, I pulled my hair into a messy bun as my headphones nestled into my neck. "Anna?"

"Yes," she replied. "It's so nice to finally put a face to the name. Everyone is so excited for you to join our teaching team."

Her thick English accent is endearing and makes me feel comfortable, though I feared my face was not registering this as I am often told I have a resting bitch face. We then began to walk toward our next terminal.

"I'm pretty excited myself. This will be my first solo teaching job."

She looks at me with confusion written all over her face. "What other teaching jobs have you had?"

"I've been a high school teacher, a teaching aide, and I did a semester of solo professorship under an adjunct professor as an intern."

"That's a pretty wicked resume."

"My husband was the real deal, though. English, economics, and finances. He taught it all, but the both of us have loved academia since we were teens. It's how we met."

"How does he feel about you leaving the country to pursue this job?"

"He actually passed away three months ago."

"I'm so sorry to hear that."

"It's okay. I am still dealing with that."

"Is that the reason you decided to take the job?"

"Somewhat. I also just needed to get away."

I thought the news would have gotten to her since I disclosed it to the school. However, she looked so sad and somewhat embarrassed for assuming that Luke was still alive.

"Hey, you look sad. It's really not that serious. You are entitled to make a mistake. You didn't know."

"I know, but it's really sad."

"It is, but I can't get stuck there right now. We have a two-hour flight to our final destination, and I want to talk about all the beautiful things we will do."

"Sorry, we can do that," she said, shaking herself out of the moment.

"It's absolutely fine."

"One more thing I should tell you. I upgraded my ticket before I left to come here. If you would like, I can see if the airlines can upgrade yours also."

"No, I don't want you to do that."

"Just hold on one moment."

Seeing as she just ran afoul of the situation with Luke, I felt there was no other way to pick Anna up than to upgrade her seat. As I walked to the gate agent's counter, I stood and waited for the agent to finish her call.

"Hello, do you speak English?" I asked.

"Yes, I do. How can I help you?"

"Is there any way that I can upgrade her seat to first class?"

"Can I see your seat?" the gate agent asked, looking at Anna.

"Mr. Westmore-Miller, actually, you are in luck. The seat beside you is open."

Delighted by the fact, I waved her over. She lightly squealed and hopped over to the gate agent.

"Give her your ticket so that we can pay the difference."

"The difference is going to be two hundred euros."

"Marcus, you don't have to do that."

"I want to," I said, taking out my wallet and handing the gate agent my platinum AMEX.

She prints off a new boarding pass and hands it over to Anna. "Standby; you are going to be boarding in the next five minutes."

"Thank you so much."

"Marcus, thank you so much; you didn't have to do that."

"It's more for me than you. I really don't like flying, and with you sitting next to me, you can distract me with conversation for the next two hours."

"We will now begin boarding Lufthansa sixteen sixty-eight. We are boarding in two sections. First Class and Business to the left, Premium Economy and Economy to the right," the agent called into the speaker.

As we boarded the plane, I watched as Anna texted someone with vigor while looking up at me.

"Who are you texting?"

"I just reached out to the Director to make sure everything was good for you."

"Okay, you aren't going out of your way, are you?"

"Absolutely not. I told her that you upgraded my ticket and that you were going to be a great addition to the school. The entire town is buzzing about a new teacher coming. I think many of the people are going to be shocked when they see you, though."

"Why is that? Because I'm black? Tall? Have long hair?"

"No, because you are a man. The only thing said was that it sounded like an heiress was coming to town at the direction of the monarch."

"But you knew I was a man."

"Actually, I found out only moments before I called you. I don't know why they've been so secretive about everything."

"That does seem a bit strange, but the entire situation is odd if you want me to be completely honest."

"I know that the school is very sensitive about private information being shared."

"I mean, that isn't such a bad thing. Can you tell me about the make-up of the staff we will be working with?"

"Well, many of us are from the UK. So, most of us speak English, and some speak English and Romanian. But even the Romanians are picking up English. Hence the reason they brought you in. We don't have an English as a second language teacher."

"Okay, that's great. How about the Inn where I am going to be staying?"

"The Inn is run by a local named Kraven. He is a charming guy. I know some of the ladies from the school are sweet on him, but he doesn't seem very interested. He seems very focused on working."

"That's not a bad thing. What else does he do?"

"Well, he owns the Inn and is also a local tour guide. He will likely take us around, showing us the town when you get settled in."

"Okay. Last question, I promise. Can you tell me about the monarch? I read that the monarchy was disestablished, but I see that he still has a significant amount of pull in the town," I asked as we took our seats.

"Well, I don't know much about the monarch. I've only met him once. He is a strange man, very secretive. But I think that's because of his lineage. He is the great-great-great nephew of Vlad the Impaler. Something like that. The family is independently wealthy. Stays to himself. There are often months on end when we won't see him at all. However, on some of the night celebrations, he will make an appearance. We have a large gypsy population, and they don't particularly care for him. There are legends that the town has told for many years that make him seem very scary. Well, at least his family."

"Legends?"

"Yeah, the Vlad the Impaler, Vampire thing. They said he came to visit the family one winter evening, and the next morning a number of the townspeople were dead. Drained of all of their blood. It's a piece of lore that lent itself to the legend regarding Vlad the Impaler being Dracula. The family even carries the Dracula last name."

"That is strange and exciting. To be in a place that has a history like that. I think it's the creative writer in me that finds it interesting."

"Well, then you will fit in just fine."

The Captain calls overhead, "Crew, prepare for take-off."

"Well, Anna, I am going to put on my headphones and take a quick nap. I know the flight is only slightly over two hours, but I need the rest. I don't want to get to town completely jetlagged."

"Go ahead. I will wake you as we descend. The views are amazing."

"Thank you."

As I placed my headphones back over my ears and rested my head on the window, I looked out upon the beautiful architecture and thought to myself: Why didn't we do this together before you left? Sleep then clouded my vision, and I was gone.

As instantly as I closed my eyes, I was staring at a beautiful stone castle surrounded by fog. As I looked up towards the gargoyle-riddled steeples, I noticed a murder of crows. The door to the castle opened for me, and I looked around before walking in. As the door slammed behind me, I was suddenly jerked awake by Anna's hand on my shoulder. My adrenaline was pumping as there was slight turbulence going into the landing. But the sight out of the window was absolutely stunning. The patches of lush green grass next to the brown farmland make an almost checkered pattern into the landing.

"We're here."

"Two hours?"

"It was more like an hour and thirty. I think the pilot wanted to get us here earlier. It's not much to look at now, but wait until you get to our small town; we are surrounded by mountains. It's stunning," she said, almost squealing again.

As we begin the descent, I pull my hair out of the messy bun and comb through it with my hand, taking care to get the stray pieces from the back of my neck. I then placed it in another messy man bun on the top of my head. It's just easier that way, allowing my headphones to rest about my neck and not become caught up in my hair.

"I can make out the mountains in the distance."

"I can't deny nature here is something out of fairytales. Just wait until you go on some excursions. Kraven picks out some of the best places to take tourists to."

"I can't wait."

For the first time since we had been together, Anna saw me smile, a genuine smile. The plane landed, we disembarked, and didn't wait long for our luggage as there weren't many people on the flight. Only moments later, we were greeted by a tall man. He looks like Jason Momoa with greyer hair and splashes of grey throughout his long, clean beard. He is holding a sign that reads Westmore-Miller. As I walked toward him, holding up my hand, I was nearly knocked off balance by Anna, who came barreling down toward the gentleman.

"Luca!" she screamed, running over to hug him.

"Anna, what are you doing here?"

"The school sent me to meet Mr. Westmore-Miller in Munich."

"That was very kind of you."

"It really was," I said, extending my hand. "Marcus Westmore-Miller."

Luca shook my hand for what felt like an eternity as he looked at my face as if he'd known me in a past life. I looked into his eyes and recognized the inquisitive look on his face surrounding the strip of gray hair blossoming from my forehead. I was born with a birthmark right above my hairline. This caused a piece of my hair to grow grey from the very spot where my birthmark is located. I always wanted to dye it as a kid, but now as an adult I embrace my difference. I feel like it adds to my unique qualities.

"I promise you this isn't a fad thing. I was born with it. Mom says it grows out of my birthmark like this."

This shook Luca back to the conversation. "No, it's just a very unique look. It's very fitting."

This caused me to look down, somewhat blushing. "Thank you."

"Follow me; I want you both to get comfortable in the car. I will come back and grab your bags."

"I only have one suitcase and my small carry-on, which I'll hold for the ride. The rest of my things were delivered to the Inn about a week ago."

"Okay, what does your bag look like?"

"It's the Vintage Hard Shell Luggage that looks like this," I replied, holding up the twelve-inch vintage tote.

"Anna, do you have any luggage?"

"No, just this carry-on bag."

"Okay, well, make your way to the car. We can make our way to town as soon as I get his suitcase. It's a bit of a drive, and I know Kraven is waiting."

Anna and I made our way to the large SUV and got in.

"So, Anna, who is that?"

"That's Luca; he's Kraven's father and the Gypsy King. He owns his own company, that's like Uber. Kraven's company is somewhat of a subsidiary of the company which handles clients' tours and excursions."

"Oh, okay, and how do you know all of this?"

"Well, I dated Luca's middle son Stefan before he moved to London. He told me all about their family. They have ties back to some old money. Oh, and I am kinda nosey too. I can't help myself. I love finding out about people."

"That's good to know. I would hate for my business to be floating around town."

"Marcus, I would never."

"It was a joke. I expect people to be a little inquisitive about me. Being an outsider, coming in at the start of the school year, in addition to being black."

"You mean and being wealthy."

"Who told you I was wealthy?"

"I told you I overheard the director discussing that you didn't need this job. You had come into a bit of money. I.e. heiress or not so much because you are a man. I didn't know that it was money that came following the death of your husband. I just put those two things together after. You know what? I am going to stop talking now."

"It's not a problem. I really don't need the job, and Luke did set me up well. However, I would return all that money to have just one more day with him."

"He sounds like a special guy."

"One in a million," I replied as the truck door opened and Luca placed my suitcase in.

He jumped into the car, adjusted his mirror, and sent a text message before starting the vehicle.

"Are you hungry?"

"No, sir. I'm just in need of a shower."

"To the Inn it is."

"Thank you."

"So, Marcus, where are you from?"

"Portland, Maine."

"Were you born there?"

"No, sir. I was born in Venezuela. It's a fascinating story. I was technically born in a nursing pool on the shores of Lake Maracaibo. Have you heard of it?"

"Yes, and please call me Luca. You make me feel old when you call me sir."

"Sorry, Luca," I replied, pulling a piece of stray hair from my face.

"Yes, I have, though. It's known for its electrical properties."

"Electrical properties?" Anna asked.

"Yes, it's literally one of the most electrically charged places on this planet. They literally get these lightning storms every night.

"Wow that sounds beautiful."

"Beautiful and dangerous. My mother died in a lightning storm giving birth to me."

The car jerks to a stop as three stray sheep jump into the middle of the road, causing my tote to hit the floor and almost causing Anna to slam into the driver's side seat.

"I'm sorry, you two. Those darn sheep just come out of nowhere." Luca says as he looks Marcus in the eyes through the rearview mirror.

"It's okay. We are fine."

For the remainder of the trip, Luca doesn't say a thing. He looks perplexed by the information that I've just given him. Although I wanted to ask him why he seemed so intrigued by me, I was far too taken by the countryside and the mountains as they overtook us, leading into the small town.

"We're home," Anna says as Luca parks in front of a beautiful Victorian-style bed and breakfast nestled in the heart of the town. "That's our school over there," Anna points to the small modern-styled building which stands out amongst the traditional structures of the town.

"That's perfect. I almost thought I would have to buy a bike to make it to the school."

"Nope, it's a simple walk. My apartment is a few streets over, so if you need anything, here is my address. Stop by anytime. I love visitors."

As we hopped out of the car, she hugged me as if she would never see me again.

"Thanks again for getting me here."

"That's no problem. Thank you for flying me first class for the first time in my life."

"Now, that wasn't a problem."

Luca removes my bag from the car and places it on the curb. "I hope to see you around, Marcus. You are always welcome amongst the gypsies if you don't feel comfortable with the locals."

"Thank you, Sir...Luca."

We shook hands, and Luca whistles so loud that it reached me to my core. In that instance, I stood back, looking up at the beautiful building, placed my hand on my suitcase, and took it all in. The wind blew lightly around me, and it was fresh and cool. Welcoming. Like it was welcoming me to new adventures. Then I saw him. One of the most beautiful men I'd laid eyes on since Luke.

"Dad, what have I told you about the whistling thing? I am not an

61

animal."

"It got you out here, didn't it?"

They share a laugh and a hug.

"This is Marcus Westmore-Miller."

"As in the old lady that's supposed to come here to teach Westmore-Miller?"

"As you can see, son, he isn't an old lady."

"I'm so sorry, Mr. Westmore-Miller."

"Don't be. Call me Marcus."

"Nice to meet you, Marcus," Kraven said, extending his hand.

"You must be Kraven. I've heard wonderful things about you."

"I heard you were an older heiress," he continued, smiling, slightly blushing.

His smile was captivating, his canine teeth seem a little more elongated than the average person, upon his face a short beard cleanly tapered, and his eyes. They're the color of teak.

"That's what I heard. I can only imagine what people will think when they see a tall black man with a streak of grey hair," I mocked with a straight face.

"You're black? I never would have guessed," Kraven continued to mock.

Is he flirting? I smiled for the first time, looking him up and down, trying my best not to be noticeable. He is solid, not fat, but not annoyingly muscular or slender. His arms, however, are massive and accompany his huge legs.

"It smiles," Kraven continues.

I cover my face out of embarrassment as I feel I have been caught ogling this man. "So, this is the inn?"

"Yes, you can make your way inside."

"Thank you."

As we look at one another, a young man skateboarded by and attempted to grab my bag. He is instantly caught by Kraven and yanked from the skateboard.

"Cairo! We talked about this. You can't snatch bags in front of the inn."

"You can't snatch bags in front of any establishment, Cairo," bellows the voice of Luca as he walked up to the young man.

"Marcus, meet my little brother Cairo."

"Nice to meet you, Cairo," I replied, extending my hand. I'm guessing Cairo is the youngest of the bunch, but clearly a teenager.

Kraven releases him, and Cairo shakes my hand.

"Cairo, this is no way to make a first impression. He is going to be your English professor," Luca explained, towering over the young man.

"I apologize, Mr. Marcus."

"It's Mister Westmore-Miller, but you can call me Marcus."

"Sorry again."

"Go get in the car. I am taking you home," Luca said, angrily pointing to the car.

"Marcus, again, I am very sorry."

"It's not a problem, Luca. Thank you for getting me here."

As I attempted to grab my suitcase, Kraven grabbed it. The moment our hands touched, a slight shock caused us to drop it back on the ground, and we stood back and looked at one another. I was surprised. The last time I felt that shock was when Luke and I touched. Every time we kissed or touched, we were shocked. Yes, even then. This was the first time I'd felt that shock with someone other than him.

"You make your way in; I will take this for you. I need to have a quick chat with my dad," Kraven replied as his face becomes slightly more serious and somewhat confused.

"Okay, thank you."

Walking into the Inn made me feel like I was stepping back in time. I felt like one of the Von Trapp children. I turned, noticing the two of them talking, which caused me to smile. I couldn't hear the conversation, but the two of them looked at me as I tried to look away as if I weren't just staring in their direction moments before. Kraven hugged his father and walks into the Inn, closing the door behind him. I made myself a cup of tea to distract myself from the fact that I was being nosey.

"I hope the tea is nice."

"It's perfect. Not too sweet and not too tart."

Kraven blushed as I once again explore his body.

"Let me take you to your home for the next year."

"Okay."

We walked up the stairs, and Kraven attempted to engage in small talk.

"So, where are you from again?"

"I was born in Venezuela but raised in Portland, Maine, with my adopted parents and sister."

"How do they feel about you being here in Romania?"

"It's my life. They would have preferred that I stayed home, but honestly, I needed to get away."

"Why is that?"

"My husband died three months ago."

"My condolences. I am so sorry."

"Nothing to be sorry about. Hit by a drunk driver. I survived, and he didn't."

"Mr. West..."

"Marcus... please call me Marcus," I pled.

"Marcus, if you don't want to talk about it."

"It's okay; I think I am finally coming to terms with it. It's taken me some time."

"So why do people think you're this rich old lady?"

"I don't know. My husband did leave me a sustainable nest egg. But I... I'd rather have him than the money. He was my... best friend."

"Again, Marcus, you don't have to talk about it if you don't want."

"No, you seem like someone I can talk to. I mean, I am going to be living under your roof for the next year. You probably want to know if I'm a psychopath or not," I said as Kraven placed my suitcase on the floor, pulling a set of keys from his tight pants pockets.

As he opened the door, my mouth dropped. The room was made up in the old Victorian style. The sleigh bed with canopy lent to the appeal. The room faces the back of the Inn, which gives a view of a beautiful mountain and a magical river, and nestled in the corner, one can make out the castle that belongs to the monarch.

"This is so beautiful."

"I'm glad you like it," Kraven said, looking me up and down, exploring my body now.

Over the last couple of months, I've slimmed down a bit due to the lack of food and sleep. I'm not thin, but I am the right weight for my tall, athletic frame. I pulled my hair out of the messy man bun; I noticed the veins in his neck tensed up. It was something that I had only seen in movies but thought nothing of it. As I turn to him, he seems slightly uncomfortable.

"Are you okay?"

He breathed heavily, "Yes, maybe a little winded by the stairs."

"You know you could have given me a cheaper room. Or I can pay full price. This has to be like the presidential suite."

"I will do no such thing. My brother will be in one of your classes, and I expect him to learn perfect English."

"Like you? Where did you study?"

"My dad sent me to a boarding school in the UK while he worked on a crabbing vessel back in the day. A lot of people think we are independently wealthy."

"Why do people think that?"

"Because my middle brother is a liar and loves getting into the teacher's pants. Thank God he is in London now."

"That's awesome and funny."

"Well, let me go through everything with you."

"Okay."

"There is no curfew. Those keys will get you in and out of the house and into your room. The big key is for your room, and the smaller key is for the inn. I live here; my quarters are downstairs in the basement. I make breakfast upon request of the guest. In addition, we have a spa; if you don't feel comfortable with me, we have a local masseur who can come with a moment's notice. Besides that, this is your room; as you can see, you have all of the amenities you will need, including internet for working from home. Here is your bathroom; it has a stand-up shower and a basin bathtub which was built to fit two," he said while trying not to turn red.

"Finally, you have a private balcony where you can take your coffee; there is a Keurig and Nespresso maker in the kitchen with plenty of pods. I do provision runs three times a week, so if there is something that you need, please let me know, and I will add it to the list. I can get you a small refrigerator for your personal items if you would like, but feel free to store anything in the main fridge. I want this to feel like your home. We will have guests from time to time. Normally tourists stay only a night or two. Do you have any questions?"

"How do you maintain if you only have a few guests?"

"Well, the school often hosts lectures and teachers who only teach for a semester or two. Other than that, it's through my travel business."

"No modeling?" I asked jokingly and instantly regretted it as Kraven turns deep red.

"Unfortunately, I have a face only my parents can love."

"That's a lie," I tried to catch the words before they left my mouth, but it didn't work. The comment came flowing out of my mouth like a waterfall. Kraven again went beet red. "I apologize if I've been rude."

"Not at all. It's been a while since I've been complimented by…well, anyways."

I wanted him to continue. I wanted to hear what else he was going to say at the end of that sentence. However, he seemed as if he felt confused and conflicted. These feelings were also strange to me. It had been so many years since I'd flirted with a man.

"Well, I should probably wash this fourteen-hour trip off of me."

"I am sorry, yes. I need to bring you towels. I wanted them to be fresh; hence the reason I missed your arrival. I'll be right back."

"Thank you."

I looked around the room in a continued state of disbelief. I placed my suitcase on the bed. I walked into the bathroom and took my clothes off. After letting the water run, it's the perfect temperature. The faucet rains down from overhead with the ideal amount of pressure. As I step under the water, I let out an orgasmic moan as the water massages my muscles. The steam encased me, fogging the mirror as Kraven walked in with my towels. He stood there, watching me for a moment. I could feel his eyes upon me. I could tell by how his head is turned he can make out the curves of my body. I turned, looking at him as he bumped into the bed.

"I am placing your towels on the edge of the bathtub."

I feigned a jump to hide the fact that I knew he was watching me and stuck my head out of the shower, my silky jet-black hair clung to my neck and back. "Thank you so much."

"No, no, no problem," replied Kraven, stuttering. As he made his way out of the room, I called to him.

"Kraven."

"Yes."

"Can I take you up on one of those massages?"

"Of course. Let me know when you are ready."

"After this shower. I will be ready."

"The spa is downstairs. I will meet you in the room."

"Okay. Thank you again," I said, smiling and covering my face.

I could feel him smiling on the other side of the door. There is something about a new feeling of flirtation. But I don't even know if he is gay or not. I can only assume that he has a boyfriend, which I would hate to be made a fool of. As I got out of the shower, I did my hair. It's naturally curly, full-bodied, and hangs well beyond the back of my neck. Typically, it doesn't take this long to dry, but making Kraven wait is also exciting. I stood at the foot of the stairs wanting so badly to turn around, return to my room, and read a book. I had no business going down to get a massage from this man that I could already tell that I was physically attracted to. However, my legs kept moving forward. As I entered the foyer, I opened the sliding wooden doors adorned with stained glass windows. Kraven stood there, his eyes widened, and I didn't know exactly how to take it.

"Wow."

"What?"

"Your hair."

"What about it?"

"It's beautiful; I'm sorry this is so inappropriate."

"No, it's not."

"Well, let's hope that this massage makes you feel better. Please lay down."

As I nervously moved toward the table, I laid on my stomach and placed my head in the hole at the top of the table.

"It's been a while since I've treated myself to a massage."

"Not very many people take the time for self-care. That's one of the reasons I bought this place. It sat at a perfect angle with the beautiful river and overlooks the forest, hills, and mountains."

"That sounds amazing."

"Well, now we are going to stop talking; I am going to turn on some music, light the aroma therapy candles and incense, and begin. What kind of massage would you like?"

"What is your specialty?"

"I specialize in a number, but my take on a deep tissue basalt stone massage is the most popular."

"That sounds amazing; let's go with that one."

"As you wish."

As I closed my eyes, the room filled with the aroma of eucalyptus and citrus. I allowed my body to go limp in complete relaxation. I could hear the oil splashing into Kraven's hands as he lathered them; he then placed the stones on a warm cloth at my side. I could feel the warm rocks close to me; they juxtaposed the cool air seeping into the room from the window. Kraven started by lifting my left leg, bending it at the knee as he started with my feet. The pressure caused me to choke back a moan. I felt my body becoming warm. It wasn't the usual kind of warm; this felt different. Am I having an anxiety attack?

"Does that hurt?"

"No, I apologize. It's just been a while since someone has touched … No. It doesn't hurt."

Kraven smiled as he made his way to my right leg. Again, I did my best to maintain my composure so as to not let another moan come creeping out of my lips. The strength of Kraven's strokes melts away my pain. It's a feeling unlike anything I've ever felt. Strong, yet gentle. Firm, yet kind. Kraven worked his way to my right thigh and added additional pressure, followed by the deep strokes with the hot stone. He moved to my left thigh and did the same. He maneuvered the towel and noticed that I still had on my boy shorts. There is a good reason for this. It would be very unseemly for me to have a boner while I am getting a massage from a guy I barely just met.

"Do you mind if I remove these?"

"No, I apologize. It's a habit. Get out of the shower and put on underwear."

"No worries," Kraven says as he slides me out of the underwear, folding them beside the stones. "If you aren't comfortable being naked, I can put them …."

"No, that's not it. It's really a habit."

Forget that, it was a habit, but this time the habit was so I didn't get a boner in front of an almost complete stranger. Why did I feel the need to lie to him? I hadn't felt that need in months. I guess Luke's death made me a little bit of an asshole. Kraven began again working out the tension in my glute muscles. He then moved to the small of my back. When he reached this area, I could hear subtle cracks as if Kraven was setting my body back in alignment. The stones were an added pleasure as they rested in the sore places. Kraven finally finished with the upper back and neck, allowing the stones to rest there for a moment. As he allowed me to sit there, a faint snore startled me awake. Had I fallen asleep? I guess I'd fallen asleep on this man's table, and I don't have any shame. If you had felt what I just did, you would be sleeping too.

I nodded in and out of sleep. As I noticed that he had stopped, I lifted my head and he motioned for me to turn on my back. Kraven started with a facial massage which caused me to close my eyes again, followed by the stones upon my softly muscular pectorals. Finally, Kraven made his way down to my lower stomach and hip flexors. My eyes opened; something was wrong because I could see things that I knew weren't there. I saw distant constellations where Gods and Monsters fought, a land where fairies reigned, planets with mythical creatures. Suddenly I heard what sounded like a crackle and Kraven was to be propelled across the room into a wall. I screamed out of fear, and my body awakened, but I could only remember what I was seeing in my mind's eye.

I covered myself with the towel and looked over at a visibly shocked Kraven. I realized at that moment that I had an erection and couldn't understand why Kraven was on the ground. However, it was all too much for me to worry about. I needed to be out of his sight. I ran furiously to my room and slammed the door shut behind me. Face planting into the pillow, screaming.

CHAPTER 6: KRAVEN

I stood up shaking myself off and steadied myself as Cairo walked through the door.

"What happened to you?" asked Cairo.

"Nothing; I need to talk to Dad. Can you watch the place for about an hour?"

"Can you get Dad to unground me?"

"Yes, but you will work here for a week. Deal?"

"Deal."

I grabbed my jacket and walked out of the front door gripping my side. Blood was beginning to appear through my flannel shirt.

I sped through the winding country road and came to an impasse of trees. I closed my eyes and lifted my left hand, which caused the trees to move; a hidden route appeared before him. I turned down the road, and the trees closed behind me. As I made it to our encampment,

I saw my father standing by a house. I stepped out of the car, limping, holding my side.

"Come in; what happened to you?" Luca asked, assisting me into the shack.

"He's a lot stronger than he knows."

"What do you mean?"

"His abilities are governed by his emotions right now. He doesn't understand what's going on, and I don't know if it's the right time to explain to him what's happening. I legitimately believe that he has no clue who or what he is."

"Kraven, you know this land has magical properties. He is only going to get stronger the longer he stays here. He isn't going to understand it, so you are going to have to stay close to him."

"I know that."

"Stop it, you two, come here, my child, lay down," my grandmother said as I looked into her eyes, the color of diamonds due to the calcium buildup from the cataracts. As I laid down on the table, she lifted my shirt. I have a scar across my ribs; it's healing slowly. She touched it, which caused me to wince in pain. "I have something for this."

"I won't heal on my own?"

"You will, but you are going to need a little assistance. If he is the one from the prophecy, he is born of the first. His powers are beyond this world."

"Curara, what do you mean?"

"Give me a moment, child. Let me mix these things together, or you will have a leg growing out of your tummy. Then I will explain it to you."

She hummed as she took plants and oils and combined them in a mortar and pestle. She then brought the concoction over to me.

"Hold on to the table; this is going to burn."

I did as I was told, and as she applied it to the side, my body instantly changed, turning blue, and I could feel my fangs sliding through my lips as I opened my mouth and screamed. My breathing became heavy as she wrapped my stomach.

"I thought your father told you about the prophecy?"

"He did."

"Then why doesn't he understand?"

"Curara, it's been a long time. I honestly don't think these children believe in the prophecies anymore."

"Did you never think this would happen during your lifetime, Kraven?"

"No, we were never given a timeframe of when he was going to come or if he would even be a he or a she."

"Kraven!"

"I'm sorry, Dad."

"The reason why you won't heal fast from this scar is because we all come from his father."

"From his father? Are we related?"

"Yes, his father, and no, you aren't related in that sense," replied Luca.

"Again, Marcus's father had something to do with the creation of our people?" I asked.

"Yes," Curara said as she sat in a rocking chair beside a dimly lit fire. "You see, his father is one of the original Gods, Pontus."

"You mean to tell me that a Titan got his mother pregnant?"

"It's not the first time a God has impregnated a human woman out of lust. Poseidon, who is also a relative of his by marriage, created many demigod children."

"Curara, how am I going to tell this man that he is a demigod?"

"My child, only you know that. The prophecy doesn't allow for interference. The fates will come soon, but until then, you have to gain his trust. He is going to need you to guide him through this world and the many others that he will have access to as royalty."

"Kraven, the sun is going down; you need to get back. You know you can only trust your brother for so long."

"Okay. Curara, can I bring him here?"

"Not now, my son, but soon. You will know when the time is right."

I kissed her on the forehead and walked outside to his car. My father grabbed me by the forearm. "Are you okay with all of this?"

"I always thought it would be you," I said to him, looking sadly into his eyes.

"Why?"

"You are brave and strong and have been on this earth long enough to know the things that I don't."

"Just remember your lessons. You will be fine, son. I know it," he said, pulling my head into his chest.

"I hope so," I said, getting into the car. "I really hope so."

CHAPTER 7: MARCUS

As I waited for Kraven to return, I caught the aroma of marijuana gliding into my room from my open balcony door. I slid into a pair of UGG slippers and walked downstairs to the back. The moon is casting a beautiful reflection on the turquoise river, which is flowing so seamlessly that it almost looks as if the moon is dancing in the night sky. Sneaking around corners, I finally made my way to the patio and noticed Cairo sitting there smoking. He jumps up, attempting to hide the weed.

"It's okay. Can I get a drag?" I asked, trying my best not to sound like a desperate housewife.

"It's not a cigarette, it's...."

"Cairo, I know what it is. Can I get a drag?"

Cairo hopped up on the railing, took a drag, and passed it to me. I took the longest drag I could, which did nothing but send me into a fit of coughs.

"You good?"

"It's been a while," I replied as I struggled through coughs. Despite the slight coughing, I took yet another drag. This one went down easier as I exhaled. It was just like riding a bike. The first time I smoked weed was with Luke, and he was an expert. He would make donuts, blow the smoke out of his mouth, and inhale it back through his nose. After his parents died, he started smoking again. I didn't mind it because high sex was out of this world with him. He knew how to do things to my body. Oh snap, I just drifted away into my high mind.

"There you go," Cairo remarked as he handed the joint back to me. "You can't tell my brother about this. He would kill me," Cairo said as he passed me the blunt again.

"Your secret is mine to keep. Just as long as you hook me up every now and again."

Cairo laughs, "You aren't what I thought you were going to be like."

"What do you mean?"

"Like as a teacher. You aren't stuffy like the others. You seem...relatable."

"I'm sure they aren't that bad."

"Okay, you will see tomorrow."

I laughed at him, particularly because he has a handle on the English language, but hearing him speak slang like in his thick accent just sounded so adorable.

As we talked, I stared out into the beauty of the night. I don't know if it's the weed or if it's the location, but I can sense something different about this place. Something almost mystical, magical, but it feels like where I'm supposed to be.

"How are you taking things in?"

"That's a loaded question from a kid."

"You seem like you are struggling with something."

"I don't know. Something happened today, and I didn't feel...like myself."

"What did you feel?"

"It felt...otherworldly...powerful."

Cairo looked at me. It was a look like he knew something that he didn't want to talk about, or he couldn't talk about.

"What is it, Cairo?"

"I need to tell you something, but it's not for me to tell."

"What is it?"

"I can't say. The only thing I can say is that you must keep an open mind while you are here."

"What does that mean?" I asked, taking another drag.

Cairo jumped as car tires stopped in the distance. "That's my brother. I can't say anything else. Please promise you won't say anything, and..."

"The weed is mine. I promise. Maybe we can talk sometime next week?"

"Sure," Cairo responded as Kraven comes walking around the back porch.

"Cairo!"

"It's not mine."

"It's mine. It's mine," I said, grinning clearly high off my ass.

"Cairo, it's time to go home. Dad is waiting for you. I'll see you tomorrow after school."

"Okay, bye, Mr. Miller."

"Have a good night, Cairo," I said, winking at him. "Is he going to be okay in this darkness? Y'all don't have much light here?"

"He'll be fine. Y'all. You are very American," Kraven says mockingly as he walks toward me.

"I guess I am."

"You know I know that's his," Kraven exclaimed, taking the blunt from my hand and taking a drag. He winces in pain.

"Are you okay?"

"Yeah, you just kicked the shit out of me earlier, but I think it was an involuntary muscle spasm, nothing serious."

I clearly looked concerned as I took another drag, "I'm so sorry about that. I never meant…."

"You didn't hurt me. It's fine," Kraven replied, taking another drag.

"It's a beautiful night."

"That it is. How are you liking your stay?" he inquired.

I looked over at Kraven; the moonlight bounced off his beautifully tanned face. He turned, looking at me, noticing me staring.

"It's been wonderful."

"That sounds wonderful."

For about five minutes, neither of us said anything. We just passed the blunt back and forth until there was nothing left. My eyes were redder than the blood pulsing quickly through my veins. Kraven then turned slowly, looking at me. Well, at least it felt like it happened slowly. Everything at this moment felt like a Spanish telenovela.

"I don't know if I am high as a bird, but I want to kiss you," he said to me.

"That's quite forward." I replied, laughing, unable to control my giggle-box.

"I'm sorry. I shouldn't have..."

I stood up because I wanted to walk away. I needed to walk away from him. I would give him all of me in this state, and I didn't want to do that. I wasn't ready to do that with anyone. I turn in an attempt to walk into the house; Kraven grabs me by my forearm and pulls me in.

"Don't you want to kiss me?" he asked, my eyes became cloudy.

"I don't know. Something is just drawing me to you, and I don't know what it is. But I've felt this before...with my late husband."

"I don't..." Before Kraven was able to complete his sentence, I moved in slowly, pressing my full lips against his.

I opened my mouth, allowing Kraven's tongue in. As their tongues danced, an electrical charge ignited something in me; I was taken to that state that I was in when my body felt unusual earlier. I could feel my body becoming warm, and I saw hands reaching out for him again. A voice screams, "You will be mine!" This causes me to push back from Kraven, hitting the sturdy wooden deck.

"What is happening to me," I asked myself as I took off to my room.

"Marcus!" I could hear Kraven call out to me, but I closed the door and placed my back on it.

Kraven knocks on the door, to no answer. With my back against the door, I slid down and placed my hand over my mouth. I couldn't explain to him what I just saw while I was kissing him. He would have thought I was crazy. Hell, I thought I was crazy.

"I'm sorry," Kraven said on his knees; it sounded like his head bumped and pressed against the door.

Hearing him outside my door like this broke my heart, but I didn't know what just happened, and I was starting to scare myself. I didn't know if this was a warning from Luke from the grave or just a guilty conscience. Whatever it was, it didn't want us together.

"You have nothing to be sorry for. We should get some sleep. It's late, and I have an early morning."

"See you in the morning."

I cracked open the door.

"Good night."

Kraven smiled at me and walked away, rubbing his lips.

He looked back, and Marcus closed the door again.

CHAPTER 8: MARCUS

T he following weeks went by like a flash. I was quickly integrated into the school and was finding myself popular with the students. With the help of Cairo, I quickly became the cool teacher. One that the students would sit with at lunch and want to talk about everything American. However, amid the hustle and bustle, Kraven and I have had very little interaction with one another. What I once thought could be a roaring fire seems to be nothing but smoldering embers.

"Mr. Westmore-Miller," Sybil, the director of the school, called for me out from the hallway.

"Please call me Marcus, Sybil. Do you need something?"

"Yes, as a matter of fact. Your presence has been requested by the monarch."

"Why does he want to speak with me?"

"I don't ask why the Prince wants to speak with one of my teachers. Especially not one that he paid good money to hire."

"Oh, I see."

"When does he want to meet with me?"

"Are you available this evening?"

"I guess. Does he often want to meet with people at night?"

"He prefers the night. He seems to be very busy during the day."

"Okay, I won't ask any questions. If he is bringing money to this amazing institution, then I'll do my part."

"We thank you. Well, Kraven Dariav will help you get to your destination."

In my mind, I was saying perfect, an opportunity to see if we still had it or if he is done with me after the weird weed interaction.

"Okay, do I need to report back tomorrow?"

"That won't be necessary. He just stated that he wanted to meet with you this evening before he heads out of the country for business."

"Okay."

*****

Later that evening, as I locked the school doors, I waited outside. The night sky flashed as lightning danced through the clouds. A horse-drawn carriage stopped in front of me; I look around, and Kraven stepped down in front of me.

"You've got to be joking," I scoffed, laughing to myself.

"Unfortunately, I'm not. This is the only thing that will make it up that mountain without tearing up tires. You should also know I am the only person who is going to take you up there this late at night. The gypsies are afraid of that man," he replied as I looked into his beautiful eyes, watching his lips as they moved, looking him up and down as he held his hand out to me.

"Kraven, I feel that we need to start again."

"Why?"

"We haven't spoken in weeks; I felt like you were mad at me."

"No, I've been giving you your space."

"It's just been very busy."

"I completely understand, so I felt that I would give you your space."

"Okay."

"We can start again." He finally replied, with the biggest grin on his face.

I smiled back at him as I placed my long curly hair into a ponytail and hopped up in the front of the carriage, "What's your name?" I jokingly asked, smiling back at him.

"We're starting back that far?"

I grin, "Not necessarily."

Kraven shook his head, chuckling, "It's Kraven."

As he jumped beside me, we started our ascent up the mountain. The path is heavily laden with wood and rocks, which rocks the carriage back and forth, causing our shoulders and hands to touch. As we ride, it's as if the sky is afraid to let a droplet fall upon us.

"Why won't anyone come up here?" I asked.

"There are legends of the pale man that lives in the castle. Since the abdication of the monarchy, he's lived there and still enjoys all of the privileges of his title. However, there are tales that he never ages; he never dies," Kraven replied, trying not to look into my eyes.

"What you are saying is completely crazy," I replied, looking at Kraven questioningly. I noticed, however, as Kraven told of the legend, his face doesn't change.

"You asked me why; I told you why."

"Why are you taking me here if everyone is afraid?"

"Cairo loves you. He said you are his favorite teacher. So, when I heard you were being called upon by the crown, I knew no one was going to be willing to take you." Kraven replied, looking over at me coyly. "It also gives me time with you, and at least I know you will make it home safely. I mean, I missed you too."

"Then why don't you take me to a gelato shop? Vice..." I was stopped by the sight of the monstrous castle coming into view. I didn't even realize that it was going to be this otherworldly. As it came into view, I'd inhaled sharply and breathed it out slowly.

The castle was different from what I had expected. White, the slightest tint of grey, aged by time, enormous pillars topped by French gargoyles. Massive lion statues lined the paved path from the monstrous gate which led to the front door. As we stopped, I looked at Kraven with uncertainty in my eyes. Kraven ran to my side to help me down. His strong hands gripped my left hand as the other slowly grabbed my waist.

"I'll wait for you." He said as we stand dangerously close to one another, staring into each other's eyes.

The door opened, and the valet walked out.

"Mr. Westmore-Miller, the Prince is waiting for you in the library."

At that moment, I didn't realize I was holding Kraven's hand until I attempted to walk away. I turned back, looking into his eyes again. They looked as if he were saying let's just leave.

"1 hour," I said.

"I'm setting the alarm."

I laugh softly to myself, "Then gelato?"

"All the gelato you can stomach." Kraven smiled.

As I walked through the vast entryway, I turned around again, looking to see if Kraven was still there. A drop of rain landed on my cheek as I watched Kraven get inside the carriage. My heart fluttered as a smile traced my face. The door closed, candles seemingly came to life. I looked up at the massive door before turning. There standing before me like a beautiful porcelain statue was the Prince. Shocked, I place my hand on his chest, laughing nervously. His valet clears his throat, and I bow.

"Did I scare you?"

"I wouldn't say scared, your majesty, but it was definitely a shock seeing as your butler said you were waiting for me in the library."

"Valet."

"I'm sorry?"

"Winston isn't a butler; we call them valets."

"Oh, like on Downton Abbey. Got it."

The Prince smiled, amused by my forwardness. "I forgot you were American for a moment."

"Not by birth, but by adoption."

We began to walk towards the foyer. I was captivated by the grandeur of the castle.

"Would you like a tour?" the Prince asked.

"I'm sorry, your majesty, but what am I even doing here?"

"My name is Ciprian; please, you don't have to be so formal."

"Ciprian, I am …."

"Marcus," he responded before the words could leave my mouth.

"Now that we have gotten that out of the way, why am I here?"

"Well, it's customary for the monarch to meet new employees of the school. We are the ones who provide the means for the school to continue at no cost to the townspeople."

"That's wonderful and alarming at the same time. I almost feel like a prize cattle."

"I don't mean to alarm you."

"No, I'm sorry. I am being rude. This is one of those situations in America that we wouldn't do. It's like being hired by a firm and the CEO asking you to come to their home late at night. Everyone knows that's a recipe for disaster."

"Well, I don't want you to look at me as your boss. The money came from an old endowment that the family kept up even after we disestablished the monarchy."

"That's kind of your family."

As we walked into a vast library, there were books as far as the eye could see, and my mouth dropped.

"You like?"

"I love...being an English teacher. I can only imagine this is the library that was described in Beauty and the Beast."

"I've always hated that book. It gives such a bad connotation to royals, especially young men like myself."

This statement caused me to turn so that I could look at Ciprian. This was the first time that I could actually make out his face in the light of the fire. He isn't old; clearly in his early thirties, his eyes seemed to change color in the light. They seemed to go from blue to silver in the shadows back to blue. It was strange, but I guess not all that unusual. He was very attractive. He had cleanly coiffed hair, and his smile was captivating.

"Why are you smiling?"

"Why are you looking at me like that?" Ciprian asked in response.

"I just wanted to see what the allure of the Prince really was. I heard you never age, and your hands feel like ice."

"Oh, that legend they have been telling about my family for years to keep kids from coming into the forest. I know you don't believe in those fables."

"I can't say they eased me on the ride up," Marcus explained as Ciprian laughed to himself as he held his hands closer to the fire and then placed his palm up to my face.

His hand was warm and soft like fresh snow. I smiled, feeling the warmth, but I also felt the cold. It was as if it unlocked my guard.

"Can I ask you a question, Marcus?"

"Sure."

"Can I take you out sometime?"

I looked back at the library door. Winston stood there in the shadows. The only thing I could make out of him are what look like silver eyes. At this point, I could only think about Kraven.

"That would be nice."

"Great, when I return, I will send for you."

"Okay. Well, I have to go. With this weather and the mode of transportation down the hill, I want to make sure that I make it to our date."

"Okay. Yes, it's a date. Winston will show you out. It was a pleasure meeting you," Ciprian said, reaching back for my hand and kissing my knuckles.

In that moment, I noticed what people had mentioned. His hands were freezing. As I walked out, I kept looking back at Ciprian. I was somewhat captivated by him. I waved one last time before shuffling out of the front door. The rain was now coming down fiercely, and the lightning skipped through the clouds overhead. Kraven runs from the carriage holding a cloak covering himself as we ran back.

"I'll get you down this hill safely and then gelato."

"That sounds ..." I looked back up at the castle and could faintly make out a figure in the window looking down at the two of us. "That would be great."

I couldn't stop seeing Ciprian's face in my head the entire ride back. I shook my head, but I still saw him. With his pink lips and his beautiful eyes, he was something to behold. I wasn't expecting to like him, but there was something there. But I'm about to get gelato with another beautiful man.

"What am I doing?" I muttered to myself. All I can hear in my head was my sister's voice. "You are enjoying life."

I don't know if I'm exhausted or going crazy, but suddenly I feel the carriage stop and, with it, the rain. When I look outside the carriage window, we are in front of the Inn. I smile to myself as Kraven opens the door with the biggest grin on his face.

"I have so many different flavors of gelato and toppings as far as the eye can see."

"This is perfect."

"Well, let me return the horse to the stable out back, and I'll be in."

CHAPTER 9: KRAVEN

I went to the stables and locked up the horse, placed a bucket of feed by the door. As I made my way into the house, I noticed that the lights were all still out. I walked upstairs to Marcus's room, and he was lying on the bed with one shoe on and one shoe off. I smiled and helped take his other shoe off. I then proceeded to help him out of his clothes. Marcus didn't even move. When he was undressed, I pulled him up towards the pillows and covered his body, and kissed his forehead. I received a light shock in return. I touched my lips as I walked out of the room, closing the door behind me.

As I made my way down the stairs to my room, my scales lifted on my arms. I could feel that something wasn't right. I could hear a rustling coming from Marcus's room, which caused me to shoot back. As I got back to his room, I saw Ciprian standing at the foot of his bed. The veins in his neck began to dance in excitement as he opened his mouth displaying his healthy canine fangs. I didn't storm into Marcus's room because I wanted to see what his body would do. The closer Ciprian got to him, Marcus's body began to glow brighter and brighter. As I stepped a little closer, a floorboard creaked, which caused Ciprian to turn into a dark fog which bolted from the balcony window. I ran into the room, closing the door. As I looked down, I saw him standing in the middle of the street smiling the most sinister smile.

CHAPTER 10: MARCUS

Marissa just stared at me as I paced the floor. The morning sun came creeping into my room.

"Why are you so angry?" asked Marissa, sitting up in her bed in a dark room.

"Are you serious? Are you serious?"

"Yes, I'm serious."

"I literally just told you that I went to the castle to meet with the Prince, and everything that took place in there creeped me out. Your response back to me was? Is he cute?"

"Yeah, I wanna know if the man is fine or not?"

"I'm about to hang up on you."

"Why would you treat me like that?"

"Marissa, I am in this strange country, trying to navigate my life after Luke's death, and you want to ask me if the man is cute. I thought you were calling to see how I was doing."

"I mean, I am, but it's not often I get to talk to my brother about meeting a man. I mean, you and Luke were high school sweethearts. That was all the family knew. Luke this and Luke that. Not to speak ill of the dead, but I really felt like you should have been out there exploring life with another man instead of settling down so young."

"Marissa, you know that shit is hard for me to talk about, so I don't know why you always play like that."

"Marcus, who is playing? You were literally 19 years old when y'all got together, and that man literally insulated you with a beautiful life. Don't get me wrong, I am sure he wouldn't want you over there as a widower. Hell, you are only 36."

"Marissa."

"Marcus, you can huff and puff and call my name all you want. I said what I said. You can't stay stuck in the past. It's been almost nine months, and that man is gone. I am sure if he loved you as much as he showed you he did, he wouldn't want you out here living a life of seclusion, teaching at a school in some remote town in Romania."

"I know." I replied, sitting down in the chair as the tears overran my eyes.

"Stop that crying mess."

"I'm not crying."

"Boy, I can see you."

"Marissa, I just don't want to like this man. I mean, the Prince, but there's something about him. I wish you could have seen the way he looked at me."

"Oh, how did he look at you?"

As I looked at her in the video screen with the same expression that was written across Ciprian's face, she sat up again in the bed.

"Daaaamn, not he was looking at you like you were a snack." Marissa joked.

"See, that's why I don't tell you anything; you always making stuff into a joke."

"I'm not joking. That was a look of pure desire. So why won't you let yourself explore it?"

"Well, it's complicated."

"Marcus, what is complicated about it?"

"I can't explain it. Something seemed off."

"Off how?"

"It was weird. I guess you can say it was like he's known me for years. The weirdest part about the entire interaction was that his voice was familiar to me."

"Now that is weird."

Kraven knocked at the door and poked his head in. Marissa sat up again, and I could tell that she had seen his face. He continued to walk toward me as I turned around.

"Hey there." Kraven said, waving.

I closed my eyes trying to avoid her skeptical look.

"Well, hello there. Who are you? And why are you walking into my brother's room so early in the morning?"

"I'm Kraven, the Inn Keeper here. Just checked to see if he wanted anything for breakfast before he headed off to class today."

"Oh, well look at that. The complication."

Kraven smiled, exposing his beautiful white teeth. I opened my eyes again, looking at Marissa as he touched my shoulder, causing a slight shock. This time, Kraven doesn't move.

"Well, sis, I gotta go. Can you call me tomorrow just to check on me?"

"You know this time difference is crazy, but I will do my best."

"I love you."

"I love you too, big head, lil boy."

"Hang up first."

"You are such a weirdo. Bye, boy."

"Byeeeeeee."

I closed the computer and turned to look at Kraven.

"She seems wonderful," he exclaimed as I stood in front of him. Our faces just inches from one another.

"She is."

"Your sister? Friend?"

"Sister Marissa."

"That's wonderful that she called to talk to you."

"Yeah, I just wanted to talk to her about the interaction with the Prince."

"You didn't tell me anything about it?" Kraven responded as I attempted to slide away from his eyeline.

"I don't want to ruin what we have going…"

"But?" he continued for me.

"But I think I need to explore whatever this is."

Silence crept into the room.

"I'm not going to stop feeling what I am feeling for you, but if you want to explore this I will be here."

I turned and looked at him. He looked hurt that I would even mention dating someone else. I should feel bad about it. So many of the women in this town would have killed to be in a relationship with Kraven. But I am sitting up here trying to figure out if I want to date him or some disestablished royal. When did my life turn into one of the legendary Queen Charlotte?

"I don't want you to. I don't think I could stop feeling what I feel about you either."

Kraven walked over to me and placed his hand upon my waistline as he leaned in, giving me the warmest hug.

"I just want you to be happy. Happy here."

I can feel his lips touching the anterior part of my neck, slightly behind my ear. It causes my heart to race and the hair on my arms to stand on end. Instantly, a gust of wind causes the left balcony door to slam shut, sending glass shards cascading across the room. Kraven turned me so quickly that one would have thought he'd expected that to happen, as he blocked me from the midst of glass particles, covering my head with his massive arm as my head slid into the crease between his arm and chest. It was as if everything was happening in slow motion.

"What the hell?"

"Sometimes the wind does that. I will fix the window today. Just get off to school."

"Damnit, you are alright," I grabbed his face, noticing small scratches and specks of glass caught up in his pectorals. "I'm gonna be late, but we gotta get this cleaned up."

"Grab a bowl of oatmeal. I made it with fresh berries. There is a lunch bag on the table."

"Let me at least help you clean this arm and your face," I urged as I softly ran my hand down his temple.

"No, I'm fine. I got this. Don't be late for class. I'm a big boy," his statement was made with such humility that I didn't know what to say.

"You are the best," I replied, kissing him on the cheek as I ran downstairs, grabbed my lunch, and headed toward the door. Before I left out, I turned to Kraven who looked down from the top of the stairs. I couldn't help but notice the concerning look upon his face.

CHAPTER 11: KRAVEN

A s I spun around, wanting nothing more than to keep him safe, I saw it...the fog. Ciprian was becoming more and more emboldened and powerful with every breath that Marcus took. The fact that Marcus had chosen to see both of us is going to continue to strengthen him. At some point, Ciprian will be able to do the same thing to Marcus that his family did to Oannes.

"Let me help you clean this," Marcus said, looking confused.

"No, you have to get to school. Don't worry about this. I will get you a new door, but until I do, you can sleep in my room. I will sleep in the loft next door."

"Kraven, that's too kind. Let's talk about this more when I finish class. I don't want to put you out over something that you can temporarily fix with some plastic. Anyways, I love the night breezes here. They are cool, which will make it even better for sleeping."

Marcus kisses me on my cheek, and I want nothing more than to turn my head so that he can plant the kiss on my lips. He sprayed on a cologne that fills the room and lingers as he bolts out of the door. I couldn't help myself. The smell of the room causes my scales to ripple across my arms. The timing is perfect because he is well on his way out of the front door and down the street. I watch him from the broken balcony door and can see the fog traveling back towards the castle. I feel my fangs extend as I close the door in anger behind me.

CHAPTER 12: MARCUS

"Good Morning Class!"

"Good Morning Mr. Westmore!" The class responds in unison.

"I have an exciting assignment for you all today."

"An American movie?" Cairo blurts out in excitement.

"No, no movies until the day before spring break. That means next week."

They all moaned in disappointment. Cairo looked up at me and shrugged as if to say; I told you they wanted to see a movie.

"No, today you all are going to show me the progress you have made with your English."

As I turned my back to write the assignment on the board, I could hear one of the students boo behind my back. This made me smile because they didn't know what they would be writing about.

"Today you will create your own story. This story can be a legend, a fairytale, it can be true, it can even be a part of your family's history. Whatever you want to write about. The only thing I am going to be grading on is imagination and the use of English. How does this sound?"

They all look at me for a moment and then pulled out their notebooks. The classroom buzzed as they talked amongst themselves about what they were going to write about. I look over at Cairo and he seems like he is conflicted.

"Hey, are you okay?" I squatted next to him.

"Yes. I just want to write about something, but I think it's going to make my dad and brother mad," he replied as I took a chair next to him.

"Why would it make them mad?"

"I want to write about the gypsy history? A gypsy legend."

"That doesn't sound that bad. How about this, you write about it, and I will read it and won't tell a soul about what I read. When I give it back to you, you can throw it away or hide it. You can do whatever you want with it. We got a deal?"

Hesitantly, Cairo replied, "Deal."

As he took out his notebook and began to write, I walked away looking out of the window at the castle.

"Hey Marcus, can I bother you for a moment?" Anna asked, creeping up behind me.

"Of course, Anna. Class, keep working. I will be right back."

"So how did it go last night?"

"It went well. The Prince is a nice guy. He asked me on a date."

"Oh, my God. You are going on a date with the Prince? Where is he going to take you?"

"Hopefully nowhere."

"Oh, my dear. He doesn't do nowhere dates. He likes to take people on night trips to places in his private jet."

"I should have known you would know. You Brits love your royals and any type of royal news."

"Hey, can you blame a girl? I don't have a man, and all I do is read and scroll through Instagram and TikTok."

"Well, I will let you know as soon as I find out."

"Okay."

My phone vibrated. It was as if Anna spoke him up.

Hey, I would love to take you for the best pasta you've ever had in your life. I'm going to have a car pick you up at 5. Are you cool with that?

"Anna, you spoke him up."

She runs over looking at my phone. "What are you going to say? He is going to take you to Rome. I just know it."

"It is Friday, so I guess this would be the perfect timing for a date out of the country."

"Please say yes."

"I am kind of nervous."

"Why?"

"I don't know. The meeting was a little weird, but he is very captivating. Like, I want to get to know more about him, but I should be scared also."

She just stood there glaring at me.

"What?"

"Marcus, you are literally living one of my fictional fantasies. Please let me live through you."

I rolled my eyes. Thought about Kraven, and texted back.

Hey, that sounds like a plan. Should I pack a bag?

He replied back quickly.

No. While I am away taking a meeting you can do all of the shopping your heart desires. On me of course.

This sent me reeling because I'd never thought of myself as a kept man, or someone that could be bought.

"Anna, I don't know if I like that."

"Marcus, it just sounds like he really likes you. Don't take it personally. Maybe he doesn't know that you don't need his money."

"I guess so."

"Tell him that you want to talk to him about it tonight. You can let him know then that it didn't land well with you."

I texted back,

I don't know how I should take this, but okay. We can talk more about it when we meet tonight.

He responded again quickly.

Deal. See you soon beautiful.

I didn't know what to say so I sent him the heart-eyed emoji.

He sent me back the blushing emoji.

Anna stood there looking down at my phone. Her face beamed with light and optimism. Something I wish I felt in this moment. However, all I felt were the butterflies sinking into the pits of my stomach. Butterflies for the excitement, dropping like stones due to the thought of having to tell Kraven.

"Okay, I gotta get back to the kids."

"Please tell me how it goes."

"Will do hon."

She walked quickly back to her class, as I walked back to mine looking down at my cell phone before I placed it back in my pocket.

"Hey everyone. How are the stories going?"

"Goooood," they lingered over the word as I sat down at my desk watching them.

I pulled out my computer. I looked up at Cairo who looked as if he was frantically writing. I opened up Instagram and typed in Prince Ciprian. His page opens up and the display name is Prince Ciprian Dracula with a dragon emoji next to it. As I scrolled down there are photos with him boating, jet skiing, and sun tanning on the beach in places like Rome, Paris, and the Maldives.

As the bell rings the students came running up, placing their papers on my desk as I slammed my computer shut. Cairo is the last student to bring his paper up, and I looked into his eyes. He still seems pretty nervous as he clung to the two pages.

"Cairo, we made a deal. I won't renege."

"What is renege?"

"I won't go back on my promise. I will read it and bring it right back to you."

"Okay," he says, letting the papers go.

During my free period I read his story.

The Legend of the Sons of Oannes and the Lost Boy

Thousands of years ago, there existed a land where mankind and mythical creatures lived in co-existence. Atlantica, also known today as Atlantis. Atlantis wasn't an ordinary civilization. They had grand armies, superior technology, and the people were scholars who wanted nothing more than to protect this planet that we call Earth. One of the most notable of them went by the name Oannes. He was one of seven princes who was far more scholarly than his other notable brothers. In addition to being a scholar, Oannes was known for his great abilities as a warrior, in addition to his love of the land. Learning from a young age how to grow and maintain crops made him valuable to his father and his people.

One night the King and the Goddess of Light got into a vicious argument about the level of technology coming out of the empire. Some of their pieces were making their way to the shore and man was becoming more and more intrigued. They were starting to send more and more advanced vessels on voyages to find this place. In an attempt to foul man, the Goddess created a portal which would send the ships to what we all know as the Bermuda Triangle. Saddened by the cries of the innocent men who would lose their lives in this forever prison, the Goddess begged that the King consider moving the island.

The King declined the offer, which sent the Goddess in a rage. Not known to be vengeful, she called upon her grandson Pontus to sink Atlantis. There would be one catch. The moment that the civilization reached the water, they would turn into Merpeople. She was not sinking the civilization to murder them, but to send them through the portal. Oannes heard about this and tried to warn his father. When he didn't listen, Oannes enlisted the help of three of his friends. As a consequence of his father not heeding his warning, as the sunset upon the beautiful civilization, it shook with the force of several earthquakes. The land underneath detached, and the civilization began to bounce across the Atlantic. Oannes found himself packing a bag, but before he could leave a tidal wave pulled them under.

As the island sank into the deep, its inhabitants could be heard screaming and moaning as they too were enveloped by the ocean. Their legs merged into fins like those of dolphins yet covered in dragon-like scales. Their necks burst from the sides, giving way to ridged gills. Finally, their arms and breasts became plated like that of their tails. As Atlantis hit a huge underwater sea lake, many of the mermaids and mermen swam in other directions, while others swam back to their homes in Atlantis. The underwater lake swallowed the civilization, transporting it to another dimension.

One of the inhabitants that didn't swim back was Oannes and his three companions. They took to the waters in their new bodies and swam all over the ocean, mapping it and finding merpeople who decided to settle in places along the way. The merpeople realized when they got on land they would turn back into their human form, shedding away the tail and their blue skin. Oannes and his new tribe finally made their way through rivers and into the Black Sea. Here they came in contact with a new nation of people, my people, the Gypsies. They liked that the Gypsies considered themselves travelers.

The Gypsies realized how much help these new strangers were as they had the strength of five or six strong adult men, even the women. They integrated, and Oannes ended up falling in love with a beautiful

Gypsy woman named Paquette, my many great grandmother. Oannes taught the Gypsy people the ways of the Atlanteans and also gave of his blood so that those who were not born of Atlanteans could themselves live as Atlanteans. He placed his blood into a bowl, which never goes empty. Legend has it the bowl will continue to fill until the Atlanteans find the lost boy who can return Atlantis to its rightful place in this world.

Oannes is no longer with us. He was killed by Vlad Dracula. Vlad wanted Oannes's powers from the day that he heard of them. He called upon Oannes, requesting he come alone to the Southern Carpathian Mountains. Inside a cave, he slit Oannes's throat and drank of the blood. However, he didn't know that in order for the blood to work, it had to be given, not taken. The blood turned Vlad Dracula into a blood-thirsty savage that wanted nothing more than to kill everything in sight, and he did. He toppled armies with his strength and killed every night. The taken blood made him live as a recluse. Over the years, the Dracula bloodline lived on and the taken blood was given to all those who wanted it at the age of 16. If they did not take the blood, they would have to sacrifice themselves to the family during the Maiden Festival.

The Maiden Festival is when offspring of those who have taken the blood meet at the hosting Dracula's castle. They plot how they are going to attack the unknowing townspeople. Many locals stay in their homes as no blood taker can come in without first being invited.

The lost boy doesn't know that he is the son of a First or original God. It is said that the lost boy will have the features of night, with a streak of white hair which illustrates the light coming from the darkness. The legend doesn't know when he will come, how he will come, but it does state that the Oannes clan is here to fight with him, protect him from the blood seekers. If they fail and his essence is taken, Atlantis will never rise again, and the one who takes his essence will be the most powerful blood seeker in this cosmos.

"Hey, what are you still doing here?"

"Huh," I responded, lost in a daze from reading the piece.

"Why are you still here? We let the kids go early," knocked Sybil.

"I was just catching up on work."

"Although I love your dedication, get out of here. Enjoy your weekend."

"I will," I said, looking around for my bag.

As I pulled my reading glasses from my face, I looked outside and it was getting late. I shuffled the papers into my bag. I quickly made my way out of the school and run straight into him. Kraven.

"Hey."

"Hey."

"Cairo said they let the kids out early. I was checking because you were still here."

"Yeah, I just wanted to check on a few things."

"Okay. Well, I was able to get a tarp up on the door. So if it's too uncomfortable for you to sleep in my room, you can always sleep in yours."

"I've been meaning to tell you something... I won't be there tonight. Ciprian is taking me out and I don't think I will be back until tomorrow."

"Oh... Ciprian."

"The Prince?"

"I know who you are talking about, Marcus. I just don't understand why a man as smart as you with your means would want to be whisked off by a royal."

"Kraven, he's not a royal anymore."

"You're right. He comes from a long line of thieves."

I attempted to grab his arm, but he yanked it from me. "I'll see you when you return."

"Kraven!"

"What was that about?" Anna walks up from behind.

"Anna, I don't want to talk about it. I have to get back to the Inn and pack at least a clean pair of underwear."

"Have fun."

"Okay."

The entire walk to the Inn, all I could see in my head were the mystical illusions of what Cairo wrote. Is this what he wanted to tell me?

CHAPTER 13: MARCUS

T he flight in the private jet was lost on me. I kept going back in my mind. Why would Kraven get so angry? We talked about me seeing Ciprian just earlier that morning. He acted as if the entire situation came as a surprise to him. It wasn't my intention to hurt him in any way. As I sat there looking out at the beautiful night sky, I wondered if I should have just stayed.

"A penny for your thoughts?" Ciprian holds a glass of white wine.

"I'd rather not."

"Did I do something wrong?"

"No, I am going to take the wine. I would rather not tell you about the thoughts lingering in my head at this moment."

"If you don't want to tell me about that, at least tell me what you wanted to talk to me about earlier."

"Oh yeah."

"I don't know how I feel about you offering to buy me clothing or other things."

"I want to apologize for that. It completely escaped me that you are a man of your own means."

"Man of my own means. What a way to say it," I chuckled, sipping on my wine.

"You know what I mean. I don't want to say anything that scares you off."

"Let me tell you one thing about me. I find very little frightening."

"Is that so?"

"It is."

He moved to the seat beside me and I could feel the butterflies again. Now I can see him. Fully lit by the overhead lights on the plane that I requested stay on despite the night sky around us.

"So, if I wanted to buy you something nice you wouldn't wear it?"

"It depends on what it is. I think it's too soon for jewelry. If I'm being honest, I'm the guy that it would be wasted on because I don't wear more than these studs in my ears."

"Clothing?"

"I'm not a super designer guy. I like what I like. Now shoes…I love a good shoe, but again, where am I going other than school, the inn, and maybe a little light hiking now and again."

"That's understandable."

"What about you? I saw from…"

"No, no, don't stop now. Keep going. You saw from what?"

"I IG stalked you today."

"I figured as much. I would think you were weird had you not."

I almost choked on my wine.

"I know you saw a lot of jet setting. But I also hope you saw all of the work that I do around the world."

"Yes, I did."

He turned and looked at me, and for a moment his eyes sparkled, and I found myself feeling as if I was weightless. It's like my body became warm and I could feel something. He went to touch my hand, and I fully expected a shock, but there was nothing.

"Is everything okay?" he asked, as I assume my face displayed some level of disappointment.

"Yes, everything is fine."

I smiled as he held my hand the remainder of the flight. His hands were ice cold, but I figured there was nothing to it because I normally run pretty warm. I could feel him watching me. Examining me.

"Hello, this is your pilot speaking. We are making our final descent into Roma Urbe Airport. Here you will take a helicopter to Cagliari Elmas Airport, Sardinia."

"You flew me to Rome so you could helo me to Sardinia for dinner?"

"It's something about you."

"I felt like I was super awkward during our first meeting, so I was only assuming I would get a dinner at the castle."

"We were both awkward. It's not often I meet a gay guy that's not after me for my money."

"I didn't even know if I wanted to go out with you, let alone trying to gold digger you out of your money."

"See, that's the reason I would give you the world."

I inhaled heavily. Give me the world. I don't know if it's his old school upbringing or if he's been sheltered due to this money. This kind of talk took my breath away. It'd been a long time since a man told me he would give me the world. The last man who did that ended up being my husband.

"Before we get off the plane, I have a confession," he said, looking at me as Winston retrieved a large box from the chair.

"What is that?"

"I know that you weren't expecting this kind of lavish dinner, so I brought you a suit."

"That's not just any suit, Ciprian. That box says Dior."

"It's the classic black with the scarf. I too did some internet sleuthing, and you were very specific: classic black with black, red, and white scarf...and size 11.5 black classic Christian Louboutin's. Yeah, you said this was your dream suit and you even gave your sizes in case anyone wanted to buy them for me."

I had completely forgotten about this. Thinking that Luke would buy the outfit for me, but he didn't. He couldn't. He died. I can feel the rush of emotions coming over me. My eyes want to let the tears out, but I took a couple of deep breaths. I take the wine bottle and turn it up to my mouth, drinking deeply.

"Is something wrong?"

"I left that message for my dead husband. I completely forgot I put it up there."

"I'm sorry, Marcus. If you would like to wear what you are currently wearing, it's fine."

"I just need a moment. I'll be fine."

As the plane lands, Ciprian continued to look at me. Concern is written on his face, and although I wanted to assure him that everything was fine, I couldn't. I wasn't fine. This opened up a wound that I thought had a tough enough scab over it.

***

As they waited for me on the tarmac, I got dressed. The suit fit like a glove. The shoes too. Is this what Cinderella felt like going to the ball? As I walked off the plane, he waited for me by the stairs.

"You are a vision."

I smiled as I pulled my hair back into a half ponytail.

"Thank you. Let's get this show on the road. I am starving."

As we flew over the city, it's beautiful. I could see everything. Ciprian pointed out all of his favorite landmarks that he wants to take me to. I couldn't remember laughing or smiling so hard. As we landed, a car pulled up, and as we went out, Ciprian placed his arm around my neck, keeping my head low as we ran over and got into the town car.

"How was that?"

"It was my first time in a private jet and in a helicopter. All I can say is that anyone after you is going to really have to step it up."

Ciprian laughed, "Wait until you taste the pasta."

Winston jumps into the front seat beside the driver, and the car proceeds. They make their way through the city to a restaurant nestled upon a hill which overlooked the white sand beach.

"What is this place?"

"Somu. It's one of my favorite restaurants," Ciprian exclaimed.

"Okay."

As we got out of the car, we are greeted by a waiter. As he walks us to our table, which is surrounded by candles, Ciprian smiled at me.

"What are you thinking?" He asked.

"I don't know what I should be thinking at this point. It's beautiful," I replied, trying my best to maintain my composure.

"Well, now that we are alone, maybe I can get to know you a little better."

"What do you want to know?" I asked.

"I want to know everything you want to tell me."

"Well, ask away."

"Do you have siblings?"

"Yes, a sister. I was adopted."

"Where is your family?"

"Well, I was told that my mother died during childbirth, and my father gave me up for adoption."

"How does that make you feel?"

"I don't really know how I should answer that question."

"I'm sorry. Was it insensitive?"

"No, just different. No one has ever asked me how I felt being adopted. My adoptive parents even hate when I mention my adoption."

"Why do you think that is?"

In that moment, I stopped, which was the opportune time for the waiter to come over to the table.

"Ciao, can I offer you both something to drink?" He asked, smiling in my direction.

I couldn't help but notice that Ciprian also saw this. I smiled back in an attempt to be kind.

"I'll take …,"

Before I could answer, Ciprian replied to the waiter, "Do you have a Valdicava Brunello Di Montalcino Riserva Madonna Del Piano?"

"Your Italian is very good," the waiter replied in his thick Italian accent.

"It should be, with all of the business I do here. Do you have the bottle?"

"Let me check."

"Okay, until then can we get sparkling water?"

"With lemon," I asked, causing the waiter to look back at me smiling.

"Coming right up."

"Aren't you popular, Mr. Westmore-Miller?" Ciprian joked.

"I think people like him are only interested when they see me with a man like you. I think they instantly become intrigued. It doesn't hurt that I am American and Black."

"Well, back to our conversation."

"What was your question?"

"Why do you think your parents hate that you mention that you are adopted?"

"Oh yeah, that question. Why don't you let me ask a few questions."

"Be my guest."

"Do you kill people?"

Ciprian didn't flinch. He didn't move. He just watched me. Eerily, I didn't turn my gaze from him either.

"Two sparkling waters, one with lemon."

His eyes slowly left mine and looked over at the waiter. Again, he was looking at me with a slight grin on his face.

"What's your name?"

"Massi, Tomassi."

"Tomassi, either ask him for his phone number or do your job. But it's very unprofessional to look at my date in such a manner in front of me."

"I'm sorry, sir. We have a 2013 Valdicava Brunello Di Montalcino Riserva Madonna Del Piano."

"Thank you. I would like it and two glasses."

"Would you like a menu?"

"Unfortunately, I don't have an appetite. How about you, Marcus?"

"Glasses of wine it is. I'm good with a slice of pizza."

"As you wish. I am very sorry about that, sir."

As the waiter walked away defeated, I looked over at Ciprian. The look in his eyes was familiar, yet distant.

"Are you okay?"

"I don't know. This is the first time I wasn't the center of attention, and yours was the only attention I wanted."

"You have it."

"If you don't mind me asking, how much is this bottle of wine?"

"I don't mind. It's a little over two thousand American dollars."

"Well, I guess expensive wine is offset by inexpensive pizza."

The waiter brings the wine and pours two glasses. He looks over at Ciprian with distaste.

"Again, sir, I would like to apologize."

"It's absolutely fine."

As the waiter walked away, Ciprian ran over to him and had a conversation. I sat at the table waiting for him to come back to me. I didn't realize how fast I was drinking the wine, but it slowly began to creep up on me quickly. I then noticed Ciprian handing the young man a tip. He patted him on the back and walked back to the table.

"What was that all about?" I asked.

"I don't like feeling like a bad guy."

"You aren't a bad guy. You just stood your ground and I liked it."

"Oh, you did?"

"I think I might be slightly drunk."

"First or second glass?"

"You were talking for so long. I haven't had a drink in a while, so it's probably my second."

Ciprian takes the bottle and turns it up to his mouth, finishing it up.

"Just figured I should probably catch up."

As I smiled, Ciprian stood before me holding out his hand.

"Let's go grab that pizza. There is a little spot within walking distance."

As he grabs my hand, his hands are ice cold despite the warm temperature of the night. I look down at his hand, and he looks at me. In that instance, it was almost before my very eyes that a piece of his hair turned grey.

"I know they are cold. I want to answer the question you asked me earlier."

"Before you answer that question, did you always have that streak of grey in your hair?"

Ciprian looked at himself in the spoon.

"Yeah, it creeps out every now and then. I will dye it tonight."

"It just looked like it turned right before my eyes. Maybe I am drunk," I said laughing.

"Maybe. Back to your question."

"What question?"

"You asked me if I kill people?"

There was a moment of silence between us as we walked. Then he stopped.

"Let's enjoy pizza."

"As you wish, your highness," I replied jokingly as we walked into the small restaurant.

We ordered our pizza and walked down the street back to the car. He fed me a piece of his margarita pizza and I let him taste my white pizza. We laughed like kids. I hadn't felt like this in quite some time. I guess it's because I got into a routine. A routine to forget about Luke.

"What are you thinking about?" he asked.

"I'm just having a really good time. You aren't the monster that everyone makes you out to be."

"I don't think they intend on making me out to be a monster. It's just my family. They are very secretive. The older generations told stories to following generations, and those stories became lore."

"And you are left alone at the top of the hill."

"Not alone. I have Winston, and during the festival season my whole family will be coming to town this year."

"But for the most part you are alone."

"For the most part, I'm hardly ever home. I keep that castle for sentimental reasons."

As the car pulls up beside me, he opened my door and I got in.

"That's honorable. Do you want a family?"

"I don't know if that's in my future, but I would love someone that I can share my life with," he replied, interlocking our pinkies.

I felt something in the pit of my stomach. The butterflies. The same ones that I felt when I met Kraven, but no shock or spark, however, it was something I wanted to continue to explore.

"There you go again."

"Huh?"

"You do this thing where you are here one minute and the next minute you are gone. Your body is present, but it's like your mind is a million miles away."

"I apologize. I just get caught up in my thoughts," I replied, yawning. "Excuse me."

"Are you tired?"

"I am a bit. I had a long day."

"Would you like to fly back tonight or would you like to stay? I reserved a villa close by."

"I'd love to stay."

"Then let's head in," he replied, tapping at the backseat of the driver.

I could see the villa in the distance as we drove up the hill. It was beautiful, and there looked to be a small path that led to a beach.

However, my eyes began to get heavy. I couldn't think about going to the beach. All I wanted was to get in the shower and slide into a clean bed. Ciprian looked at me smiling. I felt the butterflies again. As we pulled up to the villa, I got out of the car and stood waiting to retrieve my things.

"Come with me. Let's get you into bed."

I followed him. At this point I even lost the desire to take a shower. I just wanted to lay down. I'd never felt like this. He didn't drug me, did he? No, he couldn't have. He is such a kind soul. Or at least he's being the perfect gentleman to me. He unlocked my room and I felt like I was walking into one of the bedrooms at Versailles. Its beauty wasn't lost on me or my tired eyes. I instantly started taking my shoes off and stripped out of my pants and shirt until I was only in a pair of boy shorts and my tank top. I turned to look at Ciprian and he had his back turned to me.

"I'm sorry. I'm just really tired, and I think I might be a little drunk."

"It's not a problem."

I crawled into bed so he didn't have to see my partially clothed body.

"You asked me earlier?"

"Mmmhmm," I replied, laying my head on the pillow.

"I want to give you your answer."

"Okay."

The room went dark.

CHAPTER 14: CIPRIAN

I am a killer."

I turned to him fully expecting him to leap from the bed and take off running down the hallway. But he didn't. I turned to look at him and he was asleep. The vintage wine had done a number on him. He's absolutely beautiful. I walked over to him and placed my hand upon his face, pushing his hair away. He slightly woke up.

"You were talking," he said.

"Get some rest. We will talk tomorrow. I have meetings in the morning, so I will only be able to meet you before we head back."

He nodded his head and rolled on his side. As I looked upon his neck, I could see the blood pumping through his strong, healthy veins. I turned from him and caught my own reflection in the mirror. The veins around my eyes were prominently displayed in red as the sockets looked almost black. I walked out of the room quickly. How am I going to get him to love me if this is the creature that he sees looking at him?

"Your Highness, the boy from the restaurant is downstairs,"

Winston groaned as he lurked toward the end of the hallway.

"I'll be right down. Give me a moment to get myself together."

"Yes, Sir."

When I reached the bottom of the stairs, I could see him standing on the patio of the villa. His hair slicked back like an Italian James Dean. I made my way to him and he turned, looking at me.

"I was a little surprised when you told me to meet you at the villa. Seeing as you lectured me for looking at your date."

"Don't worry about him. Would you like to take a walk with me down by the beach?"

"Yeah. Not really attracted to white guys, but you said you would make it worth my while."

I looked back at Winston, and he nodded at me.

"He will have three thousand euro when you return. But let's go have some fun."

"Okay."

"Do you like your job?"

"Naw, I'm saving money to move to the States so that I can become a model."

"Oh, really?"

"Yeah."

As we made it to the beach, I could feel his veins pumping blood. He was several feet in front of me, and with my speed, I closed that gap quickly. He turned to me, and before he could utter a word, my hand was over his mouth and my mouth latched to the side of his neck. He fought me with all of his might. However, being hundreds of years old comes with its advantages. His strength was nothing compared to mine; it was like a teddy bear fighting against a rock. His blood was warm, tasted like bread topped with warm garlic butter as it slid down my throat, chin, and neck. I sucked him completely dry and flung his lifeless body into the water. I could feel my skin becoming younger as I rinsed my hands in the ocean water. The blood slowly glided off my hand, turning the water a light pink. I slicked my hair back with the residual water as my skin became firmer and more youthful as I touched it.

CHAPTER 15: MARCUS

W hen I woke up the next morning, the night was a subtle haze. I remembered getting drunk. I remembered going and getting pizza. I even remembered getting into bed. Everything that followed was a blur. I quickly looked under the covers to make sure that I still had on a stitch of clothing, and I did. By my bedside lay a note from Ciprian. It read:

I am sorry that I can't be there to see your face this morning. Please enjoy the breakfast provided by the staff. I noticed you were looking at the beach, and the water is exceptionally clear this time of year. Please take the swim trunks on the table and enjoy it. I will see you later tonight. If you need anything, please call my personal assistant, Anastasia.

Yours Truly, Cip

The note made me smile. It reminded me of the notes that Luke would leave me around the house. He would leave these similar little colorful sticky notes. They said things like "don't forget your lunch," "don't forget to floss," and "if you are running late, you are already late." I missed him still. Thinking about him still stung.

I took a deep breath, got out of the bed, and walked over to the swimming trunks. They fit, but were small and tight. I guess he was into that European style. As I made my way downstairs, covered in a robe, I was greeted by the cleaning staff. They all spoke Italian, so I didn't bother them. I made my way to the veranda and helped myself to breakfast. Sitting alone was lonely, so I decided I would call Marissa. She picked up after the second Skype ring.

"Hey boo," she greeted me with the most sincere morning smile.

"Hey."

"Is everything okay?"

"Yes, everything is fine," I assured her.

"Where are you?"

"I'm in Sardinia."

"What?"

"With the Prince, Marissa."

"Whaaat? How did that happen?"

"I don't know. I was asked to meet with him that one time, and then he asked me on a date."

"To Sardinia?"

"Look, I was thinking that I was only going to be going back up to the castle for a dinner."

"But the man took you to Sardinia, Italy?"

"Yes, girl, get past that part."

"How did you get there?"

"Private jet and then helicopter."

"Marcus, stop playing with me."

"Marissa, I promise. I wasn't expecting any of this. I didn't even sleep with him," I whispered into the phone.

"Oh, I know you're lying now. That man did all of that and you ain't give up no ass?"

"Marissa! No!"

"Whatever you got, can you bottle it up for the rest of us? I mean, damn."

"Anyways, I wanna show you the views."

I picked up my phone and turned my view so that she could see the beautiful water and the path leading down to the private beach.

"Well, I be. Where is he at?"

"He left me a note. Said he had meetings today and would come for me tonight."

"That was very Pretty Woman of him."

I couldn't help but laugh at the joke because it was actually pretty funny.

"Anyways, I don't want to keep you. I just didn't want to sit here eating in silence."

"Well, what are you about to do for the entire day? Don't say tan, you already black enough as it is."

"Please don't come for my beautiful mahogany skin. After breakfast I am going to go for a swim. Then I might do a little shopping, maybe see some things."

"Well, please enjoy this little getaway."

"I will. I'll call you when I get back home tomorrow."

"Tomorrow?"

"Bye, Marissa, you doing too much," I said laughing at her.

"I love you."

"Love you more, girl. Talk soon."

"Byeeeeeee."

"Byeeee."

The phone conversation made me feel so much more comfortable being here by myself. I at least thought I would have been able to see him before he left. Nevertheless, I was excited about this beach.

"Ciao, I am finished. I am going to go down to the beach. I will be back," I said to one of the females in the kitchen as I left my plate in the sink.

She nodded at me, and I was off. I grabbed my towel and began my walk down towards the water. The waves lightly crashed upon the sand. I was in heaven. Or at least my version of it. I laid my towel down on the white sand and ran toward the water. It was warm; I had expected it to be freezing. I dived in and began swimming out. When I got far enough for my own comfort, I stopped and turned on my back and just floated. I looked up at the blue sky, which went on forever.

As I backstroked, I could hear nothing but the silence of the water. Suddenly, I was jolted out of my serenity by a bird pecking at something behind me. I hadn't noticed anything in the water before, but then again, I wasn't looking either. As I turned, I saw it. The waiter from last night. His lifeless body bobbing up and down in the water, surrounded by all types of small fish.

My chest went tight, and it felt like I imploded. This caused my body to become submerged as I kicked to get away from him. Completely submerged, I looked up at him; the expression on his face was one of shock. His jaw hung from where I kicked him. It slowly detached and fell toward me. The fish around the body were getting bigger and bigger, which prompted my flight sense, and I began kicking and swimming back to the shore as quickly as I could. When I reached the shallows, my legs felt like they were being weighed down by fifty-pound weights. I hit the ground, gasping for air, but it didn't seem like I could get air into my lungs fast enough. I couldn't scream. I couldn't call for help.

My head began to spin, and I threw up. As I crawled away from my vomit, I landed in the sand near my towel, and everything went black.

CHAPTER 16: MARCUS

Ahhhhhhhhhhhhh Lui è morto. Entrambi sono morti.

I was awakened by the screams of one of the women on the staff. My back was on fire from the sunburn I was developing, and I could taste granules of sand in my mouth. As I lifted myself from the ground, my arms gave way, causing me to once again faceplant into the sand. I wiped the sand from my face, and it felt like shards of glass. As I turned my head, I could see the young man's body had washed back ashore and was covered in small crustaceans.

I screamed, "No, no, no, no, no, no."

As the woman made her way to me with four men running down the hill behind her, I yelled out to her.

"I'm not dead. I don't know who did this. Call the Policia."

That they did. I was questioned for hours as one of the women applied aloe to my back. They wanted to speak with Ciprian, and the only thing I could do was give them Anastasia's contact information. The police ruled me out as a suspect and let me go. The officer gave me his card.

"Can I trouble you for a ride back to the main island? I can't stay here waiting on the Prince."

"That's not a problem."

We rode back to the main land with the body in a body bag positioned at the back of the boat. I looked back once and instantly got sea sick again.

"First time seeing a dead body?"

"No. First time seeing a dead body like this, yes."

The officer looked at me weird.

"My husband died earlier this year."

"My apologies."

"No worries. I've just never seen a body like that."

"I would love to say that it's my first time, but it's not. I was on the force when the mob ran a lot of Italy."

As we docked, I got out of the boat and made my way to an Uber. I messaged Kraven that I needed him to pick me up at the airport. In the time that it took the police officer to question me, I was already booking my flight back. When I got on the plane, I didn't sleep. I stayed up. I didn't want to close my eyes. Every time I did, I was back at the bottom of the ocean looking up into his lifeless grey eyes. The flight attendant brought me a vodka tonic, which helped take the edge off, but it wasn't enough. I needed to see him. I needed Kraven. He was safe.

What could do that to a person? I just kept thinking to myself. As the plane landed, I made my way off and headed directly to pick up.

There standing was Luca and Kraven. I must have been a terrible sight because Kraven bolted toward me like a track star running hurdles. Before he could reach me, I busted into tears and fell to my knees on the concrete. I didn't mind the shooting pain. At this point, feeling anything would be welcomed. He wrapped me in his arms and picked me up off of the ground. Examining me, pulling my hair back, looking at my neck.

"What happened, Marcus?"

"The waiter of the restaurant that we went to last night was killed. I found his dead body."

"What?!"

Kraven looked back at his father, and Luca shook his head. They got me into the car, and I said nothing else the entire ride back. I just peered out of the window at the now night sky. Then it happened. My WhatsApp began to buzz. It was Ciprian.

Where are you?

Why are you not responding?

Are you okay?

I didn't reply. I turned my phone off. When we made it back to the house, Kraven walked me up the stairs like I was crippled by the experience. He placed me in the bed, and I winced at the pain, turning on my stomach. He lifted up my shirt, and my dark skin was already starting to peel.

"We will take care of this tomorrow. Sleep now."

But I couldn't sleep. I heard him and Luca talking outside of my bedroom door.

"We need to bring him to her. She can help with the healing."

"No, Kraven. I think it's time that we take him to the Garden."

What was the garden? Where were they trying to take me? In my state of confusion, I guess I fell asleep.

CHAPTER 17: KRAVEN

I pulled the door closed, noticing Marcus had fallen asleep.

"Are you sure it's time to take him to the Garden? We haven't even talked to him about us."

"If Ciprian is bold enough to kill and discard a body in his father's sea, then it's time," Luca said, pulling me away from the door.

"I'm just ..."

Boom, boom, boom, three quick pounds landed upon the Inn door. We made our way down slowly so as not to wake Marcus up. As I flung the door open, my fangs became prominent. It was him...Ciprian.

"Is Marcus in?"

"How dare you show your face here?"

"Kraven, I don't wish to fight. I was told Marcus had a pretty traumatic experience today. I wanted to make sure that he was okay."

"You mean he found the body that you just carelessly flung into the sea. Yes, he did. The first message before boarding the plane was to me."

"Can you tell me that he is okay?"

"He is with us, so he is fine."

"Can I come in to see him?"

"I will not give you permission to cross this threshold. In addition, a gypsy priestess has made it so you can no longer enter via the balcony either."

Before I knew it, he was face to face with me. Me inside of the house, him standing inches before the doorway. The veins in his eyes bulged in anger as his canine teeth were also now on full display.

"You aren't going to be able to keep him from me. I will visit him in his dreams. He will come back to me."

"Not if I have anything to do with it."

"Kraven, he will come because he is going to have questions. And when he does I am going to give him all of the answers."

"Don't forget how we killed your dear old uncle Ciprian."

"Kraven, you don't forget how we killed Oannes and your mother."

When he said my mother I leapt, turning into a tiger. My father grabbed me and held me, shutting the door.

"Kraven, now is not the time. I know how you feel about Marcus, but you must control yourself. Ciprian is a lot stronger than his uncle who was almost completely exsanguinated when we caught him off guard. Ciprian has recently fed, and you know that means he's at his most powerful."

I turned back into my human form after being calmed and made my way back upstairs. As I opened the door I saw Marcus looking down toward the street. I walked up behind him resting my head upon his shoulder. He placed his hand on my face.

"What was that sound?"

"I was angry and pushed a table. It sounded like a roar I know. That's this big old furniture."

Marcus and I watched Ciprian walk back towards the woods. He stopped, looked up into the window, and Marcus looked at him for a moment before turning his back, placing his hand upon my chest right before getting back into the bed.

"Is there something that I can do for you?"

"Can you stay with me tonight? I don't want to be alone. The memories are going to haunt my dreams. I just don't want to be left alone."

"I can stay with you."

Luca walked into the room with a glass of water and placed it at Marcus's bedside.

"I think it would be wise of me to stick around tonight also," Luca said.

"You can have my room, Dad. See you in the morning."

He came over and rubbed the back of Marcus's head. "We will take care of your back tomorrow."

Marcus cried into the pillow as Luca walked out of the door, looking back at me. I wanted to make everything alright, but I knew he was in both physical and emotional pain right now. I laid on my back and eased him onto my body. I placed my hand upon his back and he winced at the pain. I could feel the heat coming from his sunburn. As he fell asleep on me I stared at the ceiling, praying that everything would be okay.

CHAPTER 18: MARCUS

T he next morning we were awakened to the sound of construction equipment. I looked over at Kraven as he rubbed his eyes. He mistakenly touched my back, and my eyes rolled into the back of my head.

"I'm sorry. Let me help you up," he said, sliding from underneath me, walking around the bed helping me to my feet.

The entire back of my body felt like someone just ripped my skin off. I slowly walked to the window and noticed that the construction equipment stopped at the edge of the forest. There was an army of men.

"They're going to make a path to the castle," I said.

"Yeah, he has the money to blow, and he wants to make it easier to get you back up there."

"Why would you say that?"

"Because he came here last night asking about you."

"That's why I pushed the table. We were about to fight. I was trying to protect you."

"Protect me from what?"

"You mean who?"

"No Kraven, I mean from what?"

I handed him his brother's story and allowed him to read as I watched in silence. I watched his eyes scan the paper reading every single word. Then he looked up at me.

"Marcus, do you believe this?"

"It doesn't matter what I believe. I know what I saw. I saw a man who looked like he had been drained of every drop of blood in his body," I closed my eyes and I could picture it all over again. "His face was sunken in, and when the Policia got to us they said it looked like he had been dead for over five years based on the state of the body and decomposition."

"What are you saying?"

"Don't make me say it."

"Are you asking me if Ciprian is like his uncle? The uncle that you Americans have made movies about? Glorifying the atrocities leveled upon man."

"Yes," I screamed. "Tell me if he is a direct descendant of a Vampire!"

Luca came into the room. "Whoa, let's temper this conversation. Marcus, you aren't in good shape, and I would like to take you somewhere."

"Where?"

"We need to take you back to our home."

"Why?"

"There is a woman there who can heal you."

I didn't know what to say, but who was I to argue with Luca. On a Sunday of all days. We all got into the car and I sat far away from Kraven. I just looked out of the window the entire ride, my back writhing in pain. Then we approached a thick grove. I watched Luca hold up his hand and the trees parted. My eyes widened as Kraven looked at me, sitting up in his seat as if he was waiting for me to jump out of the car.

"I'm fine."

Kraven sat back and took a deep breath. Although I said I was fine, I was freaking out on the inside. My heart was racing. I had never seen trees move like that. After we drove through, they closed back as if cloaking us from anything trying to follow.

As we made it to a clearing, I am astounded by the beauty. The gypsies have created their own community, surrounded by beautiful trees. I guess the trees are meant to protect them. From what I am sure I will soon find out. As the car pulled up to a small cottage, an older woman stepped out and stood on the front porch as if she were waiting on us.

"Who is that?"

"My grandmother," Kraven replied somberly as he opened the car door and got out.

I guess I could be a little nicer. As I slowly eased out of the car, he came to my side, giving me his hand, not looking at me. Oh, he's mad. That's fine. I'm in no shape to be catering to this man's ego right now. My entire world is systematically being turned upside down. As I walked up to the older woman, I bowed. I don't know why I did it; I just did.

"Honey, you don't need to bow to me. I am just the mother of the Gypsy King. Either way, it's lost on me," she said as I looked down into her cataracts.

"I'm so sorry."

"No need to apologize either, but one thing we must take care of immediately are your emotions. You are spiraling and I can feel it."

"I'm trying to take deep breaths," I replied as tears welled up in my eyes.

"He's not mad at you. That's just Kraven."

Kraven interjected, "She is a telepath. The elders get these abilities when they get to a certain age, right before they lose a certain sense."

I couldn't help but think that isn't intrusive at all.

"Baby, it's very intrusive, but I can't help it. Your thoughts come to me as clear as your voice. So honestly, without sight, I can't tell if you are saying things out loud or if you are saying them in your mind. Nevertheless, I have a calming tea for you. It will also act as a temporary sedative so that I can fix your back."

"Okay."

"Luca and Kraven, you are going to have to wait outside."

"Why?" I asked.

"Darling, I can sense the pain that you are in. You are going to have to be completely naked for me to address all of the problem areas. Is that okay?"

"Yes ma'am."

"Okay, boys, out."

Kraven looked at me. I know my face read fear, and I know it was killing him.

CHAPTER 19: KRAVEN

W e waited two hours. I could hear Marcus's moans of pain, but after a while, everything went silent. I paced the porch.

"You are going to walk a hole in your grandmother's porch. Calm down, my son," Dad says, looking back at me.

"I'm trying."

"Have you imprinted on him?"

"No."

"Then why does it feel like your emotions are so interconnected?"

"I don't know. He slept on me last night. I know he was in a lot of pain, but now I can't hear anything."

The door slowly opens and I can make out the bandages wrapped around Marcus's chest, abdomen, and legs.

"We are done, son."

"How are you feeling, Marcus?" asked Dad, standing to his feet.

"I feel like a person again."

"Has he not activated his powers?" Grandmother asked.

"Curara!" I screamed.

"Kraven."

"Marcus, I don't think you're ready."

"Excuse me? I just spent a night in the house with a vampire. Woke up, went to the beach, and swam with a dead body. You literally just drove me through trees that moved like Crouching Tiger, Hidden Dragon, and now I can feel my back healing at a rapid rate. If you don't trust me at this point, then I need to pack my shit up and leave."

"Marcus."

"Kraven, it's not your decision. Marcus, come with me," said Dad as they made their way through the encampment towards the lake.

The lake was still, and then I saw his tail. The water rippled as the object got closer. Then out of nowhere, Cairo jumped out of the water. Marcus clung to my father's arm. His tail had transformed mid-air, but his skin remained blue and covered in an almost translucent layer of scales. Marcus turned, looking at me. I put my head down in shame, because I wished I had told him a lot earlier.

"Marcus," Cairo said, shocked to see him standing by the lake.

Marcus walked over to him as his scales began to dissipate under a layer of skin. He touched his face.

"Marcus, we are the children of Oannes, also known as the children of Atlantis. We are shapeshifting vampiric merpeople who happen to take up the ways of the gypsies when Oannes founded this colony."

"Did you say vampiric?"

"Yes."

"So you all are vampires?"

"Technically yes, however, we are pescatarian," Dad stated, trying to lighten the mood.

Marcus pinched his mouth with his pointer finger and his thumb, as if he were trying to keep himself from asking any more questions.

"I knew something wasn't right with me."

"What do you mean?" I asked.

"My entire life I never felt regular. From how my mother died, to this streak of white hair coming out of my birthmark. I don't know, I just never felt regular."

"Marcus, that's where things get interesting," Luca continued, pulling him away from the water as a group of teenagers jumped in. "Come with me."

I knew exactly where my father was taking him. We walked to the home of Oannes, which is now my home, or at least where Dad resided. Yes, we are direct descendants of Oannes. As we walked in, Dad pulled up a chair for Marcus, and he sat down. Still pinching at his mouth. Dad placed the written history in front of him and turned toward the back.

"I can't read that."

"You can't read it yet. Because your powers have not been activated. I will explain everything to you."

"Dad, you don't have to do that."

"Why not?"

I took a deep breath before continuing. The look on his face registered confusion.

"Cairo already did it."

Dad looked back at Cairo, who looked at the floor, kicking at air.

"Up until what part, Cairo?"

"I didn't say anything about how he was going to save our people," Cairo responded.

"Excuse me?"

"Marcus, the way the legend goes, the moment the figure with the streak of white shows up, the blood will no longer flow until he or she activates their powers."

"What blood?"

Dad brought over the bowl which was still filled with the blood.

"It looks full to me."

"Marcus, this blood heals our soldiers and helps our wounded. If I take three scoops, the levels will drastically decrease."

"Is that not normal of anything placed in a bowl?"

"Not this one. It never gets low. However, when you got here, it hasn't replenished itself."

"So is there something that I need to do?"

"Marcus, tomorrow Kraven and I will explain more. This is already a lot of information. If you have any more questions, Kraven can talk you through it. I just wanted to give you time to digest what you've already learned."

Marcus turned to me.

"Is this what happened when you were giving me my massage?"

"Marcus, I really think Dad is right. It's a lot of information."

"Kraven, come here."

He pulled me by my arm away from Dad and Cairo.

"You don't get to hide stuff from me now. I am starting to think whatever is coming is going to mean life or death for me. Now can you please tell me the truth?"

"Marcus, you have an electricity inside of you. Your eyes turn blue, and the electricity is some sort of protective system inside your body. The day of the massage, a pulse of energy came from your body which sent me flying across the room. The thing about you is that you can hurt me, unlike many other mythical creatures. Merpeople have tough skin. The pulse cut me," I said, lifting my shirt and revealing my still-healing scar.

"Kraven," Marcus said, placing his fingers upon my scar. His soft, warm, delicate fingers upon my bare skin made me flinch.

"I'll be fine. I will explain more later on tonight. I'll make you dinner."

"Of course. But there is something I have to do when I get back."

"Okay."

"I don't want to hide anything from you. So I am going to tell you now, I am going to see Ciprian."

"Why?"

"I need to know more. I want to know if he killed that boy."

"Marcus, that is dangerous."

"You have to trust me. I will be okay. I just have this feeling that he wants something from me. He's not going to kill me."

"I know what he wants. He wants your blood at your full power."

"Why would you say that?"

"Because it's the thing that kept him from becoming the most powerful vamp on the face of this planet and many others. My father is currently the most powerful because he killed his Uncle Vlad Dracula with the help of Professor..."

"Abraham Van Helsing," Marcus completed his sentence. "All of that is real?"

"Yes, it's all real. Abraham was a part of a society that was created to keep the mystical world hidden from normal people. Abraham was killed by Ciprian's vengeful mother."

"This is exciting and terrifying at the same time. The sun is going down, so we should probably head back."

"I think that's a good idea," I replied. "Dad, can I borrow one of the cars to get back to the house?"

"Of course, Kraven. I'll pick it up in the morning. Drive safe."

Marcus ran over to him and gave him a big hug. "Thank you so much. Thank you for telling me the truth and opening my eyes to this new world."

Marcus looked over at Cairo and patted the top of his head.

"Hey, you owe me a conversation."

"I'll come see you tomorrow morning," Cairo responded, smiling.

Marcus smiled at him as Dad threw me a pair of keys. We hopped in the car and made our way to the trees. When we got to them, I held up my hand and they parted for me. Marcus's eyes opened wide, still in complete disbelief as we began through.

CHAPTER 20: MARCUS

I didn't know what to say on the ride back. I just kept thinking about everything that had just been told to me. The fact that there was more to tell had my mind buckling under the pressure. However, I knew that I needed to have a conversation with Ciprian. Sooner rather than later.

When we made it back to town, the construction workers had made a lot of progress, clearing most of the brush from the manmade path that already existed to get to the castle. As I got out of the car, Kraven sat there staring forward.

"I know that you're worried. Please don't be."

"Marcus, I can't help but be concerned. You're literally going into the den of someone you suspect of killing a human."

"Kraven, you said it yourself. He's waiting for me to come into my full power. Luckily, I'm not there."

"I understand, but it's in you."

"Whatever it is has yet to be activated. I can't even make it happen. See."

I focused on electricity, hoping that I could get some sparks out of my fingers as I held up my hand, and nothing happened.

"I will come back to you tonight. Unharmed. I promise."

"You promise?"

"Kraven, are you flirting with me again?"

"Marcus, from the moment I saw you, I've wanted to be with you. I want you to give us a chance."

"I have to see this through before I can commit to anything. Can you agree with that?"

"I don't have to agree with it. It's what you want, so I will not push the issue."

I kissed him on the cheek, got out of the car, and proceeded toward the mouth of the woods.

CHAPTER 21: CIPRIAN

"Winston, I can hear someone coming towards the door."

Boom, boom, boom.

There came a heavy knock, and Winston made his way toward the door. I stood in the hallway, looking to see who was revealed on the other side. As Winston opened the door, I knew exactly who it was. I could smell his honeysuckle and rhubarb cologne as the door slowly opened. Winston didn't turn to me because he knew I was standing in the shadows of the hallway.

"Prince Ciprian, it is Mr. Westmore-Miller."

"Winston, let him in."

I walked forward to meet him halfway. He didn't look afraid of me, which instinctively made me nervous. I didn't know what the gypsies had told him about me.

"Ciprian, we need to talk."

"I agree. I tried to come see you last night."

"I was in no place to see anyone last night. Today, after some things were revealed, I am in a better place."

"What was revealed?"

"That doesn't matter. Can we talk in the library?"

"Of course," I said, holding out my hand, ushering him into the room.

As he walked in, he avoided my line of sight. Now I was becoming more and more concerned that this meeting wasn't going to go well.

"Let me have it."

"Ciprian, I want this to be a mutually beneficial conversation. I don't want you to feel like I'm attacking you. You can't see me if you're going to hide parts or all of yourself from me."

"Okay."

"Ciprian, are you…"

He paused, and I could hear the fire crackling behind him.

"Are you a vampire?"

He didn't even stutter over the word. I was so shocked by his boldness that I didn't know how to react or how to spin it. I wanted to lie to him, but something wouldn't allow me to. I attempted to mesmerize him, but it wasn't working. I'd never met a person who couldn't be mesmerized. I'd heard that they existed, but I'd never met one until now.

"Yes."

He didn't move back or even flinch.

"Did you kill that boy?"

I hesitated before answering and could feel Winston's irritation in the distance.

"Yes."

"Are you going to kill me?"

"No."

"Can you show me your true self?"

I didn't want to show him the true me. I was afraid it would be the last thing he needed to see before he took off running out of my life.

"I don't want to scare you."

"You just told me you're a vampire and a murderer. If I haven't taken off by now, I doubt I will take off when you show me what you look like."

I snapped my fingers, illuminating the room with chandeliers and candles. The red veins around my eyes bulged when the lights came up, and my fangs came out. I sped up, moving inches away from his face. He didn't even wince.

"You don't scare easily."

"No, I don't."

He reached up and placed his hands on my face. He took his fingers over the veins surrounding my eyes, touching my lips and taking his fingers down my canine teeth. I grabbed his hand before he could touch the tip.

"You have to be careful. Some vamps only have one set of fangs. My descendants and many of the royal families have two. Both sets of fangs allow us to drain blood. One is used to give the blood."

"The blood?"

"Yes, the blood that turns a human into one of us. We use two when we want to completely drain our prey, like I did with the young man."

"Why did you kill him?"

"I'm very jealous, and I was starting to age. Human blood restores our youth. The more you drink, the younger you get. However, it only goes back to the day you were turned."

"Is there somewhere we can continue this conversation?" he asked.

"Let's go back to the balcony."

As we walked out onto the balcony, the moon was bright, lighting up the night sky. We looked out upon the lake, and he then looked at me.

"Ciprian, can you tell me how this all came about?"

"Of course I can."

I took a deep, full-throated breath, exhaling before I replied. For the longest time, I knew there was something wrong with my family, but I didn't bother to put my finger on it. I was a continent-hopping, yacht-sailing, cash-blowing royal. I lived a fast life and loved lots of beautiful people—men and women. However, nothing could have prepared me for my 21st birthday. I knew we were descendants of the Dracula family, pronounced Dra-cul-ya, and although my great-uncle was accused of being a vampire, nothing led me to think that this was remotely true. So, it should come as no surprise that when he arrived, I was frightened out of my skin. His hair was white as days-old snow, peppered with streaks of black; his skin, although tanned—something Eastern European—was soft yet stiff and cold, as if he had been embalmed; his eyes were the most piercing blue, and his lips the color of rose as they sat upon his strong face.

"My dear sweet child. Have your parents told you what is going to be taking place today?" he asked me.

"No, but I've only come home to receive my gifts and leave to celebrate with my friends."

"Tonight, you will not be celebrating with your friends. Your entire life is about to change," he said, grabbing my face between his index finger and thumb.

He raised his hands, and the candles that lined the once dimly lit room flickered into illumination. I wondered to myself, what if he wasn't a vampire? What if he's a witch? Not knowing the entire time, he could hear my thoughts.

"I am not a witch; a vampire I am. Over the years, we have been adorned with gifts. The gift of flight and manipulation of the elements is the oldest and the hardest. But I've had some great teachers over almost 500 years on this Earth."

I said nothing. I could feel my eyes swelling with tears that refused to leave my eye, but I said nothing. He let me down, licking a rogue tear from his thumb.

"You are about to receive the blood. Your mother has received the blood, and so has your father, as their mothers and fathers also did. However, I need to warn you there are three stages by which we have to observe."

"What are those?" I asked.

"First is if the blood takes. If the blood takes, your eyes will turn

160

from the brown they are now into the blue your parents and I share. If the blood does not take, your eyes will turn green, and this means that you are something other than a Dracula. The final stage is the worst—the blood takes, and your eyes turn red. This means you have the blood lust. Blood lust is an unquenchable thirst for blood which often makes vampires ravenous creatures."

"There are more like you?"

"Oh dear, yes. The first vampire can be dated as far back as the Atlantean Empire. Following its collapse, this vampire made its way to Europe to a land called Mesopotamia, evolving into a creature who loved land but also loved the water. The fishermen named his daughters the Sirens. His name is Oannes. But you will have time to learn all about this…if the blood takes."

"What do you mean?"

"The agreement in my consortium is that all newly formed vamps will come with me for their first decade so that I may train them on living in the in-between."

"The in-between?"

"Yes," he responded. "The world between this mortal world and the hidden world of vampirism and the mythical."

"Okay," I replied, holding my mouth wide, ready to take in the blood that I was sure he was about to give me.

"What are you doing, my child?" he asked, looking at me in confusion.

"You aren't going to feed me the blood like a cult?"

"No."

He opened his mouth, and his fangs flexed like that of a snake.

"This is the reason you have to be trained; in your fangs, you hold the venom that is the sacred blood and an additional set of teeth to help drain a prey completely dry. Give the blood to turn, the second set to kill."

As I opened my mouth to speak, his cold, icy lips clasped around the side of my neck. I could feel the blood enter my body, and then he snapped my neck. When I opened my eyes, everything looked different. I saw things that I hadn't seen before. This world was new. I looked over at my mother. That was the first time I'd seen her cry, and she was crying tears of blood. Uncle Vlad took me by the hand, and we were off. No longer was I the stupid young prince. That was the day that I became Prince Ciprian Dracula.

I looked over at Marcus. He didn't say a thing. He just looked at me.

"Thank you."

"For what?" I asked.

"For telling me the truth and the entire truth. I do have one more question," he said, looking out at the water. "Did your uncle kill Oannes?"

I hesitated. "He did."

He took a deep sigh and pushed back from the brick wall. He walked closer and closer to me until we were inches away.

"Can I kiss you?"

Shocked by the question, I stumbled over my words.

"Uh, um, yes. Please."

He leaned in, placing his rose-petal soft lips upon mine. I could feel his heart pounding, and the blood in his veins was racing. I could feel the veins in my eyes beginning to bulge again. He opened his eyes, looking at me.

"Are you hungry?"

"I am, but I won't hurt you."

I noticed that he paused in contemplation.

"Can you give me a little bit of the blood to see if I am one of you?"

I pushed back from him.

"Marcus!"

"If you don't want anything else from me, let me see."

"Marcus, if I give you a drop, it will only last for about an hour."

"Let me see."

I hesitated because this request contradicted my plans, but he didn't need to know what I was up to. I opened my mouth, and a drop of blood left my right canine tooth. Marcus opened his mouth, and it dropped on his tongue. His eyes instantly widened, and they turned green.

"Marcus, the blood isn't going to take in you. At least not from me."

"What does that mean?"

"Your eyes. They are a fluorescent green."

He walked over to the window and looked at his reflection in the window pane. His eyes were green. I knew he was thinking back to the story. He then looked at me, and I could tell he could see me in my true form. The human form was stripped entirely away. I looked like an aged hairless giant golden crowned flying fox. At this point he knew that I had lied to him again. I showed him the glamorous side of vampirism, not this side.

"Ciprian. I have to go."

He rushed toward the door and walked in, running toward the front door. I sped to him before he could get out, grabbing him by his forearm.

"Did I scare you off?"

"Absolutely not. I just need to get back. I have dinner plans with Kraven."

"Are you dating the both of us?"

"Ciprian. I am dating neither one of you. I am trying to figure things out."

"Okay. I understand."

"I'll come see you tomorrow night if that's okay with you."

"That would be perfect."

He leaned in, kissing me on the lips again before sliding out of the door.

CHAPTER 22: MARCUS

A s I walked outside, I wiped my mouth. It was like kissing a dog. All of my senses were heightened, and I kissed his true vampiric form.

Why did he lie to me again? He looked like the vampire of old horror movies. He looked like a bat big enough to carry me away. I asked him to tell me the truth. I have to think that he should have known that I would see him in his truth.

As I walked down the street, everything felt different. The world felt heightened. The lights looked brighter. I could see the moon in its actual hue. He walked out as I approached the Inn, and I could feel him. It was like a tingling, which in concert with the cool breeze, made the hair on my arms stand up. Although I wanted to know what this felt like, I also felt a sense of disappointment in myself. Even my emotions were heightened.

Then I saw him in his true form. He was blue; I could see his gills on the side of his neck. His eyes were golden like medallions. As he walked toward me, he looked shocked. As I placed my hands on my cheek, I touched what I thought were watery tears, and it was blood.

"Kraven. I did something."

He ran to me, observing my neck. He thrust my head from side to side like a father looking for a hickey on his daughter.

"He didn't bite me, but he did give me a drop of his blood."

"That's why your eyes are green. His blood didn't take. Thank God."

"What does that mean?"

"It means that you are something else. My blood won't even take."

"Is that a bad thing?"

"Not necessarily. Come into the house."

The house was filled with the aroma of fresh pasta and baked bread as we walked in. I looked over at the table and became instantly famished. With everything going on, I hadn't realized that I had not had anything to eat.

"This food smells so good."

"I'm going to warn you. With the blood in your system, everything is going to be heightened. You are going to smell on a higher level. Your taste is going to be on a higher level. You are on a higher plane. It's almost like being high."

Before he could finish, I was already sitting down to eat. He was so right. Everything was elevated. I moaned in pleasure as every bite hit my tongue. He laughed at me.

"What?" I asked with my mouth full of food.

"It's funny seeing you like this. But I am still mad. You did something stupid. You don't know what the results of that could have been."

"I know," I said, continuing to feed my face. "But I told you. I was going to come back. I think the tears of blood scared you more than anything else."

"You are right."

"Can you stay with me tonight?" I asked.

"Are you sure about that?"

"Yes, my body is healing, it no longer hurts. I need you to be next to me. I'm still having dreams about the boy in the ocean."

"Is that the only reason?"

"I want you to record me on my phone. I want to see if something happens to me if I have the dream. I want to see what my body looks like when it feels like it needs to be protected."

"Marcus, I can do that. However, you need to understand when Luca and I take you…"

I looked up at him. I wanted him to finish the sentence. I wanted him to tell me where they were going to take me. I wanted it to be anywhere but in my mind. Because that was the only place that I was going into tonight. Back to the place where I saw the boy floating, looking at me with his grey eyes.

"When we take you to your true home."

"Where is my true home?"

"Marcus, I can't tell you that yet. But I do need you to keep an open mind."

"I've seen a dead body that I now know to be the victim of a vampire; I found out the man I am falling for is also a shapeshifting Atlantean vampire and that the prince who used to be a monarch is also a vampire. In addition, I learned that both of these men's families or even bloodlines have a feud based on the death of their monarchs, and I haven't taken off running. I haven't said a single thing to another human being."

I stood up from the table, wiping my face. I took my plate to the sink and walked up to Kraven. I could see the shimmering of his scales underneath his skin. He is gorgeous. I touched his face and could feel them on my fingertips.

"I think…I've kept a pretty open mind."

He looked at me as if he had seen me again for the very first time. I smiled at him.

"So, are you going to sleep with me?"

"You don't want me to sleep with you. You want me to observe you, so I will do that."

I took him by the hand and walked him up the stairs. We walked into the room, and he sat in a chair across the room from me, his entire being masked by darkness. I slowly took off my clothes. Starting with my shirt. I slowly dragged it and the tank top over me, exposing my stomach and then my chest until it was over my head.

"Can you help me remove my bandages?"

"Of course," he replied, slowly turning me around like the perfect gentleman. He laid them beside my shirt.

Breathing heavily behind me, he began unbuttoning my pants, letting the zipper down. I slid them down past my knees, bending at the waist, sliding them over my feet, and dropping them on the floor.

As I stood before him, his golden eyes somewhat shimmered in the moonlight like an animal's reflecting light in the darkness. As he moved in to see me, only a piece of his face could be seen. His nostrils flared as if he were trying to catch my scent. I slid my socks off and also threw them on the floor. I stood before him in a single article of clothing as I placed my hair into a messy bun. He closed his eyes and smelled the air as I laid in the bed.

Having him in the room put me at peace. I honestly didn't want to sleep alone tonight. I knew these new revelations were going to send my mind wandering. I didn't want it to wander back into the ocean. I slowly lost sight of him as I faded to sleep. When I reopened my eyes, trying to catch myself, I was back where I didn't want to be. In the ocean. However, this time, the young man was floating directly in front of me. He reached for me. I slowly held my hand out to him. He grabbed me by the arm, spinning me in the water as he moved near my ear.

"You are a disgrace. Falling in love with a murderer!" he screamed.

A great white shark barreled toward me. I tried to swim, but nothing happened, and the shark's mouth was opening. I closed my eyes and awaited the end.

CHAPTER 23: KRAVEN

A s I watched him, he quickly fell asleep. I guess the day had gotten to him. In that moment, I saw his body begin to glow as it rose from the bed. He looked as if he was suspended in water, or swimming in the air. His hair moved about weightless around his face. He thrashed about as the glowing became brighter. I figured I should wake him, but I didn't, not knowing if it would result in another microburst of energy, or if it would render the same effects as waking up a person who sleepwalks, so I stood and got closer to him. As he held his hands up to block something from himself, I decided to wake him up.

"Marcus," I said, shaking his leg as the field around him vanished. He suddenly dropped from his suspended state and opened his eyes. They were still green.

"Why are you holding me?"

"Can you tell me what you saw in your dream?"

"I saw the boy again. We were floating in the water; he spun and chastised me for my continued relationship with Ciprian. A great white shark then almost attacked me until you woke me up."

"Wait here. I have a tea for you. Curara used to make it for me when I was a kid."

As I laid him down in the bed, he sat up, looking at me like a lost child with his glowing green eyes. He waited, and I mixed the tea. Lucky for me, I remembered the ingredients. I brought the tea back up to him.

"Drink this."

"What is it going to do?" he asked, smelling it.

"I had horrible nightmares as a kid. Curara made this for me so that I could sleep without them. One day Dad said in order to be able to fight the real enemy, I would have to fight the enemy that existed in my mind."

He took a sip of the tea. "So what happened?"

"That first night, nothing happened. I think the tea was still wearing off. The second night the nightmare came for me like a demon from the pits of hell. I wet the bed. On the third night, I defeated my monster. From that day forward, I was fine."

"So, are you trying to tell me that I must defeat the boy?"

"In your own time. However, tonight I would rather not see what happens if you can't defeat him. An electronic pulse can be so strong that it takes out an entire floor. I don't want to see that happen."

"I completely understand," he said as he finished the tea. I slid my clothes off and slid into the bed with him.

"Now that you've had your tea, rest on me. I got you."

I pulled him close. His light mustache tickled my hairy chest, but I enjoyed him nuzzling his head into the pit of my arm as he fell asleep again. For about an hour, I watched him before I allowed myself to fall asleep.

CHAPTER 24: MARCUS

I rolled over and inhaled his aroma. I looked at his face from my vantage point on my chest pillow. He was slowly beginning to wake up. I slid out of bed and made my way into the bathroom, then turned on the water. As I looked myself in the eyes, I noticed they were still green at the top and my usual brown at the bottom. I rubbed them both, but nothing happened. I turned, looked at my back, and it was completely healed. I stood there with my hands clenched to the sink as if I were about to fall over.

I could only assume that a shower would be so welcomed by the world at this point. The pain from my burn kept me from the shower for about two days. As I slid in, I allowed the water to wash the dead skin from my back.

"How are you doing in there?"

"I'm fine," I said, even though I was lying through my teeth.

Every time I closed my eyes, I saw him. The water.

I could feel Kraven as he hovered around the bathroom door. "You don't have to lie to me. If you want to do this on another day, we can."

"I've been waiting to uncover the truth about my birth since I was a kid. You are about to open up an entirely new world to me. No, I am not waiting another day."

He reached in and smacked me on the butt. "Then hurry up. We have to meet up with Dad soon."

I smiled as I ran the water over my face again. I closed my eyes and inhaled the steam. As I slowly opened my eyes, Ciprian stood before me.

I screamed.

I could hear Kraven drop something and take off running.

"What are you doing here?" I asked him as he stood there almost as clearly as a mortal form.

"I'm not physically here. I shared the blood with you, so I can speak to you through your mind's eye."

"So what do you see?"

"I can only see you."

"What do you want? Kraven will be here soon."

"He won't see me; he will see you in a trance-like state."

"Get out of my head."

"When are you going to come see me again?"

"It will have to be tomorrow."

"What about tonight? Come to me tonight."

"No. Ciprian. I have things to do. I still have a whole job, and I have papers that I need to get graded before class tomorrow."

"Okay."

Kraven came around the corner as Ciprian released me from my trance.

"What happened?"

"Nothing."

I know he knew I was lying, but I had to hope he only thought it was related to the dead boy.

"Get out of the shower. I am making breakfast."

"I am," I replied, as I turned the water off and held the towel lengthwise. I hid my body from him.

"Oh, you wanna hide your body now. You didn't have any shame showing it to me when we first met."

"Listen here, get out," I said, giggling.

He gave me this look that drove me crazy, like, yeah, mmmhmm. I got out of the shower, changed, and descended the stairs. My hair still clung to my neck as some pieces came free from the headwrap I had on.

"Well, don't you look like an old-school gypsy medium?"

"My name is Mr. Marcus. Call me now!"

"You are silly," he said, sliding me a bowl of oatmeal with fruit. "Eat it all; you are going to need all of your energy today for where we are going. The trip there is always hard and long. The trip back is always shorter."

"Plane?"

"No, boat."

"Kraven!"

"I know how you feel about water right now, but I am going to be with you. I promise I am going to keep you safe. Please trust me."

The level of anxiousness made it difficult to swallow. He sat down across from me.

"Ask me some questions so that we can take your mind off of this until it's actually time to do it."

"Are there other merpeople other than the Children of Oannes?"

"Absolutely. There are tribes all over the world, from the Arctic to the Antarctic and everywhere in between. Most of them left when— well, it will make more sense after today. However, most left when the Goddess of Light sent the mythical creatures from this Earth. Most of the mythical creatures that are still here are those that can survive and assimilate here."

"Assimilate?"

"Yes, they can either take on the form of humans or animals. Not every shark is a shark. Not every man is a man. There are mythical creatures walking around us all the time. A lot fewer in these regions because of your friend up on the hill, but in other locations, yes."

"Is he like the strongest creature?"

All of my life, I knew we weren't the only things in this cosmos. However, I wasn't expecting all of this. I guess I was waiting on that one day when someone revealed to us that aliens existed. Now it sounds like they do, but maybe what we think are aliens are just mythical creatures traveling from other galaxies and visiting a place they or their ancestors once called home.

"Not by a long shot. To be completely honest, the Children of Oannes are the strongest, only to be surpassed by full-blooded Atlanteans. The best way I can describe the difference: the Children of Oannes are about as strong as two or three men. Atlanteans have been described as having the strength of four or five of Alexander the Great's warriors."

"That is a stark difference. I only knew that because I had a thing for the…"

"Sacred Band of Thebes," we both said in unison.

"Yes," I replied.

"I didn't know you were a history buff," Kraven stated, almost in a state of shock.

"Undergrad dual major."

"That's awesome. History was my major in undergrad."

For a moment, I looked at him, and I saw something in him that I hadn't before. He wasn't just an amazingly handsome man. There was a depth that I hadn't yet tapped into. His rugged exterior hid his smarts.

"What?" he asked, blushing.

"Can you hear my thoughts?"

He paused for a moment and looked at me.

"Why would you ask me that?"

"Because Ciprian stated that he could hear thoughts, but he couldn't hear mine, which was something unique about me."

"No. I can't hear your thoughts. Oannes believed that the skill of listening to people's thoughts was intrusive and asked that we never use it. We can feel human emotions."

"So."

"To answer your question, Ciprian is correct. There must be something covering you because I can't feel anything. However, Dad can, and so can Curara."

"Curara?"

"Gypsy for grandmother."

"Why do you think that is?"

"It's something that happens before we..." He stopped and stood from the table. "I think it's time for us to go."

He attempted to walk away from me, but I wasn't about to allow that to happen so easily. I grabbed him by his massive bicep and stopped him.

"What are you not telling me?"

"I don't want to say anything because I want the choice to be yours independent of how history has written us."

"Written us?"

"Marcus, the thing that is not written in Cairo's story is the bond between one of the Great sons of Oannes and the savior."

"What about them?"

"The Great son of Oannes and the savior bond in such a manner that the Great son of Oannes is with him until he dies."

"Are you trying to say I am the savior, and you are that Great son of Oannes?"

"I'm trying to tell you what my people believe. I will not force you to believe anything, but you will see a lot today."

I stood there looking into his eyes. He looked sad. Like I had told him I didn't want to be with him. But, after losing the love of my life, I didn't want to experience that again. I didn't want someone to be beholden to me for the rest of my life. Losing someone that close is very hard to come back from.

"I think we should go."

"Okay."

As we sat in the car, I didn't say a word. I didn't know what to expect, and I was honestly too afraid to ask any more questions. I just found out that most things these conspiracy theorists talk about are true. How was I going to come back from that?

"You don't have to be afraid. Dad and I won't allow anything to harm you. I do need to ask you: do you know how to swim?"

"Yes. But why would I need to get into the water?"

"In order to make it to the Garden of the Gods, we are going to have to take two different portals. One is a land portal that will take us to the sea. The next will be an underwater lake that will take us through a vortex to the Gates of the Garden."

My breathing quickened.

"Marcus, are you going to be okay?"

"Yup, I just need to keep breathing."

"There is another thing that I need to tell you."

"Okay."

"Your father is the guardian of the underwater lake."

"Stop the car!"

The car came to a screeching halt, and I got out. I could feel my head spinning. It was like I had vertigo. I wanted to be level, but everything was spinning, and it felt like I couldn't get my footing. That's when his hand grabbed me and pulled me in.

"Breathe with me."

My rapid breathing was overpowered by his heaving breaths. Slow and almost melodic. I allowed my breaths to slow down. It took a little while, but everything eventually stopped spinning. Our breathing harmonized.

"I would give up my life for you. Savior or not."

I gripped the back of his shirt. Words couldn't express my gratitude.

"Before we finish this drive, I need you to explain how all of this is going to go down."

He opened up the flatbed of his truck. I sat down, and he sat next to me.

"Let me know if any of this becomes too much."

"I will."

"First, we will be teleported through the Tree of Destinations. The portal is opened by the blood of Oannes. In addition to its healing properties, that's the reason that we need the blood to continue to rise in the bowl. After we are teleported through, we will end up right over the Mariana Trench. You already know this is the deepest part of the ocean. We will then get out of the canoe and travel to the Challenger

Deep. That is the name of the ocean's bottom."

"I'm sorry, I have to stop you there. How on Earth am I going to get down there? I can't breathe underwater."

"Well, you asked about merpeople earlier. One thing I expected you to ask about was what happened when the sirens pulled men underwater."

"Well, what happens?"

"Most people thought that mermaids killed men when they pulled them under. This was only somewhat true. There is a race of mermaids that loves the taste of human flesh."

"Come on now. You aren't making things better."

He smiled, knowing that I was already scared.

"Well, merpeople have been endowed with a mythical property called the Amphibia. This is the ability to live on land and sea. In addition to having this ability, we can give this ability by blowing into a person's mouth when they are fully submerged."

"So you mean to tell me, once I am under the water, you or Luca can breathe into my mouth, and I will be able to breathe underwater?"

"Yes, you will actually sprout gills. They explode out of the side of your neck, which sounds more painful than it really is."

"I'm about to throw up," I said as he caught me.

"Marcus, you are going to be fine. After that subtle transformation, you will watch Luca and I take on our merman form. We will then swim to the Challenger Deep, which is where we will hit the lake. The lake is covered by a layer of toxic gases. Deadly to non-mythical creatures. Before we are going to be allowed to pass through, your father Pontus will appear."

"Pontus?"

"He is the God of the Sea."

"I thought that was Poseidon."

"He will be present also. Poseidon serves at the pleasure of the God of the Sea. There is a lot that you don't understand, and you won't understand until the Gods explain them to you in their own way," Luca replied. "I've only witnessed it once. It's like an unblocking of the mind."

"When will that happen?"

"When we make it to them."

"You will feel more like your true self in the Garden. At this point, you don't know who you are. You are who people have told you you are."

I sat there, trying to digest the information. But I guess I didn't have time on my side. It was time to do it.

"Okay. We can go," I said.

"You don't seem very excited anymore."

"Kraven, I am terrified."

As I sat in the passenger seat, he looked over at me and took me by the hand. "If you weren't afraid, I would be scared. There is a healthy amount of fear in everything that we do in life. We are asking you to abandon everything you thought was real, true, and simple to expand your mind beyond human imagination. You should be scared."

Tears began to fill my eyes. I lifted my head, breathing in deeply. They slowly escaped. He wiped them away.

"I told you. I will die for you. Present and future tense."

I smiled, placing my head on the window as he started the car, and we drove on.

As we made our way to the Gypsy encampment, I could see Cairo, Luca, and Curara waiting for us by the cabin. Stepping out of the car, Kraven looked visibly tense.

"What took you so long?" Luca asked in a stern voice.

"Dad, what we are asking him to do is a lot. He had additional questions, and I wanted to make him as comfortable as possible."

I watched as Luca took a deep breath. A team of men pulled a huge wooden canoe-type boat and placed it in front of a massive tree. I couldn't tell if the tree had been gutted or if it were two trees that had grown together. Luca walked over to me and looked me in my eyes.

"How are you doing?"

"I'm better. I had a moment of panic, so please don't blame Kraven. It was really me. I needed him to stop so that we could talk through what was going to take place."

"Now that you have talked through it, are you okay?"

"I can't say I'm completely okay, but I am a lot better than I was a little while ago."

"That's good to hear," he said, placing his large hand on my shoulder. "Cairo, it's time. Grab a ladle of the blood."

As we stood before the tree, Curara placed her hands on my face. "You will be fine. This is what you've been waiting for your entire life. Those recurring dreams you had as a child of the water will all make sense after today."

Her hands were soothing, like my mother's. Her face reassuring and strong. Cairo brought out the ladle and poured the blood in the dark crevice of the tree. In that moment, it was as if the tree came to life. Green lush leaves blossomed, and it began to unfurl. Beautiful blossoms and fruit sprang about. The blood slowly moved toward the center, filling the void between the two seemingly separate trees. The blood cleared, revealing a massive body of water.

"Marcus, please take a seat," Luca stated, as he grabbed my hand, leading me into the large canoe.

As I sat down, a team of men pushed. When the canoe was halfway in, Luca and Kraven jumped in. The canoe was instantly pulled through the void and into the body of water. I closed my eyes, feeling like I was in the front seat of a roller coaster. My body jerked back as my stomach was filled with butterflies. Then I felt a splash of water hit my face, which caused me to open my eyes as the sight of endless ocean overtook me. I looked back at Luca and Kraven; they were both smiling as they picked up oars and began rowing. The momentum caused my body to jerk again, almost causing me to fall backwards.

I allowed my hand to drift out as it glided across the water's surface. It felt like heaven. Deeply cold, but it made me feel a rush that I had never felt before. I closed my eyes and was instantly confronted by the shark from my dream. I rose up, which caused Kraven to stop.

"What's wrong?"

"Sharks, and other predatory ocean animals?"

Luca and Kraven laughed.

Luca responded, "Have you seen any National Geographic documentaries?"

"Yes, sir."

"Well, then, you know when other predatory animals encounter an apex predator, they scatter. The moment Merpeople get close, predators scatter."

"And if they don't?"

Kraven held up a sizeable metallic spear and exposed his fangs. "They don't make it away alive."

"Okay, and the bends?"

"Marcus, some things just don't apply to mythical creatures."

"I'm not."

"You technically are."

As much as I wanted to just trust what they were telling me, nothing in my logical mind would allow me to do so. But I needed to get it in my brain. I needed to get it there sooner rather than later because the canoe was only gliding at this point. We drifted there for a moment, and they looked at me. Luca was the first to go in. He placed his body on the side of the canoe, allowing his back to hit the water first. When he came back up, his chest revealed a red ombre breastplate and shoulder armor that looked like it came from a dragon. His blue skin was absolutely stunning, and his yellow eyes glowed like Kraven's golden medallions.

"Not what you were expecting?"

"Not at all," I said, smiling. Nervous but not as nervous as I was before he went in.

Looking at Luca distracted me until I felt the boat rock again. Kraven was sitting on the edge of the canoe now. He allowed his body to fall in the opposite direction. It took him a moment, and he returned to the top. He had a similar cobalt aquamarine colored breastplate and shoulder armor. He rested his forearms on the side as he looked into my eyes.

"It's time, Marcus."

"Okay, what do I do?"

"Sit like we did and just allow yourself to fall in. It will take away the initial shock of the cold. It will also diminish any fear of the deep that you initially have."

I turned, placing my behind on the back of the canoe; after taking a few deep breaths, I let go, allowing myself to hit the water's surface. It didn't take away the sting of the cold, but I rose to the top, quickly gasping for air.

"Shit! That was fucking cold."

Luca and Kraven laughed at me as I spit the salt water out of my mouth.

"You lied, Kraven," I said as my teeth chattered in the freezing cold.

Kraven swam up to me; his merman form was twice the size of my body, and standing six-two, that's saying something. He pulled me in and looked deeply into my eyes.

"Are you ready to go down?" he asked me.

"Yes," I replied as I continued to tremble.

"The shaking will stop soon."

We slowly drifted down into the water. I inhaled as much air as possible before becoming completely submerged in the vivid cerulean. Kraven's hair swayed weightlessly as he stared into my eyes.

"You can understand me?" he asked, and it came to me like I had echolocation.

I shook my head up and down as he grabbed me by my neck. My neck instantly became warm, and for a moment, there was a sharp pain that caused me to close my eyes. He quickly blew into my mouth. Our lips touching warmed my body. As he removed his hands, I saw a small amount of blood drifting about my face.

"Speak to me like you would if we weren't in the water," Kraven said.

"Can you understand me?"

My voice came out somewhat normal but with a slight echo. What I hadn't expected was the horrid taste of salt water. I touched my neck and felt four gills. Kraven turned quickly, as did Luca; something significant in size was coming close to us. I couldn't make it out at first, and then I had a flashback to my dream. I knew exactly what it was—a great white. Kraven pulled me by the arm, pulling me down. As the shark got closer, Luca speared it, causing the creature to drag him.

"Stay here."

"Where else am I going to go?"

Kraven took off. As Luca turned the beast into Kraven's path, he speared it in the top of its head. They both bit into the creature. I floated there as small marine animals swam by me. However, I felt like something else was out there. Down there. Something that didn't want me in the ocean. Kraven and Luca pulled their spears and allowed the shark to sink. They frantically made their way back to me. I floated as if I were suspended in place. I watched them and completely understood what Luca meant. They were apex predators and the most beautiful creatures I'd seen in my entire life. Their slick bodies were adorned with large side fins.

"Now that we've eaten, it's best that we begin moving. Your blood is still in the water, so more predators will be on their way," said Luca as he and Kraven interlocked arms with me and began swimming toward the abyss.

The speed at which we swam was disorienting. The deeper we got, the darker it became. It was in that instant the darkness began to lighten around us. I looked at both my hands, and my body glowed a bioluminescent blue.

"What is happening to me?" I asked as we continued down.

"That is how I knew you weren't ordinary. It's your body's protective reaction when it feels like it's in danger," replied Kraven.

"We're here," replied Luca as we touched what looked like the ocean floor.

"Something is here with us."

Kraven looked around as the light illuminating my body caught a shadow. It moved like a snake but was the size of a seven-story building.

"Who dares disturb my slumber?" asked a bellowing voice as the sea floor shook.

"Pontus, my Lord. It is us. The Sons of Oannes," replied Luca as the shadow moved slowly toward us.

"And who are you, boy?" the voice bellowed in the deep.

"My name is Marcus; they say I am your son."

"Who dares say such a thing!" screamed the beast, unsettling the sands and everything around us.

My voice trembled as I attempted to answer, but nothing came out. Kraven gripped my hand, and I could see that he and Luca became ever more guarded. Lightning lit the ocean, and I could see him. His body began to glow like mine, like all of the sea creatures that roamed the depths of this ocean floor. His body was that of a merman with an elongated snake's tail. His body was covered in barnacle plated armor. His face resembled a human with enormous crab claws that comprised his crown. He was enormous and handsome but terrifying.

"You can't speak now, child?"

"I'm... not a... child."

"But you claim just that, that you are my child."

"That is what I was told by a prophet."

"This prophet is a blasphemer. I have no male heirs. Only daughters. I made sure of that."

"Your grace, do you not see how his body glows like yours? Since he has not unlocked the full potential of his being, his abilities only appear when he is in danger," replied Kraven sternly.

"So you feel like you are in danger, child?"

"I don't know. My body is unsure. I am afraid. I will not lie to you."

He laughed at me. "No son of mine would ever fear me. Poseidon! Come forth."

As he called him, the sands began to swirl into a mighty waterspout. I covered my face to block the sand from my eyes as it dusted up around us. As the sand subsided, the God that we are taught rules the ocean stood before me. His merman form was three times the size of Luca and Kraven. He looked exactly like I imagined him. His tail was lapis lazuli blue, and his breastplate resembled an ancient dinosaur's. His face was stern but not scary, adorned with a long salt and pepper beard and a crown of rugged coral. In his hand, the trident of the seven seas.

"Yes, your majesty," he replied, standing beside Pontus, looking down upon me. For a moment, it almost seemed as if he was shocked to see me.

"This child says that he is my son. But I've killed every mother while their male child was in the womb."

"That would be correct... except for him."

"What do you mean?"

"I couldn't stand by and allow this child to die. I, too, was in love with his mother, and I thought if there was any possibility that the child was mine, I wanted him to live."

"So you saved him and his whore mother?"

Hearing this said about my birth mother brought tears to my eyes, but they had nowhere to go. They didn't leave my eyes.

"His mother was no whore. She was a woman in love with two men. One who happened to be a God." I stopped, not fully knowing what Poseidon was. "A Nephilim," he continued.

Pontus got closer to see me. "You do have the mark of the Nephilim. How are you even sure that he is mine?"

Before anyone could answer, a ray of light broke through the fog covering the underwater lake.

"Enough of this. I have heard enough! Pontus, this child is your blood. He is my grandchild, and he is here to see me! Let him enter," demanded a soft yet thunderous voice.

"Goddess of Light, as you wish," replied Pontus as he sternly stood. The lightning around his head began again, and I could make out his unhappy disposition accompanying a sinister smile.

Kraven and Luca approached the lake, and I stood there looking at him.

"I didn't ask for this. I didn't ask to be saved. My life would probably be much easier if he let me die with my mother."

"If you wish to die, child, I can make your wish come true," Pontus replied with a sinister look in his eyes, as his enormous face came inches from me.

Kraven and Luca turned; their armor stood boldly as spiked dorsal fins prominently displayed.

Light engulfed the sea floor around us as the voice bellowed, shaking the mountains surrounding us. "You shall do no such thing. Or you will pay with your own existence on this Earth."

Poseidon took me by the arm and swam with me toward the lake. I touched his hand. His scales were hard. He smiled down at me.

"Come with us. I have so many questions," I asked.

"All will be revealed to you in the place that you are going. When you return, I will come for you, and any additional questions you have, I'll answer."

Kraven slowly swam over to me, holding out his hand. I took it, looking back at Poseidon. He nodded his head as Pontus slithered away into the darkness.

"Are you ready?" Kraven asked.

"As ready as I can be."

We slid into the dense lake. As we made it down, it felt like a warm slime. Suddenly we were being sucked through a wormhole. I looked around, and we were surrounded by galaxies. We drifted by constellations and celestial bodies I had never seen before. Luca and Kraven no longer had their tails but still maintained their merman features. Kraven looked the way he looked after I'd taken the blood from Ciprian. Ciprian! With all of this going on, I had completely forgotten about him. As I thought about Ciprian, Luca and Kraven both grabbed a hand and stood straight as boards. I blinked, and we were standing on a golden walkway. I panned my face up and was left in utter shock. It was a Garden. It looked like the pictures portrayed of the hanging gardens of Babylon. There were three moons and creatures I had only heard about in legends and lore flying overhead.

"Welcome to the Garden of the Original Gods," Kraven said, smiling at me as my mouth hung open.

"Kraven, this is..."

"It's beautiful?"

Kraven looked at me strangely. I looked down; my clothes had changed. I was wearing what looked like a chiton made of golden silk. My skin... was glowing and felt warm. I felt my face and my hair. There was something in it. My hair, that is. I slowly walked over to the river that ran beside the walkway. As I peered in, I saw myself for the first time. My true self. I was glowing a fluorescent coral blue. My skin underneath appeared onyx, shining as if speckled with pieces of silver and gold flakes. My hair was straightened, half up and half down, flowing into soft curls. Sitting atop my head was a crown of olive-norma labradorite set with sanative moon crystals. I don't know how I knew that. It just came to me. Sitting upon the crystals laid metallic moon pieces displaying the moons in their forms. Kraven came and kneeled beside me.

"You are beautiful."

"Why do I look like this?"

"This is your true form," said Luca, looking around as if standing guard.

"Luca, what is wrong?"

"They know that we are here."

"Who does?" I asked, still slightly confused.

"The entire royal court."

"Dad, how do you know that?"

"I can feel it. Can't you?"

I thought the tingling feeling in my body was related to the way we got here. As we walked toward the towering structure, the three of us said nothing. Two massive Minotaurs stood guard outside of the entrance. They looked at us and went back to forward.

"Marcus, don't hold your breath. Everything is going to be okay. They know that we are here. You are in no danger."

"Luca, I trust you, but this is all still a bit much for me."

"A bit much, you say," replied a heavy voice in the distance.

I stopped; it was something unlike I'd ever heard. It was firm yet soft.

"Come, come, my child. You will not be harmed here. You are amongst family."

We made our way through a room riddled with hanging foliage and columns. We came to the center of the Garden. A small phoenix flew by my face, leaving a trail of warmth, blinding my first sight of them. When I regained my sight, I saw them. They sat upon thrones not as flesh and blood but in their elemental forms. The light that transcended anything that I had ever seen. The darkness that was so deep it almost enveloped you while standing still. Finally, Chaos, which took on the form of lightning and darkness, unlike any storm I'd ever laid eyes on or even imagined.

"Come, my child. You come here seeking a truth?" asked the Goddess of Light.

I could not respond, but my legs moved forward. I could not see them, but I could feel Luca and Kraven just outside of my line of sight.

"You do not speak?" asked Chaos.

"I do."

"Then what brings you here to the Garden of the Gods?" asked the God of Darkness, leaving his elemental form as he transformed into that of a man.

His skin was vanta black like the abyss, but his eyes were human-like but completely white; he stood about twenty feet as he sat upon his throne, still towering over me. The Goddess of Light, too, transformed into a beautiful female; she was full-figured, and her skin was metallic gold. Her eyes were black, but in the center, a single speck that shone like a star in the night sky amongst the blackness. Chaos stayed in its gaseous form and hovered around, suspended in the air.

"I do not know what I am. I was born into this world, and my mother was taken away from me by the God of the Sea."

"How do you know this?" asked the Goddess of Light.

"It has been told to him by the Sons of Oannes, your grace," said Luca, bowing as he spoke.

"How do you know this, Son of Oannes?" she continued.

"Oannes foretold of a prophecy, a tri-bred with hair of white would come upon my people to bring Atlantis back to earth."

"You believe that he is that tri-bred?" asked the God of Darkness.

"We do. Over these past several months, Marcus has shown us abilities that no human man should possess if not given by the Gods themselves."

"Come here, child," the Goddess of Light said as she stood to her feet. I walked closer to her. She became smaller, yet she still towered over my six-foot-two frame.

"Do you wish to know your past? If any of this is true?"

"I do."

"Your task will come at a price. It is painful."

"I understand."

"Do you still wish to proceed?"

"Yes."

"I will endow you with your desire," she said as she held her hand slightly above my head.

Instantly standing beside her, Chaos took on his human-like form. His skin was iron grey; he looked like a graven image plucked from the rib of the statue of David. His muscles rippled in the light of the Goddess, and his eyes were solid Prussian blue with streaks of lightning coming from them.

"I shall do the honors, sister," he said, grabbing her hand.

"Chaos, you have never wanted to do this."

"If he is who he says he is, I want to be the one to do the honors. He is a magnificent creature, don't you think?" he said, taking his human-like hands, gripping my chin.

I didn't move. I didn't know what to do in that instant. I just wanted it to be over so that we could leave. I never could have imagined what was going to happen next.

"As you wish, but do be gentle with the child. If he is nothing but a mere mortal with some elemental abilities, you could kill him."

Kraven screamed, "No, this is too dangerous."

"Silence yourself, or you will be removed," replied the God of Chaos as a Minotaur came stomping toward Luca and Kraven.

I held up my hand to signal I would be okay. Luca grabbed Kraven by the arm and held him back.

Chaos tilted my head back. "Open your mouth and breathe through your nose. This isn't going to be pleasant."

I did as he instructed as he returned to his elemental gaseous form. He then slipped into me—through my mouth, the sockets of my eyes, and my ears simultaneously. At that moment, I was both in my body and existing within the astral plane. I could see what was happening around me, but Luca and Kraven could not see me. I could tell that the Goddess of Light and God of Darkness could, as they stood beside one another, whispering in what looked like delight. My body, limp from its intruder, slowly rose in the air, emitting a brighter fluorescent blue aura. That's when it happened. I screamed in pain.

Something was happening. Suspended in the air, I balled up into the fetal position, gripped my hair and head in agony. It felt like hundreds of tiny bottle rockets going off in my brain. Memories started rushing back to me. Coming to Romania, Luke's funeral, fighting with Marissa, our wedding day. Back in school when Luke and I would sneak up to my room to kiss. The day we met. When I would wake up in a cold sweat after seeing the demon in the water. The day I was adopted. When Poseidon saved me. My mother murdered by Pontus. My birth. I saw beyond my life. I saw my mother healing people with her mystical abilities. I saw her loving a man. But I also saw her loving both Pontus and Poseidon. Then I saw myself in my adult form floating above the water, larger than I am, with my wings keeping me suspended. Finally, it was as if my brain had expanded so much that I felt like I was in a dense ocean of stars and celestial bodies. I felt myself inhale, and everything instantly closed in on me, and I could feel my body again.

A black tear streamed down my face. I caught it in my mouth, and Kraven screamed, "No!"

The Goddess of Light, with one motion of her hand, sent him flying back into Luca's arms.

"I told you not to interfere!" she demanded.

Suddenly a piercing pain came from my shoulder blades. They felt like they were protruding through my skin. I spun around myself to see what was happening, and I was amazed at the sight of wings. My body began to grow almost twice in size. Chaos ordered my body straight, and my arms and legs shot out. No longer six foot two. Now about twelve feet tall. My wings slowly flapped before my body returned to the ground underneath me. My mouth opened as my feet touched the ground, with my arms still splayed open wide. The God of Chaos slowly left my body. As he turned back into his human form, I slowly fell to my knees. My wings covered my body. I shook, still in pain.

Kraven ran over to me. As he touched me, my body began to shrink again, and my wings went back into my back.

"He is the tri-bred of the prophecy of Oannes. His mother was a witch, his father the God of the Sea, and his savior a Nephilim. He is an amazing creature," Chaos said, standing over me. "Your life will no longer be the same. While inside you, I unlocked the multiple syntaxes in your brain, which seemed to be under some dormant spell. This has unlocked knowledge that normal humans would not be able to remember. You can now go back in your mind to times before you were born. You can see back to a time when you never existed. These have lived through your blood. This power that has been unlocked has always flown in the blood. From every small electronic object you fried in a state of fear, to the fires that were started when you didn't know it was you. It was always inside of you."

I looked up at Kraven. "Will his eyes return to their normal color?"

"Yes," Chaos replied. "Slowly, his eyes will return to their normal color. He can still see."

"How do you feel?"

"I don't know. I feel different. Like he unlocked something in me."

"I did. You now have access to your full elemental heritage. You can cast spells like your mother, control storms, summon lightning, and manipulate water and air like your father, and you also have your Nephilim abilities from Poseidon, which consist of your wings and strength. When you call your wings out, you will also grow so that you can support the weight of them. Your natural human form cannot."

As I stood there with Kraven and Luca holding me up, the Goddess of Light walked over to me again. She smiled.

"You are among family now. If you wish to stay here, I can swipe the minds of those that know you. It will be as if you never existed."

"No, I want to go back. I don't think I'm ready to stay here. At least not yet."

"That is understandable. I am slightly concerned with the amount of power you have, letting you go back to Earth. You know what humans do when they don't understand something."

"I understand your concern, but I owe it to the Sons of Oannes to help them. If I am the one to fulfill the prophecy, I can't do it from here."

"I understand. Know that you are always welcome here. With your abilities, all you have to do is focus on the Garden, hold up your hand, and the portal will transport you here. No more traveling through the depths of the sea."

I hugged her, which seemed to come as a shock until she embraced me back. "Give your father time. He will come around."

I turned around and saw Poseidon standing in the back against a pillar. I limped over to him, hugging his massive side.

"Will I see you again?"

"You will see me soon. If you ever need me, call for me," he said. As I backed away from him, a whirlpool of water enveloped him, and he was gone.

"My child, it's time for you to go. What feels like only moments here are hours in your world."

The Goddess of Light held out her hand, and a portal formed. On the other side, we could see the bark of the tree which we came through. As I prepared to leave, a sense of sadness came over me. This was my family. A family that I'd never known. Luca and Kraven made their way through the portal; Chaos grabbed me by the arm.

"I will see you again. That tear you tasted was me. I will always be with you. I am a part of you now," he said, kissing me on the cheek as I fell back through the portal, causing the two massive trees to coil together as they closed behind me.

Kraven came to my aid. "Are you okay?"

"As okay as I'm going to be."

When I looked up, the entire encampment was standing there. My clothes hadn't changed back to what I was wearing before we left. I still wore the clothing that had changed when I entered the Garden. Some of the elders fell to their knees, while others just looked at me in complete shock.

"Things aren't going to be the same, are they?"

"I don't think so," Kraven replied as Cairo broke through the crowd.

"Mr. Westmore-Miller."

"Cairo," I replied, smiling.

"You look like royalty."

"He is, Cairo. He is the Legendary Tri-Bred!" Kraven said, screaming, holding up my hand, causing the crowd to erupt in cheer.

"It worked!" Luca came out screaming. "The bowl is filling back up! We shall have a feast tonight."

CHAPTER 25: KRAVEN

I stood on the side and watched as people showered him with praise and admiration. Still concerned about his well-being. The events of today had to have done something to him. As I saw him walking towards the lake with a drink in his hand, I jumped at the opportunity to have a moment alone with him.

"Hey there," I said, clearly startling him.

"Hey."

"How are you feeling?"

"A little weak still and very sore, but I can feel myself becoming stronger by the minute if that makes any sense."

"It actually does. The Sons of Oannes don't reach their full potential until the age of sixteen."

"So you do know what I mean."

"Yeah, the first full moon after our sixteenth birthday, we go through a full transformation. We have to spend the entire night in the water. We get our adult body armor and begin shapeshifting into whatever we can think of. Then we start our training."

"Training?"

"Yeah, we go through hand-to-hand combat training, shapeshifting training, and we get trained on the history of our people."

"Can we train?"

"You want to train?"

"Kraven, if I don't train, I don't know what I am going to be capable of. These abilities couldn't have been given to me for no reason."

"Of course. When do you want to start?"

"Tomorrow?"

"You don't think that's too soon?"

"No. I want to strengthen my abilities. I can't always rely on you to come to my rescue."

"I'll always be there as long as you'll have me."

As we stood there, I wanted so badly to kiss him. I wanted to run my hands through his hair and massage the back of his neck. We just stood there looking into one another's eyes.

"I'll always want to be near you," he said, reaching up and placing his hand on my face.

"Can you take me back to the Inn? I feel like I need to lie down."

"Of course. Let's talk to my father first."

"Okay."

We walked back to my father's house. The lights were on, and the door was cracked.

"Dad?"

"Yeah, in here, Kraven."

"We are about to head back to the Inn."

"Marcus? Good, both of you are here. We can talk about one more thing before you leave."

"What's that?" Marcus asked, looking down at the old scrolls Luca rested his hands upon.

"You see these three women?" Luca asked, pointing down at three older women.

"Yeah, who are they?" I asked.

"They are the fates," Marcus answered.

"That's right, Marcus. Two of the sisters are good, and one of the sisters is sinister. Unlike what was told throughout Greek history lessons, these women not only tell the fates of humankind, but any mythical creature that resides on Earth."

"So what does this mean for us?" I asked.

"Soon, they will come. Marcus will need to be present. They will tell us if he will be able to fulfill the prophecy. We will also be told if there are forces of darkness trying to keep him from his destiny for our people."

"He starts training tomorrow. So he will be around, Dad."

"Good. Get some rest. You are going to need it. Training with the Sons of Oannes is intense, and we don't intend on easing up for you."

"I wouldn't dream of it. I want to put these abilities to the test," Marcus said, laughing as my dad clung to him. Marcus placed his head on his shoulder as they laughed.

I had difficulty laughing; I could still feel the pain in my chest from when the Goddess of Light sent me flying across the room. I looked at Marcus and wished that he looked at me the same. As we walked out to the car, Cairo ran up to Marcus.

"Can I come see you tomorrow? We can do that thing and talk."

"After training, I'm all yours."

"Okay, have a good night."

"You too, Cairo."

Marcus and I got into the car, and I drove toward the trees. Before I could hold up my hand, Marcus held his up, and the trees moved. This was the first time that I had seen someone outside of the community able to get the trees to move. The only difference was that his eyes were closed and I could faintly make out the subtle chanting which left his lips.

CHAPTER 26: MARCUS

As we made it back to the Inn, I felt there was something that I needed to do. I looked over at the progress that was made, and it was substantial. The entrance at the mouth of the woods had been completely paved, and now looked manageable to walk up. However, now there was something inside of me that burdened me. It was him. Kraven. As the car stopped, I looked over at him. He didn't make a sound; he just looked up at the Inn. He looked like he was in a daze, and then he turned to me.

"Why must you go see him now? You know what he is. You know what you now are. What is the point in going to see him now?"

"I don't know how to answer this question for you, Kraven. I just know that there is something telling me that I can't completely shut him out."

"Marcus, I want to tell you. I don't know how many more times I am going to be here waiting for you if you continue to do this to me."

"Kraven, if that is how you feel, I completely understand. However,

I can't lock myself down to something if there is even a thought in my mind that something else is out there. It's not fair to you, and it's not fair to me."

"He is going to be the death of you, and your death is going to be something that the entire world feels. I don't know how I can make you understand that, but if this is something that you need, so be it."

He got out of the car and slammed the door so hard the glass splintered into tiny pieces. I sat there and looked at it for a while. Feeling like it represented me in this moment. Strong enough not to break, yet still splintered into so many fragile pieces. I didn't want him to feel that I was using him, but there was something that Marissa said before I left that I couldn't get out of my head. When Luke and I got together, all we saw was one another. We didn't see anyone else. He was my first for everything. My first male kiss, my first boyfriend, my first lover, my first husband. He was supposed to be my only one of all of those things. He was all I knew. Now sitting in this car looking at this beautifully broken and splintered glass, I thought to myself that I owed it to me to see what awaited me.

As I got out of the car, I was confronted by a large sign that said Maiden Festival (Targul de Fete de Pa Muntele Graine).

"Kraven, what is this?"

Still angry, he walked back over to me and looked down at the sign.

"We must have been gone for a month."

"What?"

"This is a sign for the Maiden Festival. They pick a town to do it in every year, and this year our town was selected to host. Hundreds of young people come together to find a mate."

"They come to this small town and do what?"

"The towns that host them have lots of things to do. For us being such a picturesque town, we are going to likely have a lot of people requesting tours of the mountains and the blue lakes. In addition, there is going to be live music. It's going to be like an American fair."

"So, this city is going to be teeming with people in about two weeks?"

"Three weeks, but yes. Why is that a problem?"

"That's when..."

"His family is coming. He normally leaves around the time the fair happens every year. Following the fair, towns are plagued by grieving parents who come thinking that their children have been stolen away into sex trafficking."

"Kraven, we don't know if his family..."

"Marcus, you can give them the benefit of the doubt, but my strongest recommendation is that you keep your head on a swivel since you are going to see him tonight. You should probably verify that his family will be here. At least, we will be able to put the word out to the town. We can impose a curfew."

"I will."

"Now go. Since it's so dire that you see him right now."

I didn't know what to say to him. So, I just walked away sulking towards the woods. I looked up at the sky and it was still a faint purple. The sun had barely completely set, and I was now at the mouth of the forest. I looked back to see if he was still standing there. To my surprise he was. He quickly opened the door and walked into the house. As I walked through the woods, my body felt different. The hair on my arms stood up straight, but I wasn't glowing. This was a different type of fear.

As I made my way to the gate, I could see him standing there. Waiting for me as if he had been expecting my visit. My pace didn't quicken, but when I made it to him, he embraced me.

"What happened to you?"

"Nothing."

"You said you would come see me a month ago."

"I lost track of time."

"Marcus, you haven't lied to me before, so please don't start now. Where did he take you?"

"Ciprian, does it really matter? I am here now, and I came to see you."

"Why did you come here?"

"For some reason I can't seem to keep you off of my mind. I want to get to know you better. I want to understand you. I want to make sure that I am not making a decision based on fear, but based on facts."

A cold wind suddenly whipped around the two of us. This was unusual as it was still mid-July. I shivered because I wasn't expecting it. I suddenly looked up and noticed a small cloud forming in the night sky. Was that me? Did I summon that wind without knowing it?

"Come in. Let's get you out of the weather."

"Thank you." As we walked in, he took me to a room that we had not yet visited. His bedroom. "This is a change from our last couple of visits."

"Do you not want to be here?"

"Ciprian, why am I here to begin with?"

"You came here at night. I just thought this was what you wanted," Ciprian said as he leaned in to kiss me. I dodged it, and placed the palm of my hand upon his chest.

"We have something to discuss."

Ciprian glided quickly to the opposite side of the room as if he were upset that I didn't allow him to kiss me.

"I'm all ears."

"First, don't do that."

"Do what?"

"Cower in the corner because I didn't allow you to come in for an unwanted kiss. It doesn't mean that I don't want to. However, when I am around you my head is clouded, and I very much need to be in a place to ask you the following questions."

As he sulked from the corner, back into view, I could see the veins popping out around his eyes. He looked famished and his hair had begun to turn a hue of grey.

"I apologize. I just hadn't seen you in so long, and I didn't know what to say. I thought…"

"Ciprian, just sit with me," I asked as I sat down on the bed that had clearly never been used.

"Is your family coming in town soon?"

"Why do you ask?"

"Ciprian, I asked you a question and you are deflecting. Is your family coming in town for the Maiden festival?"

"Yes," he replied, looking down at his feet, standing with his back towards me.

"Why?"

"Every Maiden festival happens around the Transformation of a new set of vampires. My family will be here in our home for the celebration this year. It will be christened with a grand ball. Mythical creatures from around the world with treaties with my family will be present."

"Are they going to kill the townspeople?"

"Marcus?!"

"Ciprian, please just answer me."

"They have been instructed not to kill any of the townspeople, only the tourists. We have to feed."

"You said mythical creatures that you all have treaties with. Why don't you have a treaty with the Sons of Oannes?"

"They killed my uncle," he screamed as his true face barreled through.

"You also killed their monarch. Don't raise your voice at me."

He breathed heavily, waiting for me to back down. At this point I couldn't back down. I felt this was the reason that I was here.

"I give you my word. There will be no townspeople killed. Only tourists that wander into my woods are open season."

How could I take his word? How was he going to be able to stop the others? I didn't want to say anything at this point. I just wanted to leave. As I made my way towards the door, he glided over towards the door, standing between it and me.

"If you care about me, you will allow this one indiscretion. Any more feeding outside of this will be done far away from this place. If I don't feed, I will eventually turn into a statue. That is what happens to vamps that deny themselves the essence of our lives. You think those stone sculptures that stand in your museums are all made of marble? Some of those are our oldest ancestors who wanted nothing more to do with this world. They allowed themselves to be given over to the world. Now they are being destroyed by those that wish to erase history."

"Ciprian, as long as no townspeople are harmed, then I will be forced to look the other way. Until then I am going to have to reconcile with what may potentially happen to some innocent souls. I do care about you. This situation is very conflicting to say the least."

As he walked over to me, he placed his hand upon my face. "Stay with me tonight. Let me enjoy sleeping beside you."

"I can't. I have class tomorrow, and as you stated I've been out for some time."

"Well until next time."

"Walk me to the door?"

"Of course."

As we walked back, I could feel that we weren't the only ones in the house. This wasn't Winston, this was someone else. As I stood before the towering door a saddened look crossed his face.

"What are you thinking about?"

"I don't think you will ever be able to love me."

"Ciprian, continue to show up as a good person and love will come. I can't flutter into flights of fancy every time I lay my eyes on a beautiful man."

I opened the door, and he grabbed my hand. "Will you be my date to the Ball?"

"If you will have me. I would be delighted. I would love to meet your parents."

"Unfortunately, my father was one of those vamps that I told you gave way to denying himself the essence of life. He decided this after he cheated on my mother with a mortal woman and fell in love. My mother killed her in the end. So that's the only family member you will be meeting from my direct lineage."

"Long live the queen," I said as I gave him a soft kiss upon his lips. I will stop soon.

"I'll be waiting."

"Good Night Ciprian."

"Good Night Marcus."

As I made my way down the hill, I could feel his eyes watching me. A dense fog surrounded the forest, and I couldn't help but think back to the when the door shattered. As suddenly as it rose it dissipated. I summoned a wind which bellowed around me, and I continued down the hill. When I made it back to the Inn, Kraven was sitting at the table. Nothing in front of him, a dim light shined behind him. I looked at him, but the vice saying anything I continued up to my room. In the room alone I stared at myself in the slightly damaged full length mirror.

"Chaos?"

For a moment nothing happened.

"Chaos please come forth."

I heard something tapping at my window and turned my back to the mirror. When I turned back around to summon The God of Chaos again my reflection was facing with its back to me. The moment it turned I realized it was a doppelganger. He was coming to me as me. I recognized him by the eyes, black with a specs of gold for the pupils.

"Yes."

"I am going to be training for the next three weeks. Can you assist me?"

"Assist you with what?"

"I need you to teach me the ways of the Great Witches."

"What makes you think that I would know the ways of the Great Witches?"

"Magic comes from Chaos."

"Who taught you that?"

"Let's just say I am not completely unread when it comes to the occult. I wanted to be a wiccan back in my teenage years."

"So, you've always had a connect to me and this side."

"I don't know if I would say that, but now it seems like more than a coincidence that when I was younger when situations happened of course they came with no explaination."

"Marcus, you've always had these abilities. They were just dormant. I had to unlock your mind. You can do whatever you set your mind too."

"With that being said, I need your help."

I watched as my doppelganger reached out of the mirror and caressed my chin.

"Whatever you need my beautiful boy."

"Will you show me the ways of the Great Witches?"

"I need to know why I am showing you the ways of the Greats."

"In about three weeks there is going to be a festival, and I am going to need to protect the town from mythical creatures."

"From the vamps? So, you want to know a simple binding spell."

"You can call it simple, but I have never done this in my life."

"What exactly do you intend on binding?"

"I want to bind the individuals that are inside of the castle to the woods. I don't want them to be able to make it out of the woods on the night in question."

"Marcus, you do understand that death is a part of life. Mythical creatures have to live also. It's just another form of population control."

"I didn't ask you that. I asked you if you could help me."

I can hear the creaking coming up the stairs. Chaos can be heard also.

"So will you show me," I asked in a whispered voice as the footsteps got closer to the door.

"Call on me in three days. I will find a binding spell powerful enough to do what you want. However, know that ever spell cast comes at a cost."

"A cost to who?"

As soon as I asked the question then came a knock upon the door and Kraven walked in.

"Who are you talking too?"

I looked at the mirror, and the reflection was mine. No longer the black eyed doppelganger.

"Myself. I am coming to grips with the summoning thing. I think I summoned a wind tonight."

"That's great. You should probably save your strength for tomorrow. Training is going to require it."

"I will," I replied looking at the mirror again.

"Are you sure everything's alright?"

"Yeah, just a little tired and mentally spent by the day."

"Well get some rest."

"I will."

"Good night, Marcus, and I'm sorry."

"You have nothing to apologize for. It's all water under the bridge."

As he closed the door, I stood there looking at the mirror. I could tell that he hadn't moved away from the door and neither had I. I waited until I heard his footsteps again. I took off my clothes and laid down in the bed. However, I was still afraid to sleep.

CHAPTER 27: MARCUS

W aking up the next morning felt like something new. Like my body hadn't rested in some time, and I woke up to my computer Skype going off.

"Hello?"

"Hey, how you …oh my goodness. Love you look like you haven't slept in several days. What have you been up too?" asks Marissa.

"It feels like I haven't slept in several days," I replied sitting down at the desk chair taking my hand through my hair.

"Is everything okay?"

"Yeah, I'm just a little tired."

"Okay that is understandable. Being a full time teacher and juggling two men. I mean I would be tired too," she said laughing lightly.

"I wanted to talk to you about that. Marissa, this is harder than you made it seem."

"What is harder?"

"Dating."

"Boy if you don't get out of here with that foolishness."

"Marissa, I'm serious. I don't think I've ever been this unprepared to do something ever, and it doesn't help that they don't like each other."

"Marcus they know about each other?"

"Yes, I don't sneak around that's for children, and we are all grown adults."

"Boy you on some new shit. I don't think I've ever heard about two guys dating the same person knowing it."

"I believe you. However, I made it very clear that I was just getting out of something really serious, and I didn't want to go back to the same thing."

"How are they both taking it?"

"They are both vying for time that I don't even feel like I have for either of them. I am really just trying to figure out who I am."

"Have you set boundaries."

"Yeah, as clear as I can," I replied as I heard footsteps approaching the door.

Suddenly I see a hand reach over Marissa.

"Who is that?"

"Come back to bed," says a deep male voice.

"It's Kyle…from school."

"Oh wow. Well I will let you go."

"No, you don't have to let me go. I've missed you for some reason. It's felt like longer than two days since we've last talked."

"I know, but I have to get ready for school."

"Okay, well call me later."

"Will do. Love you."

"Love you more."

"Bye Marcus," says the male voice mockingly.

"Shut up," Marissa says ending the call.

Three knocks come across the door.

"Are you decent?" Kraven asks.

"I am."

"Can we talk?"

"I need to get ready for class. I feel like I'm running behind and I'm super sluggish this morning."

"Those are the side effects of time travel. You should really stay home today."

"Kraven, I'll be fine."

"Marcus you can't afford to push yourself and have a slip. Remember what the Goddess said. You have powers now, and she was already concerned about allowing you back to earth as strong as you are."

"Kraven, I will come to training today, and I will come straight home afterwards and hit the bed early. I owe it to my students to show up today."

"Why?"

"Because I've been gone for a month."

"Marcus they aren't going to remember that month that you were gone. If you haven't already noticed when the Goddess sent us back, she made it so only a few people could remember that we were even gone as long as we were."

"I understand, but I still feel guilty."

"Okay. I can't continue to go back and forth with you over this. Training starts at dusk. Cairo is going to bring you there."

"Okay. I was also thinking about buying a car. Can you give me some options please. I want to do a little traveling myself."

"Where do you need to go. I can take you."

"I know you can Kraven, but sometimes I just want to explore stuff on my own."

"Did I do something wrong?" He asks walking up behind me. I could feel his breath upon the back of my neck.

I turned to him, and we were inches away from one another. "You did nothing wrong. I honestly wanted to go to a suit maker and have something prepared for the Ball."

"What Ball?"

"The Ball the Dracula will be hosting during the Maiden Festival."

"So, they are hosting a Ball for the festival."

"Yes, but we can talk more about it later. I need to get in the shower and head to class."

"Okay," he says placing his hand on my face.

"You really need to get some sleep. If you aren't up for training this evening just let me know, and I will get you some options for suit makers, and a car. However, I would feel more comfortable if you allowed me to come with you."

"I understand how you feel. We can discuss this more later today."

***

When I made it to the school everything felt different. For the longest this was what I desired. I wanted nothing more than to be a teacher. However, now I find myself distracted by the ever growing powers within me. I could feel the energy at my fingertips and I throughout the day I found myself distracted by the visons that were given to me my the Gods. Yet, I felt as if I had only scratched the surface.

"Mr. Marcus," Cairo called for me jerking me out of my distraction standing in front of my desk.

"Yes, Cairo."

"Is everything okay?"

"Just got a lot on my mind."

"Well class is almost over. Are you still coming to training this evening?"

"Yes. I wouldn't miss it for the world."

He smiled at me and walked back to his desk. I looked at the classroom of kids working diligently on their assignments. This was a place of peace. However, at this point in my life everything that I was feeling was filled with chaos. As I looked back at my laptop, I noticed in my trance I had begun writing a resignation letter to the school.

"Class, I need a moment. I will be right back. Please continue to work on your assignments."

As I walked down the hall I stopped by Anna's classroom. "Can you keep an eye out for my class. I need to step into the restroom for a moment."

She stopped and walked over to the door. "Are you sure everything is okay. You look sad."

"Yes, thanks for asking. Everything is fine."

"Okay. If I hear anything I will walk down."

"Thank you."

Proceeding to the bathroom I got inside and closed the door, locking it behind me. I allowed the water to run for a while before I scooped up a healthy amount splashing it on my face. I looked at myself in the mirror, as the beads dripped from my eye lashes, and lips. Then I called for him.

"Chaos. I need to speak to you."

For a moment nothing happened. I went down and splashed my face again trying to hide the tears that were becoming ever present as I looked at myself. When I raised my head, I was looking at my back. He again came to me in a doppelganger form. My doppelganger.

"If you keep calling me, I am afraid you will become dependent on what we have," he says staring at me with those black eyes.

"Is that you writing that letter on my laptop?"

"Unfortunately, my child I am only able to come to you in this form. I cannot take over your body in order to do the things that you really want to do."

"What do you mean…really want to do?"

"Marcus, you have a newfound sense of purpose. Something that you were unaware of prior to starting this job. It is you that wishes to fulfil this purpose."

"So, you mean to tell me that I am the one that wrote that letter in a trance like state. That I want to quit my job teaching these children."

"I won't say that you want to quit teaching the children, but I will say that you wish to do something more with the abilities that you have. You want to discover what it is that you are really supposed to be doing."

"What are you telling me?"

"I'm not telling you anything that you don't already feel. You know that you want to discover who you are. You need to take the letter and resign. You don't have time to continue these efforts as a common mortal."

"What if I don't?"

"You will find that your world begins to blur, and you aren't going to know when you can and cannot be yourself."

"Thanks for the talk. I have to get back to class."

"I'm always here if you need to talk. Just call for me."

As I reached down for the water to splash myself one last time, Chaos reached out from the mirror and grabbed my face. "You know what needs to be done, so do it."

When I blinked, my reflection was my own. I grabbed a piece of paper towel from the dispenser and wiped my face. As I walked back down to my classroom, I knew what needed to be done. I looked into Anna's class, shot her a smile, and continued into my room just as the bell rang for the end of the day.

"Alright, students, before you leave, I just want to say one thing. You all continue to make me so proud. Over these last seven months, I've learned so much about each and every one of you, and I hope that you learned something from me."

"Mr. Marcus, are you going somewhere?"

"I don't know yet, but I wanted to tell you all this... you can do anything you put your mind to, and know that I will always be here rooting for you from wherever I am."

The students looked around at each other, confused. I could feel a tear rolling down my cheek. Although these kids were older, they knew that something wasn't right about what I was saying to them. Many of them also began to tear up. As they slowly walked out of the classroom, they gave me hugs. Some even begged that I not leave. I chuckled through my tears. As I looked up, Cairo sat at his desk looking out of the window.

"Cairo, is everything okay?"

"I don't know. You tell me. You just gave a farewell speech, and you can't even tell us if you're coming back or not."

"Cairo, that isn't fair, especially coming from you."

He turned to look at me, and I could see the anger in his expression. "What do you mean it isn't fair? You literally just told my friends that you care about us, but you don't know if you can do this anymore."

I sat in a chair in front of him. "You know what's going on. I don't know if I can completely focus on this job and learn what I need to do to protect myself and my loved ones. I don't even know what I have these powers for."

"Does it really matter?"

"Yes, it does. I need to know why I've been destined to make the world a better place or if I'm destined to go live a life of solitude in the Realm of the Gods."

He looked at me, his eyes widened. "They asked you to stay?"

"They're worried that I'm too powerful to be on Earth."

"Then you know that you're going to do something great."

I stood to my feet. "I think you should head out. I need to finish this letter and give it over to the Headmistress."

"You're not just going to disappear...are you?"

As he stood, I placed my hand on his chin. "You unfortunately are stuck with me for life."

He smiled, picking up his books and bag and walked towards the door. "You have two hours before training. If I don't see you there, I am coming back for you."

"I'll be there."

"Cool."

He walked out, and I stood at my desk just looking out at the emptiness of the hallway. Not a child in sight, but I could hear them from the street. I sat back down and completed my letter. Once finished, I walked the letter down to her office. I knocked twice and she called me in.

"Hello, Marcus. How are you doing?"

"I'm doing well. I wanted to have a conversation with you."

"About what?"

"I'm afraid I need to resign."

"Resign? Why?" She asked, standing from her seat, giving me her full attention.

"Unfortunately, some personal issues have arisen, and I don't think I will be able to focus on the job at hand."

"Marcus, just talk to me. What is going on?"

"I'm sorry, Headmistress. I just don't think I will be effective doing this job. I want to resign."

"You are under contract."

"I understand, and I am willing to buy myself out of the contract."

"I'll have to speak to Mr. Dracula before I can say that is a viable option."

"Until then, I will be on leave. I need to take care of some personal things, and working is going to interfere."

"Marcus, if you need time, I can give you time. Please just don't leave."

"Speak to the Prince and let me know what he says."

"As you wish."

I stood from my chair and extended my hand. Although she had never shown much softness during my tenure, the headmistress came toward me and gave me a hug. She clung to me so tightly I could feel her heart beating. It caused my body to go warm, and tears again began to swell in the corners of my eyes.

"I will see you before the Maiden Festival."

"That's in two weeks."

"Yes, ma'am."

"I should have an answer for you by then. Until then, what do you want me to tell your students?"

"I've already said my goodbyes, but please tell them that I will see them soon."

"As you wish."

"Marcus, are you sure there is nothing that I can say or do to make you reconsider?"

"Unfortunately, right now, no."

"Okay. Well, I wish you safe travels, and if you need anything, please let us know."

"Thank you."

As I walked out of her door, Anna was standing in the hallway. I walked past her.

"Marcus, what is going on?"

"I think you should speak with the headmistress," I said as I continued out of the school doors.

***

As I walked into the Inn, Kraven sat there at the kitchen table. I walked past him and didn't say a word. He stood and followed me to my room.

"What is going on?"

"I don't understand what you are talking about."

"Cairo said you just gave the saddest farewell speech to your class."

"It wasn't the saddest; however, it was true."

"What are you doing, Marcus?"

"Kraven, I don't know! I am trying to figure it out for myself!"

I felt my knees buckle as I hit the floor. He tried to rush to me, but before he could touch me, I held up my hand and a gust of wind pushed him away.

"I need to feel this. I need to feel all of this before training. Maybe it will help me focus."

"Okay. I'll be downstairs waiting."

"I'll be down in a moment."

CHAPTER 28: KRAVEN

H e's getting stronger, using his abilities without even fully knowing their strength. As he got into the truck, he seemed despondent. He put on his seatbelt and looked at me. There was an otherworldly expression written across his face, as if the Marcus I had fallen in love with wasn't even there.

"Are you okay?"

He never replied. He just turned his head, looked forward, and placed his head against the window, closing his eyes. I started the car, and we were off. Somewhere down the road, he fell asleep. Maybe that was the problem—he hadn't been sleeping well before we left for the Garden, and I knew he couldn't have been sleeping well when we returned. I was tempted to turn the car around and take him back to the Inn, but for some reason, I kept driving.

We made it to the woods where the trees parted, giving way to the training site that lay next to the lake. It was cool out, and I could tell when I opened my car door that the breeze woke him from his sleep. It was as if the air and water were calling him. He inhaled deeply and looked at me. For a moment, I even thought I saw him smile.

"There you are," my father bellowed in his armor.

Marcus smiled at him as he pulled him in for a fatherly embrace.

"Are you ready?"

"As ready as I'm going to be," he replied, looking around at all of the warriors already immersed in hand-to-hand combat.

"Kraven, grab him some armor and a weapon," said Luca as I put my armor on.

"No weapon. I want to give these powers a whirl," Marcus exclaimed, holding his hand up and summoning wind that whipped around his entire body, pushing his hair in a whirl around his face.

"Okay. Gentlemen, take it easy on Marcus," Luca said as Marcus placed a golden breastplate over his chest.

"So how does this work?"

"You pick a fighter, and you show me what you have as far as hand-to-hand combat."

"Okay, I'll start with him." He pointed at the biggest guy besides myself in the group.

"No, absolutely not," I replied as the huge soldier walked into the center of the circle that had begun to form around Marcus.

"Kraven, he is a tri-bred. I think he will be fine."

"Dad, he doesn't even know the extent of his powers. Adonis can actually kill him."

"Adonis, you promise not to kill him?"

"You got it, but I am not taking it easy on him. I want him to scream my name," Adonis replied, smiling.

As Marcus walked towards Adonis, he held his hand out in a show of sportsmanship. Adonis smiled at him with the most sinister smile I'd seen in my life. Adonis then pushed Marcus to the ground, and at that point all hell broke loose.

Marcus propelled himself back to his feet with the assistance of a northern wind. As he began punching Adonis's abdomen, the mountain of almost human stone didn't move a muscle. He swatted at Marcus like he was a fly, causing him to spin. Marcus caught himself with another gust of wind, landing on his feet.

Pissed, Adonis came charging at Marcus like a bull.

"Western winds, hear my call, wrap him ground and all," Marcus called to the wind.

The wind whipped Adonis from his feet, un-leveling him as it shook him every which way but loose and spun him around. Marcus took that opportunity, running and landing a spin kick with the force that sent Adonis flying into the lake. The sound of the kick sounded like thunder as his foot hit his armor. Everyone around started yelling and cheering as he stood motionless, looking at the water.

Marcus held his breath until Adonis came flying out of the water tinted blue. As he hit the ground, he turned into a ravenous grizzly bear. His roar caused Marcus's hair to fly back, but he didn't move. I am sure that Marcus could feel the ground moving under his feet as I took off running towards him. I wrestled Adonis back as Marcus stood there unafraid and unmoved.

"Adonis, stand down."

As he turned back into his human form, he looked at me. His breastplate was split at the top.

"I'm so sorry."

As he calmed, he threw up his hand. I continued to rest my hand upon his chest. I told Adonis, "You won."

The crowd erupted in cheers.

"I think that is enough for today."

"I've only gotten started. Why are you treating me like a child?" Marcus asked.

"It's not good enough you bested one of our lieutenants?"

"No, I want to continue to train. You wouldn't do this to anyone else."

"Marcus, I think you should take the win and relax. You seem to be considerably sleep deprived," I replied as he began to walk away from me.

Gray clouds began to form overhead. "This isn't your choice. I want to continue." His body levitated unsteadily with the assistance of the wind, which caused me to turn.

"If you want to fight, then you will have to fight me."

"Then so be it."

The crowd erupted again as Marcus landed on his feet and took off toward me. I was ready. I blocked his first punch with my fist. He tried for a side kick, and I grabbed his leg, flipping him onto the ground with ease.

"You are not ready to fight a true warrior. You got a couple of easy shots off because Adonis wasn't expecting your powers, but I am."

He screamed, running back towards me, leaping in the air with a roundhouse kick. Before I knew it, my foot hit his chest, and the sound cracked again like roaring waves smashing upon a rocky shore. Right before he hit the ground, he kicked my chest plate with the same force that he'd hit Adonis. The blow sent me back on my feet as the ground moved underneath me. Marcus was hurled into the lake.

CHAPTER 29: MARCUS

M y body hit the water with such intensity that I was winded. As the water surrounded me, a sense of anger swelled in my body. I stayed there, suspended in the water as the lake creatures and small zooplankton surrounded me. Calling upon the winter wind, I felt myself lift from the water. As I reached the surface, I surrounded myself in a sphere of water. The sphere quickly became solid ice, closing me in. I screamed at the top of my lungs, which caused the ice to crack, splintering into thousands of blade-like shards. They landed upon the shoreline like hundreds of daggers. My head began to spin, and my body went limp. Again, the feeling of water enveloped me. Suddenly, a warmth surrounded me as my eyes closed amidst the feeling of safety.

CHAPTER 30: KRAVEN

When Marcus rose from the water in a sphere that quickly turned to ice, I knew that something was wrong. He was angry. I could feel the emotion.

"Get back!" I screamed as the sphere erupted, sending pieces down around the lake, piercing everything in sight, including tree trunks and the ground.

As suddenly as it erupted, I saw his body go limp and he hit the water. However, before I could reach him, there was a large ripple in the lake. Like a creature was coming for him. I ran toward the water but was intercepted by the wave that came crashing down upon me as Poseidon rose up with Marcus in his arms.

"Who is the cause of this?"

"It was I, but we were only battling. He said he wanted to fight me."

"Son of Oannes, are you not meant to protect him?"

"I…"

"I will be taking my son. If you try to follow me, believe me, you will be in for a battle the likes you have never seen."

As he glided back into the water with Marcus in his arms, I attempted to again run toward the water. I was stopped by my father.

"Kraven, you have done enough. He only wanted to continue training, and now you have infuriated a Nephilim who happens to be his father. Give him time. He shall return."

I looked out upon the water as the waves subsided and the lake again lay flat.

CHAPTER 31: NARRATOR

When Marcus regained his consciousness, he noticed that he was underwater, his face shielded by a pocket of air, and he was in the arms of Poseidon. Poseidon looked down at him and smiled as Marcus clung to him, allowing him to pick up speed in the darkness of the ocean.

With his eyes still closed, Marcus asked, "Where are you taking me?"

"To Petra."

"Jordan?"

"Yes, it will give us a place to speak, and I need to show you something."

Poseidon then bolts with a speed that can only be described as mach one. He was cutting through the ocean like a bullet through air. As they traveled through the Red Sea, Marcus noticed sea life he had never seen before. As suddenly as they had started, they slowed. Poseidon didn't wish to scare the fishermen off the coast of Aqaba.

As they reached the shore, Poseidon transformed into a man, holding Marcus up slightly as they slowly walked upon shore.

"How are we going to get to Jordan from here?"

"My child, we are Nephilim. We are going to fly."

As they walk to a remote part of the beach shadowed in darkness, Poseidon grabs two cloth sheets from a clothesline and drapes them over his shoulder.

"Now envision your wings."

Marcus thought to himself. However, he had never seen his wings.

"I've never seen them. Can you show me yours?"

Poseidon smiles and closes his eyes. His body slowly begins to grow, and his wings unfold from his back. They are a sandy clay color with brown tips, almost the length of his expanded body. Marcus quickly understood why he grabbed the sheets. His human clothing was decimated under the growth of his body. Covering himself, he looked at Marcus. "Your wings look like mine, but they are white with black tips."

Marcus closes his eyes and bends down like he saw Poseidon. He could hear his bones expanding, and the pain almost caused him to scream as he shuddered. Slowly he felt something touching his back. As he attempted to look, one of his wings hit him in the face, causing his nose to bleed slightly. As he stood, Poseidon covered him, ripping a piece of cloth for his face. As the two men stood looking at one another, they smiled.

They quickly turned when they heard a rustling on the beach. It was a young man. He looked at the two of them with his mouth gaped open.

"Angel."

Poseidon looked at Marcus, and he knew what needed to be done. Marcus held his hand up to the young man and began chanting.

"What you believe is true to you, what you once saw, I shall undo."

A small light radiates from Marcus's palm. It covered the young man's eyes like a ribbon and suddenly disappears into him. He turns around and walks away.

"I didn't hurt him, did I?"

"No, it's a spell that causes a person to forget the last ten minutes. I saw your mom do it, but I am surprised you know it."

"When Chaos opened my mind, I could see way past my birth. I saw my mom casting spells and healing people. I saw her fall in love with you and Pontus. I just don't understand why she kept going back to the both of you."

"My son, that was a mystery that your mother took to her grave, but we will have more time to talk about her. We have to get out of here."

Poseidon flapped his wings and shot up into the air. Marcus moved his shoulders, and it was as if his wings understood. They began to flap, and he too was off into the air. They glided like birds out of the sight of man, through the clouds. Marcus spun and dipped with the enthusiasm of a small child. He then flew to Poseidon's side.

"I can only imagine what it was like for Icarus," he stated.

"That young man had so much potential. He just wanted to fly too close to the sun. When he fell into the ocean, I even considered saving him. However, your father said no. Humans had to understand that the sea is a fickle creature and that it takes victims with ease."

"That sounds so sad."

"It is the way your father works. He didn't have the best upbringing, seeing as he was almost complicit in the escape of the Titans the first time around. That is how we, the Nephilim, came to prominence."

"The battle where Zeus trapped the Titans."

"Exactly. That part of lore was almost spot on, although my brother had quite a bit of help from the rest of us."

"This entire thing is completely captivating to me. To know that my lineage touches that of the greats."

"If you want to call us that. Now that the original Gods are back in the picture, we are nothing more than mere guardians of the Earth realm, and we can't even interfere with the lives of mortals anymore. Many of my brothers and sisters took to the cosmos, vowing to never come back to Earth again. Only a few of us that can maintain our secrecy have stayed. Myself, Zeus, and a few others."

"So why are we going to Petra?"

"I want to show you something. Something that I think will put things into perspective for you."

"Perspective?"

"Yes. I can tell by your emotions when you hit the water that you are still battling internally with what your true purpose is. I can tell you one thing: we can't afford for you to make the wrong decision. It has happened before."

"Really?"

"Yes. We are here," he says as he descends upon the temple of Petra.

As the two land, a pair of guards standing at the entrance of the temple barely budge.

"Are they?"

"They have been contracted by the Nephilim to watch over this site. Although throughout the day people are able to come and visit, after dark, this location is off limits to humans."

Marcus looks upon the pink sandstone in awe. As their wings retract, they return to their normal human form. Taking in the beauty of the night as the stars cascade across the night sky, Marcus's gaze once again falls upon the enormous temple. As he looks at the stairs, he notices that Poseidon has made his way through the entrance. He quickly runs after him. As he makes his way inside, it's dimly lit, and Marcus can barely see.

"Eyes open, bring to sight, illuminate the darkness, bring upon the light," Marcus calls out as a flame appears in the center of the room.

"You are getting good at these spells."

"I think it's the poet in me. Spells are just poetry asking for something."

"Your mom used to say the same thing," Poseidon said as he walked over to Marcus, standing by his side. In front of them was a great wall.

"This was what you wanted to show me?"

"No, my son. It's what's behind this." Poseidon placed his hand upon the wall, causing the sandstone to ooze away, revealing what could only be described as a shrine or tomb.

Stepping through, they stood face to face with two massive statues. One of a beautiful woman, and the other of a man.

"Who are they?"

"This is the tomb of Ethereal and Amir. Amir was the first ever noted tri-breed. He was born of magic. He was pronounced dead shortly after his birth. His mother took him to a cave and summoned a jinn. The jinn brought the child back to life for the mother. With her other wishes, she wished that the child have long life and be strong like a wolf. In return, upon the young man's 18th birthday, his mother's soul would belong to the jinn for all eternity. The jinn agreed, but as you know, jinn are tricky creatures. He awoke Amir from the dead, making him the first zombie. The wish of long life made him a vampire, and the strength of a wolf—" Poseidon stopped to allow Marcus to finish.

"Made him the first noted werewolf."

"Precisely. So, you have a zombie, vamp, werewolf."

"What about her?"

"Ethereal was born of the first vampire family. The first vampires are still unknown to us, because Chaos refuses to disclose the creation of the creatures, but her family is the first recorded vampires."

"So, you mean to tell me that these creatures have been walking the earth as long as humans?"

"As it was said to you before, as long as there has been magic, which was born out of Chaos, which is how long we have been on this earth."

"So, what happened to them?"

"Well, one night Amir was out and couldn't sleep. He had stumbled upon a well and took it upon himself to take a drink. When he arose from taking his drink, he was greeted by Ethereal. Her beauty was like nothing that he had ever seen. They talked for many hours, departed one another under the promise that they would meet again at the same location. They met in that same location for an entire week until the two shared their first kiss. It was then they realized that they were the same. Ethereal's fangs protruded as did Amir's. It was said that their lovemaking shook the heavens and earth.

"Well, with Amir by her side, Ethereal felt that she could do whatever she wanted. She slayed entire towns to quench her thirst, and Amir was right there with her. However, this became exhausting to him. He wished nothing more than to have a simple life with Ethereal. However, her thirst for power was unquenchable. Yet Amir could do the one thing that Ethereal could not. He was a day walker. After many conversations, Ethereal took it upon herself to try to suck the life essence from her lover. In turn, Amir beheaded her, and out of fear for his life, had them both entombed underneath these statues."

"So, the moral of the story is kill before I can be killed?"

"Marcus, if that is what you got from the story, then you missed the entire message."

"What was the message?"

"Marcus, people are going to want you for what you have. You have to make sure that you aren't being used for it. Yes, you are far more powerful than Amir, but the stories are the same. The Tri-bred is placed on earth to fulfill a mission. Amir felt that his mission was saving the people of Jordan from being decimated by Ethereal. In order to stop that, he had to kill her. Which he did. The loss nearly destroyed him. In order not to fall victim to his bloodlust and anger, he entombed himself here too."

A drop of blood from Marcus's nose lands on the ground. Yet neither of them notices. Marcus places his rag back up to his face as he feels something start to drip.

"I think we should get out of here. The temps are making my nose bleed again."

"Yes, be careful. A drop of blood can bring Amir back from the dead."

Marcus looks down and the droplet is no longer there.

"Not a drop," says Marcus as they continue out.

Poseidon places his hand back upon the wall and closes the tomb.

"Can you give me a little help?"

"Wind of the Saharan Desert, I call to you," Marcus calls as a hot wind whirls through the temple, sealing up the once gaping hole.

As the two walk back outside, Marcus looks over at Poseidon, who has a sadness written across his face.

"I promise you, I won't end up like Amir," Marcus exclaims.

"I'm not worried about you ending up like Amir. We have to part now. I just wanted to share this with you because I know you have been battling with your feelings for both men. Just please be careful. Make sure that the one you choose is there for you, not for your abilities."

Marcus looks up at him as Poseidon pulls him tight.

"Dad, can you take me back to Sardinia?"

"You want to go by water or air?"

"Air is fine with me. There is a seaside villa there. I have some unfinished business. Of course."

Before Marcus can unleash his wings, Poseidon scoops him up and flies off with him in his arms.

"It would have taken too long for you. The more you use your wings, the faster they will unleash for you."

Marcus clings to him, nuzzling his face into his thick neck. The smell of fresh seawater fills his nose as he takes in his scent. For the first time in a long time, he felt like he was around family. Poseidon looks down at him and smiles as they fly over the Suez Canal. Moments later, Poseidon can make out Ciprian's villa. He looks down at Marcus, who has fallen asleep in his arms.

"We're here," he says, waking him.

Marcus looks down as Poseidon glides down to the beach, placing Marcus on his feet. The two look at each other for a moment before saying anything. Marcus wanted to tell him that he didn't want him to leave. Poseidon didn't want to leave him either.

"I think I should go," Poseidon said, looking out toward the ocean.

"Will I see you again?"

"You can see me whenever you want. You just have to call for me."

"How do I call for you?"

"Go into the water and call my name in your mind. I will show up whenever you call."

"Thank you for showing me the Tower and telling me about the first Tri-bred."

"Marcus, Amir was not the first Tri-bred, and you are likely not the only Tri-bred either. I need you to understand you are a powerful piece of the magical world. People will seek you out to harm you."

"I understand, and I am doing my best to learn how to use these abilities for the good of everyone."

He looked at Marcus for a moment and pulled him in for a big hug. "I'm just so glad that you are doing well."

"If you could do it all over again, would you change anything?"

"Not a single thing. If he doesn't want to accept you as his child, I will. You are my son. I brought you back to life, and I intend on helping you stay that way," Poseidon says with a smirk on his face.

Marcus pushes him away as he begins to walk back into the ocean. He waves before jumping in and allowing his body to transform. All Marcus can then see is his dorsal fin as he disappears into the darkness. Marcus stood there for a little while, hoping that he would come back, before turning. There, standing before him, was Prince Ciprian Dracula.

CHAPTER 32: CIPRIAN

I am sure the Italian police had every intention of keeping me out of the country. However, the power of compulsion is a wonder to be seen—that's if you remember even seeing it. As I sat on the patio looking up at the night sky, I saw a winged creature come from the heavens, landing onto my private beach. Shocked that any mythical creature would be as bold as to come for me, I made my way down. As I got closer, I could see that the creature wasn't alone. As I hid behind stone, the figure began to look familiar to me. I turned my ear to hear the voices. Marcus. Who is this other person? Suddenly, I see the man walk into the ocean. As he leapt into the water, his body transformed into that of a merman. I slowly made my way down to the beach and stood right behind Marcus, not making a single sound. As Marcus turned, I could see the shock written across his face.

"Ciprian."

"I thought you were training with the Sons of Oannes, too busy for me," I said, smelling the air around him.

"I had to come back here. There is an Italian designer that I found on social media who is going to make my outfit for the ball," Marcus replied, slowly stepping back as I was standing so close I could feel the touch of his breath on my lips.

"I didn't think you would be going to the party after the way you left last."

"I had someplace to be. I am sorry that wasn't good enough for you. In addition, I know it was you that caused my door to slam."

I smiled to myself because he was becoming ever more emboldened, and I had no idea why. The few times we had spoken before, he always seemed to have his guard up. I wanted to try something to see if my suspicions were correct. I retracted my fangs and hissed at him. This caused his body to emit an electric pulse. He held his hands up and the wind bellowed around him as he began to rise from the ground. The ocean began rocking back and forth, and clouds formed overhead out of nowhere.

"Marcus, calm down. I just wanted to see if my speculations were correct."

For a moment, he just floated there, seemingly unfazed by my request. "Please calm down. I didn't mean anything by it."

Marcus allowed himself to come back down to the ground. The winds and waves subsided, but his eyes continued to glow.

"The transition has happened?"

"What transition?"

"Your transition from mere mortal to demi-god tri-bred."

"How did you?"

"Come on now, Marcus, give me more credit than that. Finding you was like finding the Ark of the Covenant. People knew that you were around, but no one quite knew where to find you."

As he sat on a large stone, he looked at me. "So how did you find me?"

"The electronic pulse that you released at the time of impact woke me up out of my sleep. Every mythical creature from Maine to the South China Sea could feel it. To some it came like a soft breeze, however to us vamps it came like a horn elevated by the sound of your screams."

"So, it was you?"

"It was me what?"

"You were the creature reaching out for me in my sleep. Calling to me from the wind?"

"I mean it took you long enough to figure that out. I surely thought that you would have recognized my voice after our first conversation, but you seriously didn't catch it?"

"I didn't…" He stopped speaking for a moment and just looked at me. In this moment I wished I could read his mind. I wanted to know what he was thinking. I realized that I wouldn't have to wait that long.

"You didn't have anything to do with that young boy being drunk and colliding with us, did you?"

"Marcus. I can't believe you would ask me something like that."

"Come on, Ciprian, you literally lured me here and killed a kid in this very peninsula. Please stop."

"I would never do something like that. However, I was there for every moment of your grief. That feeling of never feeling alone was because you weren't ever alone. Every creak you heard in your home came from me and or Winston."

"And the job?"

"The job was easy to get you into. The position was open, and I knew that you wanted to teach. You don't remember applying because you didn't apply. I applied for you, sent an email that stated you would interview, and that's how it happened."

"You had me thinking I was crazy."

"I know, but it was only to get you closer to me."

"Why?"

"I thought you would have figured it out by now, but I do things like this when I am in love."

"In love?"

"Yeah, you are the kindest person I've ever met. Giving of yourself in such a way I don't think people can truly understand until they are around you."

"You love me?"

"Yeah. Do you want me to scream it from the rooftop?" I asked, jumping from the beach to the roof of the villa. "I LOVE MARCUS WESTMORE-MILLER!"

As I jumped back down I was again standing face to face with him. I noticed that he was smiling.

"I…" Before I could finish my statement he leans in and kisses me on the lips. I could feel myself smiling, because I wasn't expecting it. "You mean to tell me that was all I had to do to get a kiss?"

"I mean I've kissed you before."

"On the cheek doesn't count, and all of those kisses felt like pity kisses, not like the one you just gave me."

"Well, that was a ... you are cute kiss. I can't say that I love you back because I still feel like I am getting to know you, but what I can say is this; you make me feel alive."

"There are ways that I can make you feel more alive," I responded in the cheesiest way possible.

"We are not having sex, but I wouldn't mind a little light petting and then falling asleep."

"Deal," I say, grabbing him around the waist, jumping with him to the porch of the villa. He didn't scream or make any kind of seemingly unusual sound. He just giggled as we landed, placing his face upon my clavicle. I was smitten by him. In real life.

CHAPTER 33: MARCUS

I didn't know what I was doing with him. I knew this wasn't the purpose of my trip here, but there was something about him that wouldn't let me leave his side. As we walked hand in hand into the villa I wondered where he was taking me. However, I didn't ask any questions. I allowed myself to be led by him. We walked through corridors that led us to a dark basement. There in a room where light didn't touch was a king size bed. Candles adorned the room. The walls covered in beautiful crimson silk. The silks converged onto the canopy of the bed. He began taking off his shirt, revealing his beautifully sculpted chest. His skin looked like the smoothest peachy white marble.

"Ciprian, what is happening?"

"I thought you came here for me."

"I didn't. I had every intention of coming here to meet with a suit maker who could design something for me for the ball."

"Why would you stop here then?"

"I... I don't know."

"Have you not missed me?"

"I have. However, I know that having sex with you isn't something that I want to do... just yet."

"So, you have thought about me in that way?"

"Yes. But we agreed light petting then bed."

"So why not now?"

"Ciprian, I really just need to focus on getting myself together for the ball and taking things slowly. I feel that you want things to happen faster than I wanted."

"I apologize. That isn't the case for me. I just want to know that you feel for me, how I feel about you."

"I don't know yet. I am still dealing with the entire situation. You being a vampire, and also being slightly drawn to Kraven."

"Kraven!" he scoffs.

"Don't do that. You both have to realize that I was with a single person for most of my young adult life. After he died, it felt like a string was cut. I have been walking around all this time feeling like a piece of tattered cloth. Waiting to be connected to something or someone else, like I was connected to him."

"Why not connect yourself to me?" he asks, walking up to me, placing his face into the nape of my neck. Kissing me softly. I could feel my body respond to his kisses. I didn't realize just how much I missed the sexual touch of another person.

He gripped my waist as he continued to pull me in. Our pelvises touched, and although I was confused by what was happening in his pants and mine, I was completely lost in his kisses. Kisses are my love language. Before I realized it, I opened my eyes. My head was lying on the pillows, and I was dragging my nails across his bare back. My shirt was no longer on, and my pants were slightly unbuckled. His kisses moved from my neck to my cheek and then to my lips. I would call what we were doing aggressive foreplay. He slid his hands into my pants and gripped my thighs, squeezing the top of my ass. I was becoming so enthralled I had to stop myself as he flipped me, causing me to straddle him as he took his tongue down my chest, kissing and licking on my nipples.

As this continued, I kept having visions of Amir and Ethereal. Blood-soaked bodies covered the lands and caused the rivers to run red like the Nile. When Amir turned, it wasn't his face that I saw but Ciprian's, and as Ethereal turned, I saw myself, blood dripping from my chin down my neck. This caused me to push back from Ciprian. I caught the wind and levitated out of the bed. He sat up looking at me, shocked. His eyes were unlike anything I had seen before. He wanted to engulf me, but the level of restraint caused him to look nearly demonic.

"I can't do this," I replied, reaching down for my shirt and running off.

As much as I thought he would follow me, he didn't. At least I didn't feel him. I rushed out of the house, down the street, and caught an Uber to the city. Inside of the Uber, I felt my neck to make sure that I didn't receive a bite. I hadn't quite figured out exactly what my blood would do to him. However, I felt that it was something he wanted. The visions of Amir and Ethereal made me uneasy. One thing that I know is that he can't take the blood from me. It has to be freely given in order to possess the magical properties.

However, in the state of pure ecstasy that I was in, I am sure I would have agreed to just about anything. Sex is a powerful thing. As I reached the small shop, I noticed that the door stated Serradu.

"Excuse me, sir," I stopped the Uber driver before he drove off. "Can you tell me what that says?"

"Serradu is 'closed' in Sardinian," he replied in a thick accent.

"Fuck!"

"Would you like me to take you somewhere else?"

"No, sir. Thank you," I replied, giving him a tip on the Uber app.

As he drove off, I knocked on the door. A small older Italian man walked up and pointed to the sign.

"I have an appointment. I know I missed it, but I need to try on the outfit before I fly back home."

"Are you Mr. Westmore-Miller?"

"Yes," I replied, taking a deep breath, hearing him speak a little English.

"You are late, but I will make an exception this one time. Mr. Dracula's assistant called and stated that you would be late."

How did he know where I was coming from? That didn't matter in this moment. I needed the most distracting garment for my plan to go off without a hitch.

"Thank you."

As he let me in, it was hanging from a dressing room door. The top: a hunter green Victorian tail coat. The bottom: hunter green suit pants with attached floor-length overskirt. Beside it, the most elegant full-length 75-inch hunter green cloak. I could tell by my audible gasp that the shop owner could tell I was happy. A huge smile came across his face.

"May I?"

"Yes, please," he replied as I stepped into the dressing room with the clothes.

I placed my hair in a high messy bun prior to putting the clothes on.

"Can I get a dress shirt and a golden tie to accentuate the golden buttons?"

"Of course."

After a few moments I received a black and white dress shirt and a golden tie. I went with the black dress shirt, tied the tie, and placed it on the suit. I looked at myself for a moment.

"Not bad. Not bad at all."

"Please step out."

As I walked out of the room, I saw Ciprian standing beside the shop owner. The shop owner seemed more serious, but Ciprian just looked at me. His face seemingly shocked.

"How do I look?"

"You are a vision, but I have a question for you," Ciprian replies.

"Yes?"

"Are you not afraid that people will feel that it is too feminine?"

"Femininity and masculinity when it comes to style of dress is a human construct. I don't want to confine myself."

"I understand," he replied.

Although he said he understood, I couldn't shake the feeling that he would prefer me in something more traditional. Maybe it's because it will be the first time I meet his family. In particular his mother. I walked back into the dressing room.

"I'll take it all."

"Mr. Westmore, it's already been paid for."

"If it's been paid for by Prince Dracula, please refund him his money, and I will pay for it myself."

"Marcus," Ciprian says from behind the curtains.

"Ciprian, this is not up for discussion. I will pay for my own clothing. We already talked about this. I don't need to be kept. That isn't going to win you any points in my book. Thank you, but I got it."

"As you wish," he replies. "Marco, place the money back into my store account."

I walked out of the dressing room and walked over to the counter. The shop owner Marco places the garment in a silk-lined garment bag and rings me up.

"The total comes to €5,789.57."

"Thank you," I replied, taking out my credit card and pressing it against the chip reader.

"Thank you, Mr. Westmore. Please think of me if you have any other suit desires. Here is your receipt."

"Marco, you have been a blessing. Have a wonderful evening and make sure you lock up," I said as we walked out of the store.

"Marcus, can we talk?"

"Sure, but I have to make it back to the airport."

"I can fly you back."

"Ciprian, you didn't come here for me. You came here to feed. I wouldn't dare stand in your way. Anyways, I have a first-class ticket. I can make it back."

"Did I do something?"

"No, why would you think that?"

"You left so abruptly I thought that I did something to you."

"Ciprian, I don't want to have sex yet, and if we kept going, I know I would have fallen victim to my flesh."

"Why not let yourself go? You have been so tightly wound since you've gotten back from whatever trip you went on with Kraven."

"I know. I just got a lot on my mind."

"Does this have anything to do with you being able to levitate? Yes, I saw it. Something has happened to you, and I don't know why you seem so afraid to talk to me about it."

"Ciprian, I don't know what you want from me, and that scares me."

"I want to love you," he says, grabbing my hands softly as the car pulls up.

He opens the door for me, and I don't say a word. I want this to be true. I would love for that to be the only thing, but I know what I am seeing in my mind. I don't know if those are premonitions or me seeing the past through Amir and Ethereal. As I get into the car, he looks at me.

"Do you have nothing to say?"

"Ciprian, I don't know what you want me to say. How about this: If our coming out at the ball goes well, we can discuss monogamously dating."

"Sounds like a deal."

"You say that now, but I know you have a problem with my more feminine side."

"Marcus, it's not that. I just tend to go for more masculine guys."

"Nothing about me has been completely masculine or divinely feminine since we met. I have always had shoulder-length hair, I've always had a softer body and disposition. Something drew you to me. This is what I'm talking about. You either want me as I am, or you don't want me."

"I do want you. I love you."

The words landed on my ears differently this time. Longing, more desperate than before, when they sounded almost taunting or joking. I turned my head and looked at the night sky.

"Did you hear what I just said?" he asked in a softer tone.

"I did, but I can't say it back. Not until I know for sure."

For the remainder of the ride to the airport we sat in silence. I placed my hand on the seat, and he caressed it. This was what I needed from him. This is the part of him that kept me in constant conflict with myself. His kindness. As the car stopped he didn't move, he looked at me. Sadness written across his face. I leaned in and kissed him on the lips. He caressed the back of my head.

"I'll see you at the ball."

"I'm looking forward to it."

I got out of the car and walked toward the airport.

CHAPTER 34: CAIRO

H ave you heard from him?"

"No," Kraven said in a mumble. I can tell that he is pissed, but I don't want to push him.

Marcus was taken by Poseidon, and no one has heard from him since. The waters to the lake sat still as we looked out upon it. For hours we did nothing but watch the water.

"I'm gonna turn in," I said as I looked over at him.

"Okay, I'm gonna sit here a little while longer."

"Bro, he will come back. He is safe. Don't worry."

"Cairo, that's easier for you to say you aren't in love with him."

"Kraven, I still love him. He is important to me also. We have a connection also."

"I'm not saying you don't. I'm just saying…"

"You are saying because I am younger and he doesn't see me like that, that our connection isn't as deep as yours."

"Cairo!"

I stormed into the house and ran to Marcus's bedroom, slamming the door. I jumped into his bed and grabbed his pillow. It smelled like jasmine and cocoa butter. Outside, a car pulled up, but I didn't bother to get out of bed.

"Hello?"

His voice sounded like a familiar place. It was Marcus. I got out of bed and ran down the stairs, skipping some in the process. I leaped into his arms, and he caught me.

"Well, hello to you too," he said, placing his head on top of mine.

"We didn't know when you were coming back...if you were coming back."

"Of course, I was going to come back."

I could feel him standing behind me, brooding, but relieved that he returned.

"Hey you," Marcus says to him, shooting him a slight grin.

He didn't want to show his happiness. "Where did he take you?"

"He took me to show me the past and my future if I don't make the right decision."

"You are talking in riddles," Kraven replied, a little sterner.

"Kraven, I don't want to fight with you right now. I really don't have any fight left in me."

"I can smell him on you."

"Okay, I'm done. I'm going to my room," replies Marcus, picking up his garment bag and walking up the stairs.

"What is wrong with you?" I asked, shoving Kraven.

"Cairo, you don't know him like I know him."

"Then you don't know him at all. He really likes you, and you can't see it past your hate for Ciprian Dracula."

I ran up the stairs following Marcus, knocking on his door as I made my way to his room.

"Come in," he says, sitting on the edge of his bed.

"You can't leave me again."

"Cairo, that wasn't on me. Your brother hurt me, and my father came for me. He isn't going to watch me be harmed."

"I understand, but I mean you can't leave me."

"Listen to me. Of all of the people here that I've met, you and I will always be connected. You were the first person who tried to educate me about who I was, despite being told not to and risking yourself getting in trouble. I could never just up and leave you. We are connected for life."

He stood up and hugged me.

"As a matter of fact, I got one better. Do you want to be connected to me?"

"Yes."

He began to chant while holding my hand, "Once was lost, now is found, forever connected, forever bound."

I watched as what looked like a flapping string came from his back, wrapped around us, causing us to lift off the ground. The weave pierced my back, wrapping around my heart as a burst of light came from the two of us. Kraven came bursting into the room.

"What was that?"

"I've linked myself to Cairo and the Sons of Oannes."

"Linked yourself?"

"Since Luke's death, I've felt like a tattered piece of fabric. Cairo has been the only one to really care about me in a way that isn't clouded by something else."

"He's trying to say I'm the only one that hasn't been clouded by his powers or a relationship."

Marcus smiled at me. "It's felt like the love of a younger brother, and unconditional love."

"I'm sorry my love for you has caused you so much strain."

"I love you too!" screams Marcus at Kraven.

I didn't know what to say. Marcus just confessed his love for Kraven. This was the first time that I saw my brother at a loss for words.

"I love you too," Marcus repeats, softer this time. "I did all of this for a reason. I had planned on leaving before Poseidon came. I needed to get a garment for the ball."

"What plan are you talking about?" Kraven asks, still trying to shake off the shock.

"The night of the ball, I intend on placing a containment spell on the castle and the woods to protect the people of this town."

"What are you trying to protect them from?"

Marcus pulls up his laptop. "I was doing research before I left about the Maiden Festival. Every year there are people that go missing. This isn't widespread news, but I did find details about it on Reddit. See."

He showed us article after article about people going missing following the festival. Some bodies were found drained of blood. Others weren't even found at all, still considered missing people.

"I feel that it's my responsibility to protect the people of this town. I have fallen in love with this place, and the people," he says, looking back at Kraven.

"How do you plan on doing this?" Kraven asks.

Marcus then pulls out an old book. "It's a grimoire. This was given to me by Poseidon. He said that it belonged to my mother. Inside of the grimoire is a powerful containment spell that lasts for 24 hours. It is meant to contain mystical creatures, but not humans. The moment it goes up, any mystical creature that is within its walls will be trapped there. Any mystical creature that walks into it will also be trapped. Humans, however, can walk freely through it. This will contain the vampires and any other deviant beings that wish to cause the town harm."

"Are you sure you want to do this? Won't it make Ciprian angry?"

"Ciprian goes to Sardinia to feed. He should have no feelings about this. I just want to keep those who don't have a managed hunger at bay."

"So again, how are you planning on doing this?"

"My plan is to go to the ball but leave early. The moment that I feel that they are about to do something to the town, I will make my way out. As soon as I get past the newly paved path, I will send the containment spell up."

"Do you have to go?" asks Kraven.

"I do. I feel that's where I'm going to get my sign that I've made the right decision."

"What if I don't?" I asked.

"What if you don't what?"

"If you didn't make the right decision?"

"Cairo, I have to trust my gut. I feel that if I ever give the blood to Ciprian, he is going to be unstoppable."

"Can I come with you?"

"I would prefer that you not. I don't want to be distracted," Marcus says, cupping my face.

"Then I shall come with you."

"Kraven, you and Cairo will stay here. I don't know what this spell can do to my body, but until I have gotten these new abilities in check, I need you to be my protectors in any type of vulnerable state."

"When is this happening?"

"Next week. Until then, I will resume my training with the Sons of Oannes."

"With that being said, I need to sleep. My body has taken a beating—literally and mythically—over the last twelve hours."

"See you in the morning," I said as I walked out of the room, standing by the door.

"Would you like me to stay with you?"

I peeked into the room and saw Marcus walk up to Kraven. He placed his hand upon the coarse hair that lined his face. "I would love for you to stay. Get Cairo to bed and come back to me."

"I'm sorry for today. I was just very angry."

"I understand, Kraven, but you must know that I can't make rash decisions. I was foretold of tri-breds and those that they are bonded to in the blood. One story really scared me, and with your vampiric background, I am still a little nervous. When you return to me, I will tell you all about it."

Marcus leaned in and kissed Kraven on the lips, causing Kraven to grip him tightly around the waist. As their lips parted, Marcus looked him in the eyes. "I choose you. I love… you."

CHAPTER 35: NARRATOR

T he days flew by, and the training was even more intense, but Marcus kept up. He even met up with Poseidon for a training session on the water. The two together made quite a battle on the seas. Poseidon was proud of the young man that he'd saved. He loved him like he was his own son.

The day before the maiden festival, he came to Marcus. Marcus walked down to the lake to greet him.

"What are you doing here?"

"You are about to do something good for these people. I felt that it was time for me to give you something from me."

"What's that?"

"Take off your shirt."

"Man, it's always something with you mythical folks," Marcus says jokingly.

Poseidon opens his hand, holding it out in front of Marcus. "What is that?"

"It's the scale of a dragon. When placed upon your chest, it will seal you from powerful blades. There is a catch—if the blade gets underneath, then it will slide through to your human flesh."

"Okay... so like—" Before Marcus could complete his sentence, Poseidon places the scale on his left breast. The scale instantly replicates until Marcus's entire chest and back are covered in cerulean blue scales. Once complete, the scales flex up and then lay down into his skin, giving the appearance of a shimmering, moisturized texture. "So, you just weren't going to let me ask any questions, huh?"

Poseidon laughs. "There's no need for questions when you have protection. You need to know you are going to meet people tomorrow that are very old and very dangerous. Although you are a tri-bred with multiple power sources, you need to keep your head on a swivel."

"I know. Can I see you next week?"

"It's a date."

"Love you, Dad."

Poseidon didn't know what to say back to him. He reached out and grabbed him, giving him a hug. "I love you too, son. If you need me, you know how to reach me."

"Yup."

Kraven looks down upon them from the Inn as Poseidon looks up.

"Seems like you made your choice."

"Nothing official yet, but I am sure you will know when it does happen."

"You can all but guarantee it. A lot of people are only hearing that there is a tri-bred, but no one really knows who it is."

"Let's try to keep it that way for a while."

"My sentiment exactly," Poseidon says as he glides backwards on the water in his merman form.

"Next week."

"See you then."

Marcus makes his way back up the hill to the Inn and is embraced by Kraven.

"How did that go?" he asked.

"You tell me," Marcus says, opening up his shirt revealing the dragon scale chest plate.

Kraven touches it. "Dragon scale, like mine."

"Yeah, he said something about powerful blades?"

"Yeah, there are many mythical weapons that can pierce our skin. No matter how tough, however, only the dagger of Oannes can pierce dragon scale."

"Where is the dagger of Oannes?"

"No one knows."

"Well, that isn't helpful at all," Marcus replied, kissing him on the lips, walking back into the house.

Kraven looks up at the tower and could feel that he was being watched.

CHAPTER 36: CIPRIAN

A s I run around making sure that everything is perfect for this evening, the door opens and a cool breeze accompanies it. I know exactly who this is.

"Welcome home, Mother."

"Ciprian, the castle looks absolutely wonderful."

I escort her to the Ballroom, and the space is lined with servers who have been compelled.

"This is a delightful touch. Are these for tasting?"

"Absolutely. We have fifteen, and two on tap in the basement."

"Well, I have to say that your father and I absolutely miss you. Have you found someone yet to settle down with?"

"Actually, a guy that I am seeing will be here a little later on this evening. He can't wait to meet you."

"I can't wait to meet him either. So, I've heard rumblings that the Sons of Oannes found the tri-bred."

"Yes, ma'am."

"Have you scoped this person out?"

"To be honest with you, I just want to think about tonight, and maybe we can discuss that before you leave?"

"Absolutely, darling, but I want you to make sure that you keep your options open. Our great ancestor Ethereal was the last vampire that ruled by the side of a tri-bred, and I would so like to reach that status again."

"I understand."

I think I was bred just to match the tri-bred. My family couldn't care less if it's a male or female. My job is to fall in love and be offered the tri-bred's blood so that we can rule the mythical creatures on earth. I walked outside to greet our guests, praying that Marcus would show up early so that I could get the introductions out of the way. Tonight, I was expecting a who's who of vampire royalty. The Western Coven from North America, the South African Coven, the Victorian Coven, and the Eastern Coven. All of these royal families have children they are trying to marry off. Hence the reason for Marcus showing up on time. With him here, I won't have to entertain the other children.

CHAPTER 37: NARRATOR

L ater that same night, Marcus sits in his room staring at a blank computer screen. Cairo comes up to his room, noticing this, and touches him on his shoulder.

"Are you okay?"

"Yeah, just making sure that I get mentally prepared for this night."

"Everything is going to be great, but your man is waiting downstairs for your arrival."

"Head down and tell him I will be right down."

"Okay, remember you got this!"

As Cairo walks out of the room, Marcus stands looking at himself in the stand-up mirror. He closes his eyes and calls for Chaos. "Chaos, come to me!"

When he opens his eyes, his reflection's back is facing him. He slowly turns around, looking at him with jet black eyes.

"Well, hello, it's been a long time."

"I may need you tonight. It's going to take some power to lift this containment spell."

"What are you containing?" Chaos asks.

"The castle and the forest around it."

"Well, you know magic is my thing. I am here to enhance you whenever you ask."

"Thank you. What do I need to say?"

"Chaos, I let you in. The moment you let me in, I will take over."

"Okay, and how do I come back?"

"I will release you."

"Will you release me though?"

"Marcus, I would rather not be banished by my sister. So yes, I will release you."

"I will hold you to that. I have to go."

"Okay, you look fantastic. But I don't like the color. Crimson is your color," Chaos says as he waves his hand, turning the hunter green garment a shiny blood crimson. "You also need a few stars," he says as he sprinkles in golden luster which settles around the ends of the cloak and around the hood.

"Well, look at you being my fairy godmother."

Marcus closes his eyes, and when he opens them, he is looking back at his reflection. Marcus gives himself one more look over and walks down the stairs. As he hits the middle of the stairs, Kraven stands up, staring in awe.

"How?"

"I took a little creative freedom. The green wasn't meshing with my skin, so I used a little magic to change it."

"You aren't concerned using that much magic this early on?"

"I feel fine. I promise you," Marcus says, smiling at Kraven.

"Well, you look absolutely stunning."

"You don't think I look too feminine?"

"No, why would you ask me that? You look beautiful. I would love you if you were feminine, super masculine. I would love you as you."

Marcus walks up to him and kisses him on the lips.

"Alright, alright, Marcus has to go or you're going to be late."

"Cairo, you are driving me, right?"

"Yup, don't need anyone seeing you guys make out in the car."

"Shut up. Let's go."

"Be safe," Kraven says, grabbing Marcus's arm.

Marcus hugs him tightly, whispering into his ear. "I'll be coming back to you tonight. I promise."

Marcus kisses him on the lips and walks out the front door.

Kraven sits down and breathes in deeply.

Cairo makes it up the path and is able to make it all the way to the front door. He pulls up and looks over at Marcus.

"You be safe."

"I'll be safe. We have a connection, so you will know if something is going wrong."

"That's what I'm feeling?"

"Yeah, I'm a little bit nervous. You can feel that?"

"Yeah, that's creepy."

"That means that your father and brother can feel it too."

"I will make sure that I calm down."

Marcus holds up his hand and begins to chant, "Fear here, fear there, fear released, into the air."

He gasps as a black mist rises from his chest. "Whoa. How does it feel now?"

"It feels like a calm," replies Cairo.

"Okay. Let me get out of here."

Marcus steps out of the car and walks towards the door, looking back at Cairo. "You can go, young man."

"Okay," he replies, driving back down through the forest. When he got to the bottom, he pressed on the brakes, nearly missing Kraven and Luca. Cairo jumps out of the car.

"I could have killed you."

"What happened to him?" asked Kraven.

"He released his fear."

"Did you see it?"

"Yeah, I could see it and feel it. Go back to the house, and he will be fine. We just have to wait for the sign."

"What is the sign again?"

"Kraven, the lightning," Cairo said as he gets back into the car and drives slowly as groups of people make their way to a local bar.

CHAPTER 38: NARRATOR

Marcus took a deep breath as the door was opened by Winston. Marcus smiles at him, and he keeps his austere disposition as he guides Marcus to the ballroom. As Marcus walked in, Ciprian was making his way around the room mingling, continuing to look up at the spiral staircase that leads down into the grand Victorian ballroom. A hand touches the Prince's shoulder.

"Prince Ciprian, how are you doing?" asks a handsome male with a deep South African accent.

"Prince Amadi," he says with a slight sense of disdain.

"Can you explain to me why we haven't met up? That last time was a wild night," Amadi whispers into his ear.

"Amadi, you got me so high on blood we nearly slaughtered an entire resort. I told you then I only drink blood to sustain myself. Eating that way, I've been able to maintain my blood lust."

"Why would you force yourself to do such a thing? You were wild that night. A man I could see myself with. This version of you I don't understand."

A rush of emotions takes over Marcus as he steps to the top of the stairs and looks down upon the sea of pale faces. He then locks eyes with Prince Ciprian, and in that moment, everything fades away for the both of them.

"You don't have to understand that version of me…he does," Prince Ciprian says, walking away from Amadi with his mouth half open as if mid-response.

Prince Ciprian walks to the foot of the stairs, and Marcus begins walking down. His heart is pumping so heavily in his chest that he can faintly hear the voices whispering around him. However, in that moment, the only thing he can focus on is Ciprian, who is looking up at him like he has won the grand prize. In the distance, Queen Sorina Dracula looks with contempt written on her face.

As Marcus hits the last step, he stops and does what looks like a curtsy lunge. Ciprian smiles and gets down on one knee. Marcus looks at him with their faces nearly inches apart.

"What are you doing?" Marcus asks, giggling.

"What are you doing? I understand the formality, but you are damn near lunging," he says as he holds out his hand, standing.

"You made it."

"I said I would."

"You look … beautiful."

"Not too feminine?" Marcus asks mockingly.

"I didn't mean it like that. You know that you are a vision, and I would accept you in any way that you came to me."

Marcus playfully spins him around. "You aren't so shabby yourself."

As he and Marcus stand face to face, Ciprian continues to look into his eyes. Ciprian's eye color shifts from red back to blue.

"Is everything okay?"

"Yeah, why do you ask?"

"For a minute I almost thought your eyes were red?"

Enamored, the two didn't see Queen Sorina saunter over to the two of them. "Ciprian, who pray tell is this?"

"Come, you must meet my ...," Ciprian stops as they nearly run into the back of Queen Sorina. Ciprian places his hand upon the small of Marcus's back. "Mother, I would like to introduce you to Marcus."

The tall, statuesque, blond-haired, blue-eyed, Grecian marble sculpted-looking woman turns, and her face is immediately filled with disgust. "Oh, he's ... your friend?"

"I'm sorry, is there a problem?" Marcus asks, almost accusatory.

"Ciprian, when you spoke of this creature, I thought you meant he was one of us?"

"Mother!"

"Don't be so sensitive. He didn't take offense to that. See, he must be used to it, being ..." she pauses to think about what she will say next.

"Black?" Marcus asks, as irritation was bubbling on the inside.

"I was going to say, an American and all."

"That doesn't..."

She interrupts the Prince and looks into Marcus's eyes. "So powerful, aren't you. I can feel the energy radiating off of you," she continues as she places her long manicured fingernails upon his chin, causing his body to lightly glow. "So, you are the one who has captured my son's heart. I can see why he likes you, tri-bred."

Outside, cumulonimbus storm clouds form, darkening and giving way to lightning and thunder that echo Marcus's anger in this moment.

Back at the Inn, Kraven and Cairo are startled by the sound of the lightning, which causes Kraven to drop his cup as he takes off running outside the house. The two look up at the castle.

"It's time," Kraven says as Cairo stands beside him.

Back in the Ballroom, spectators ignore the storm and continue looking on at the interaction between the Queen and Marcus.

"If he says so," Marcus replies, annoyed, curtseying. "It's wonderful to meet you," not knowing the protocol for a situation like this.

Marcus looks horrified as the party guests laugh at his display of respect.

"The monarchy has been abolished, but you would know that if you'd done some research," she says, laughing mockingly, looking at her son.

"That's enough! He has been nothing but kind, and you are…"

Marcus stops the Prince from finishing his sentence. He places a kiss on his cheek, and with tears in his eyes, he looks at him.

"I got everything that I needed to make the decision," Marcus says as his tear rolls down his cheek, landing on his cloak.

"What does that mean?" Prince Ciprian asks with concern dripping off his words.

"I think I should go," Marcus says, placing his hand over the Prince's heart, stopping him mid-sentence.

"Yes, I think that would be best. Don't want anyone getting the wrong idea about dinner," she replies, licking her lips, displaying her fangs.

Marcus looks into her eyes, not shaken nor moved by her overt display of aggression. He holds out his hand in an attempt to leave gracefully. She holds out her arms as if to hug him, and he leans in slightly, patting her on the back.

"I think you are just mad your son wants to be with a black man, vice one of these pasty inbreds," Marcus whispers into her ear.

She pushes him back and hisses like that of a crouching cat.

Prince Ciprian pushes Marcus out of the way as he hisses, causing her to step back. He turns fast enough to see Marcus's cape slide into the passageway. Not even the Prince's vamp speed could help him catch up with Marcus before he departs the castle.

Prince Ciprian screams to himself as Marcus disappears down the elaborate pathway as he catches only a mere glimpse of his cloak slipping out of the door. Marcus summons a wind and glides upon the air like a superhero. As he makes it to the end of the path, he can see Kraven and Cairo standing, waiting on him. Marcus flies into Kraven's arms, nearly knocking him to the ground.

He whispers into his ear, "It's you. It's always been you."

Kraven places his hand on the back of Marcus's head. Marcus pushes back, looking into his eyes, which are glowing emerald green. "I need you to stand back."

Kraven and Cairo step back as Marcus shakes himself off. He places his hands palms out to the sky.

"Chaos, I let you in."

Everything goes silent as Marcus's head flings back and he is engulfed in black smoke. Chaos in his male form emerges.

Kraven thrusts at him, but Cairo holds him back.

"Let him do this."

Chaos begins to chant as the wind begins to blow heavily, causing people in the city streets to take cover. Chaos rises off the ground, levitating as his arms rise above his head and slowly come down.

"Rise from the ground, contain what you might, hold mythical creature with all of your might, give way to none, hold them tight, twelve hours until the dawn's first light!"

As he speaks the words, a grey dome forms over the castle. Ciprian watches as the dome forms, and Winston takes off running. As the dome closes down on the edges of the forest, Winston gets out narrowly. Ciprian, saddened by the display, walks back into the house.

"What has happened? We felt the ground shaking," asks the Queen.

"No one will be leaving the castle tonight."

"Ciprian, what do you mean? Our guests must leave."

"These are the consequences of your actions. He has placed the castle and the surrounding forest in a dome. I am sure it's some type of mythical containment spell."

"You didn't say the Tri-bred was a witch. I never would have pushed so hard."

"You should have never pushed hard from the beginning!" Ciprian screamed, causing the room to go silent.

"I will let you have that one. If you ever scream at me again, you won't live to see dawn," Queen Sorina whispers to him. "Guests, we've run into an issue, but it's nothing we can't handle. The castle has been surrounded by a containment spell, but we aren't going to let that ruin our night. We have plenty of blood, and rooms downstairs in the catacombs. You can leave as soon as this lifts."

"Queen Sorina, are you sure it will be lifted by morning?" shouts a male voice in the crowd.

"I assure you, I've never met a witch who was powerful enough to keep a containment spell longer than 24 hours. This time tomorrow night, you will all be heading back to your respective homes to enjoy your own national delicacies."

The music starts up again, and people continue about their night.

"You better pray that he isn't as powerful as I think he is."

"For your sake, you better hope that he cares about you enough to let this thing down."

"Winston got out."

"Well, sounds like we will have our meal after all."

"What do you mean?"

"Containment spells keep us in. They don't keep humans out. Go to the woods and contact Winston. Have him scare us up some humans. These aren't going to last the remainder of the night."

Prince Ciprian leaves with his vamp speed, causing her hair to lift in the wind caused by his quickness.

Chaos slowly landed on his feet. He turns, looking at Kraven and Cairo, shooting them a wink with his jet black eyes. He holds out his hands again, palms facing the sky. "I release you."

The black smoke blooms around Marcus as his head tilts back, his mouth opens, and it goes back within him. Kraven runs to him as a single black-stained tear falls from his face. He collapses in the middle of the street. Kraven picks Marcus's limp body from the ground and carries him back to the Inn. Bystanders slowly walk out of the bars, witnessing Marcus being carried and looking on in shock.

As they make it back to the Inn, Kraven places him onto the massage table in the sun room. Cairo closes the door behind him. A group of young people preparing to leave look on in shock.

"Kraven, is he okay? What was that?"

"That was Marcus's uncle, the God of Chaos," Kraven says, wiping his face with a damp cloth. Marcus slowly opens his eyes. He desperately tries to get up from the table.

"Stop, Marcus. You are weak. Just sit here for a moment."

"Did we do it?"

"Yes, but I have another question for you. How long have you known that Chaos is inside of you?"

"I've known since we left the garden. When I tasted the tear, a piece of him remained."

"So, all those times I asked you if you were talking to someone and you lied, it was him?"

"Yes," Marcus replies, slowly sitting up as he placed his head into the palms of his hands.

"He's helped you get stronger, hasn't he?"

"Yes, I couldn't have done it without him. I knew that tonight. I could feel the power in the room, and they could feel my power too."

"As much as I want to be angry, I'm just happy that you are safe."

"Me too," Cairo replied as he looked on with his back against the sliding door.

"Can you take me to my room? I can feel myself healing, but I'm still tired."

"Of course," Kraven replies, holding him by his side.

"Cairo, keep as many people away from that field as possible. Humans can go back and forth, but anything mythical that gets in is going to have to wait until tomorrow to get out."

"Will do," Cairo replies, sending up a hand salute.

As the doors open, the group is still waiting. A young man with a strong French accent asks, "Is he okay?"

Kraven smiles and replies, "He's fine, just had a little too much to drink."

"Hey, I can show you guys to the best bar in town."

The group begins to whoop and holler as Cairo takes them out of the house. He looks back, and Kraven shoots him a wink. Kraven gets Marcus into the room and turns him around as Marcus holds on to the back of a chair while Kraven helps him out of his clothes. Once in nothing but his boxer briefs, Kraven lies him down in the bed.

"You sure you're good?"

"Yeah, I'm actually feeling much better," Marcus replies, smiling at him.

"You scared me," Kraven says, looking down into his eyes, pushing a stray hair from his face.

"That's a first. At least it's a first that you've admitted to me."

"I know. I know I am not the most open with my feelings, but that was because I didn't want to be hurt by you."

Marcus sits up soberly and serious. "Kraven, it was never my intent to hurt you. I just didn't know what I wanted. But after that, I knew the only one I could be with was you."

"You said it was me, it's always been me."

"Let me put it like this. It has always been you. I didn't realize it until I saw you standing there. In that moment, every protective thing you've done in defense of me flashed before my eyes. That's why I said it's always been you."

"Do you love me though?"

"I do," Marcus says coyly, looking down, averting Kraven's stare. He places his hand on Marcus's chin, causing him to look back into his deep golden eyes.

He leans in, kissing him passionately on the lips. Marcus places his hair in a messy bun, and Kraven's nostrils flare.

"Why do you do that?"

"It's a turn-on when you put your hair up like that."

Marcus takes it down slowly and shakes his wildly curly shoulder-length hair. Pulling it up from the back to place it back in a messy bun again, teasing Kraven. His nostrils flare again. Marcus leans in, kissing him. This time he slides his tongue into Kraven's mouth. His tongue tastes like copper and honey. Marcus slowly pulls Kraven's shirt over his head and begins kissing on his neck. Kraven grabs Marcus and lifts him out of the bed, causing Marcus to wrap his legs around Kraven's bare torso. As they fall back onto the bed, Kraven's massive body lands on Marcus. This causes him to inhale deeply. The weight was welcomed; it felt like home, like comfort.

Marcus unbuckles Kraven's pants, causing him to stand to remove them and his socks as he removes Marcus's stockings. The only thing keeping them from being completely flesh upon flesh were their underwear. As they make out, Marcus claws at Kraven's back. His scales strengthen as Marcus takes his nails through them, his eyes rolling back, his body in complete sensory overload. Kraven kisses his neck, chin, pecs, and his inner thigh as he slowly slides Marcus out of his underwear.

"Are you okay with this?" Kraven whispers in his ear, placing his body on top of Marcus's exposed, throbbing private.

Marcus reaches up with both hands, placing his palms on the sides of Kraven's face. "If we do this, there is no turning back."

"I don't want to turn back. I will devote my life to you."

Marcus kisses him and slides Kraven's underwear down his massive thighs. He then takes him and slowly slides him inside. Kraven watches the pleasure on his face as Marcus's mouth slightly opens, allowing only the smallest gasp to seep out. Their bodies became one in a thrusting motion. Marcus's eyes look as if clouds are filling them. He looks at Kraven and smiles as a tear falls. The intense intimacy causes Kraven to bury his beard and face into Marcus's neck as the thrusting quickens.

"I'm close," Kraven whispers into Marcus's ear.

"So am I."

In that moment, their bodies are lifted by the wind. A sphere of clouds surrounds them as Marcus grips Kraven's shoulder, holding on to him tightly. As they climax, the sphere cracks and sends a surge of energy from the room with a thunderous roar. The two hit the bed, holding each other tight. The trees bend. Cairo can feel the energy shift. Luca, back in the town, can feel it. Even Poseidon can feel it. Luca smiles as Curara walks outside.

"They sealed the bond," she says, looking in Luca's direction.

He replies, "Took them long enough."

Back in the room, the two continue breathing heavily. Kraven looks up from Marcus's neck. "I love you."

"I love you too."

"Let me grab you a towel," Kraven says, looking into his eyes as the clouds dissipate.

"No, let's just get into the shower," replies Marcus.

CHAPTER 39: WINSTON

I got out right before the containment spell came down, and I waited on my Master to come. I knew he would come. I knew that I could go back into the containment spell, but once I was in, I wouldn't be able to come back out. Then I saw him. He glided until he found me. I was close to a brush. A little bruised, but nothing that I wouldn't heal from.

"Winston, how did you know?"

"I don't know. I could just feel it, and when I saw him take off on the wind, I knew he was up to no good."

"Well, at least you are safe."

"I would be safer in there, to be completely honest. I am just the undead. There is nothing that they would have been able to do to me. I don't even bleed."

"I know. Mother wants you to deliver us something fresh."

"That shouldn't be so hard. Everyone here is nearly intoxicated out of their minds. Just let the vamps know they need to be ready. I will send them to you."

Ciprian places his hand on the containment field, and it ripples underneath his touch. Winston almost touches it too, but doesn't.

"I'm sorry that things didn't work out with Marcus."

"I don't think he ever really wanted to choose me, so I am going to have to get the Blood another way. Never you fret about that. Deliver us some dinner, and I will see you when this thing comes down."

In that moment, I looked into his eyes and wondered to myself exactly why he, Prince Ciprian Dracula, never chose me. I've devoted most of my undead years in his service. But I owed him. It hurt me to see him like this. Like a caged animal unable to defend himself against a man that I believe he truly did fall for. Now I can help him like he once saved me.

That night I wandered aimlessly for some time around the small town that I once called home. I even went back to my childhood home. This was a place of happiness for me. A place where I thought I would grow old, build a life of my own, love a man that I chose. However, the small-minded townspeople of that time saw different. A young man by the name of Blake took me to the woods for what I thought would be a romantic evening. When we made it to the beautiful location that overlooked the lake, his friends jumped out. They taunted me. They called me names, and then they proceeded to beat on me mercilessly, drowning me until I took what they thought was my last breath. They then threw me into the lake, where my lifeless body eventually floated towards the bottom. Eyes open, still semiconscious on the brink of death, I saw her. A lake nymph. She swam over to me and said nothing, but I could hear her thoughts.

"Winston Rosu, I cannot bring you back to life, but I can make it so that you live amongst us mythical creatures. Would you accept my offer?"

I replied, "Yes."

She emitted a light that was so intense it caused me to close my eyes. When I opened them, I was back in my bed at home, but something about me had changed. I no longer felt my heart beating. My skin was cold and clammy, and the only thing that I could think of was flesh. I walked downstairs to the kitchen and opened the icebox. There I found a piece of uncooked meat and bit into it. I gnawed on it, making animalistic sounds, until my mother came down to the kitchen and saw me. The shock on her face as she saw me, I'll never forget.

"Get out of this house. You aren't my son, you demon."

I ran out of the house back to the woods. For about a month, the woods became my home. I was dirty, rank, and starving. In my darkest moment, he came for me. Out on a hunt alone, the young Prince ran upon me in the woods. He turned his nose up at me at first, and out of fear I hid my face from him. After the initial shock, he showed me a kindness that no one had in the past month. He took me back to the empty castle, gave me a bath, and clothed me. He fed me the flesh from one of the victims that he had sucked dry.

Many over the years have wondered why I've never left his side. This is the very reason. In addition to the fact that he brought the boys who did this to me, to me, so that I could end their lives myself. As I watched him drain them and their eyes glossed over, it brought me such pleasure knowing that he was my friend. Over the years, I helped him calm his bloodlust to a point where he only had to drink a couple of times a month. Every now and again, he would feed on someone and drain them completely, leaving me the remains. Tonight would be the same. I would have a stock of meat for months.

I can see the bloodlust in his eyes. He is angry, but he won't show it until the most opportune time. God bless all of those creatures inside with him. Some will not make it out alive.

CHAPTER 40: NARRATOR

W inston, lost in thoughts, placed his hood over his head as he walked into a local pub. Amongst the bustling crowd, he was able to slip into a dark corner to gather himself for what was next. For a moment, he just listened, drowning out much of the noise until he was able to zero in on a group of unhappy singles who wanted to party.

"I thought this was going to be a little more exciting," one of the young men said to his group of friends.

"I've heard about these parties getting wilder as the night gets later," replies a female in his group.

Winston sulks over to their table and slides in. "I know where there is an exclusive party. Plenty of drinks, plenty of food, and plenty of, you know… things that get the party started."

"Who are you?" asked the girl, looking at Winston curiously.

"If you don't really want to party, then stay here," he said as he got up quickly, sliding through the crowd.

They sat at the table for a moment, and the young man who stated he wanted something exciting got up and walked out. His friends followed. When they reached the street, they saw Winston at the foot of the path. Ciprian was waiting for them.

"Hey, I heard you guys were looking for a little fun."

"Yeah," the young man replied.

"Do y'all know who that is?"

"No."

"It's Prince Ciprian. He's been on the cover of Vogue Men, one of Romania's most eligible bachelors."

Ciprian smiles. "Yes, that's me."

"Guys, something doesn't feel right," says one of the other young women as she looks up at the night sky. Lightning skips across above.

"Alana, I am going," the young man says as he walks through the containment spell, noticing nothing.

The rest follow. As soon as they have entered, Ciprian is in the distance, and they run up towards him. As they get closer to where he is, he once again disappears, and they are overtaken by the forest around them. Still on the path, but they can't see the sky above them. Strange sounds begin to surround them as the wind blows and the trees shake violently. The girls begin to scream and race back before being stopped by Ciprian. The young lady screams, and Ciprian takes his pinky nail, slicing her throat.

Winston stands at the foot of the path listening to the screams, which are drowned out to nothing by the thunder as the rain begins to pour. He turns, noticing Cairo skateboarding to the Inn. A sinister smile covers his face as he slowly begins walking towards the Inn. Marcus and Kraven sleep peacefully in bed as Winston walks into the Inn unencumbered with a group of guests. He slid up the stairs and into the room, not making a sound. As he takes a seat in a dark corner, the pupil of his eye casts a grey dime-like appearance in the darkness. He says nothing but watches the two as they sleep in an intimate embrace.

Kraven lets out a snore that awakens Marcus. Feeling like they are no longer alone, his body begins to glow. He can faintly make out the shadow in the corner.

"I'll never forgive you for breaking his heart," Winston says as he lunges from the seat, causing Marcus to summon a whirlwind which spins the bed like a merry-go-round. Kraven awakens, standing on the bed, pulling a marlin spike from his back. Winston stops as the floor beneath his feet seems to be turning in the counterclockwise direction to the bed. Marcus holds up his hand, causing the balcony door to open, but before he can send Winston out of it, the bedroom door opens and Cairo stands there. Winston leaps toward the boy, grabbing him, and takes off with vampire-like speed. Marcus stops the bed, and Kraven takes off after them.

Marcus stops him at the foot of the stairs as he is completely naked, throwing down clothes. Marcus sprints after Winston as Cairo kicks and fights with all of his might to get out of his grip. Marcus can tell with the distance between them, he isn't going to catch up with them, and they are only feet away from the foot of the forest. Behind him, Kraven launches the marlin spike, hitting Winston in the leg. He tumbles but picks Cairo back up, making it through the containment spell. Marcus keeps running as if he is going to run through it, but Kraven pulls him from behind.

"Stop!"

"No! Cairo."

"Marcus, if you go in there, you might not come out alive."

As Marcus walks up to the containment spell, which he can see with his sight, Ciprian appears. Winston is standing behind him in the distance with Cairo still kicking and grunting, fighting back.

"All you have to do is lower the containment spell. Let these vamps go, and we can make a deal on how you can get Cairo back."

He places his hand upon the containment spell. "Because from the looks of it, only mythical creatures can get in, but they can't come out."

"Why would you do this?" Marcus asks as Kraven continues to hold him back.

"Why would I do what? You thought Winston was a vamp. He is the undead, but he has a mind of his own. This bait and switch was completely his own. He had already done what I asked, and that was deliver us humans to feast upon. Needless to say, we got our fill. Now, we will take your little brother and lock him up until our demands are met."

"When I get inside, I am going to kill your mother and make you watch. Then I will kill you."

"I can't wait to see that happen," Ciprian replies as he and Winston take off into the night.

"Fuck!"

"Marcus, we will get him back. That spell took a lot out of you, and I don't want you calling on Chaos again. We will wait until the containment comes down, and then we will strike."

"I'm so sorry. This shouldn't have happened."

"Marcus, not even you could have predicted that Winston would have gotten out of the containment spell before it fell."

"I know, but I didn't make anything better by speaking so stupidly."

"Cairo needed to hear that. It's going to give him hope that we are coming for him. Now I have to go speak with my father. Can I leave you at the Inn alone, and you promise you won't go through the containment spell?"

"I honestly can't promise you that right now, Kraven."

"Then you are coming with me."

CHAPTER 41: MARCUS

I 'd done a lot of stupid things in my life, but never anything as stupid as that. From the moment these powers were unlocked within me, I was warned about the conning nature of those who operate in the dark. Never had I expected to experience something like this firsthand outside of a fight. Now I'm sitting in this car watching the man I love tell his father that I got his brother taken by the man who bears the same last name as the person who killed his father's father. As he walks toward the car, I stand outside by my door with my head down. He places his hand underneath my chin.

"Listen to me, this is not your fault."

"You have saved more lives tonight than you know."

"We will get Cairo back alive."

As he spoke to me, a cloud of smoke and lightning descended upon us.

"It's the Ursitoare."

"Luca, since you've mentioned them, I did a little research. They are supposed to come at the birth of a child to weave their fate."

"Marcus, when you and Kraven had your moment tonight that is what we call…"

Before he could finish, the Ursitoare responded. "It's what we call a bonding, but you already know about the bonding. Poseidon told you about it. We see all."

"So can you explain to me why you are here now?" Marcus asked.

"We are here to weave your fates and answer any questions you might have," one talking over another to complete the sentence.

"Weave our fates?" Marcus asked.

"Yes. You and Kraven, step forward."

As Kraven grabbed my hand, we moved closer to them. My body wasn't glowing, so I had to assume they meant us no harm. As we stood before them, and they hovered suspended in midair, they pulled what looked like a golden string from my chest and a blue string from Kraven's and began to weave the strings together. I could feel the string as they tugged some internal part of me. I then thought back to Luke. Was this the thing that made me feel so aimless and lost when he passed away? A tear left my eye as they tied the final knot, which pulled me and Kraven face to face. Our eyes glistened like golden medallions before turning back to their normal hue. He looked down into my eyes, wiped my tear from my cheek.

"I love you," he said with a slight grin on his face.

"I love you too."

"Now that your fates have been weaved together, there is a bond that cannot be severed. Between you, Marcus, and the boy being held in captivity, this paternal bond shall not be severed until one of you has died."

"Will I be able to feel it?"

"Yes, you will know."

One of the Ursitoare seemed off. More evil than the others, and I couldn't shake the way she was looking at me. As if she were plotting against me.

"Is there something that you wish to ask?"

"Yes, will we get Cairo back?" Marcus asks.

"Yes, but we cannot tell you how."

"Will he be alive?" Luca asks.

"Yes, but he will endure emotional damage that you will not be able to fix. He will have to stay with the Demi-God and his intended."

"Demi-God?" Marcus says.

"Marcus, you are no regular Tri-bred. When the God of Chaos unlocked your powers, he unlocked your potential. At your full strength, which you will not reach until you have left these lands, you will be more than a Demi-God. You will be a Tetramorph. The world has never seen a Tetramorph. The closest we've gotten by millennia have been the tri-bred."

"Is this the reason that Ciprian wants my blood?"

"Ciprian Dracula believes that you are a tri-bred and that your blood will make him immortal. Not only that, but your blood will allow him to create an entirely new race of vampires. Day walkers who are no longer cursed to walk at night. At your full potential, the Goddess of Light may not allow you to stay on earth, as you will be as powerful as she, if not stronger, after years of experience and exposure to your powers."

"We must go."

"One last question?" Marcus asks.

They nod.

"Will Ciprian die by my hands?"

"Yes."

The three women ease back into their gaseous form, and the cloud disappears before our very eyes. I hit the ground, completely taken back by everything that they said.

CHAPTER 42: CAIRO

T he cell was cold and dark. I could vaguely make out Winston in the corner. His eyes locked on me as I sat awaiting my escape. There was a bit of commotion coming from the hallway as I heard a door slam. That was when he walked into the room. The man whose family killed my ancestor. Ciprian walks toward the cage that they'd locked me in and sits Indian style in front of me.

"So, how long do you think it's going to take for Marcus to remove this containment spell?"

I didn't say a word. I just looked at him. Not noticing Winston move, a deluge of water came through the bars, knocking me on my back as my head bounced on the concrete floor. I gathered myself and stood to my feet, placing my back against the cold stone wall.

"I'm really sorry about that. Winston is from an older generation; we both are. A generation when your elders speak to you, you reply. Do you understand?"

I again didn't utter a word, and as expected, the water came. There was so much of it that you would have thought he had a hose on me. It knocked me down again as I slipped on the limestone floor. They had taken my shoes and my socks.

"We are going to try this one more time."

Before I could stop myself, I ran into the bars, displaying my fangs. "I am going to watch him rip your spine out of your body with his bare hand, and Kraven is going to lap up your blood like a wild animal."

"There you are!" he says as he walks up to me, cool and calmly. "The pup speaks, and you have the temper of your older brother, don't you."

Winston once again douses me with water, knocking me again off my feet. As I hit the floor, I felt the ground shake. It felt like a thousand horses galloping across a wild field.

"Sounds like Marcus is more predictable than you thought," Ciprian says, turning his back on me. "Winston, get him out of the cage."

The moment Winston opened the cage, I turned into a wolf and took off running toward the door.

CHAPTER 43: MARCUS

C iprian had gone too far this time. Kidnapping Cairo was the last straw, and now I had a band of warriors standing beside me. We took to the castle, and with the flick of my wrist, the doors came slamming down, landing on one of the vampires, crushing him.

"One down, a few more to go."

As we made our way slowly down the halls, I illuminated the structure, which sent vamps in all directions.

"Kill them. Leave the Queen for me."

I'd never seen what I could only describe as a medieval battle between good and evil. But I am sure this was pretty close. I watched as the Sons of Oannes tore the vampire royalty to shreds, leaving nothing but ash in their wake. As I continued towards the ballroom, a deafening silence fell around me. I knew she was near.

She ascended from the sky like a fiery goddess, landing just feet away from me.

"Oh, the little negro is back to get his revenge because some vamps were mean to him," she mocked.

"No, no, no. I am back so that your son can watch your last moments on earth."

"Marcus!" screams Ciprian as he walked out, holding Cairo by the neck, suspended in mid-air.

"Release him."

"Let her go, and I will."

"Ciprian, you have no bargaining power here."

He shakes Cairo, and I can feel his grip tightening around his neck. I close my eyes.

"Cairo, pull a pike and jam it into his side," I say to him using telepathy.

Cairo slowly reaches back and pulls a marlin spike and jams it into Ciprian's side. As he begins to run, Winston catches up with him. Cairo pulls a marlin spike and severs the head of Winston. Ciprian cried out in agony. As he watches Winston's head roll across the floor, Kraven steps on it, crushing his skull.

"Now, I told you, you would watch your mother die."

"Marcus, no!"

"I call forth the wind and rain, and ice of the arctic."

Lightning fills the room as I held her locked in place. Her body instantly turned to ice. Ciprian watches as I raised my hand to the sky, bringing lightning down upon her frozen frame, sending her shattering into pieces across the ballroom floor.

"Mother!" Ciprian screams out for her.

His body balls up, and I can hear his bones breaking. Gigantic wings come bursting from his back as his skin turns black and hairy. His screams turn into guttural growls as I look at Kraven.

"Get Cairo out of here. Get all of them out of here!" I scream as I hold up my hand, creating a stargate with the wind.

"I'm not leaving you."

"You must. This is my fight."

"Marcus, we can't leave you," Cairo says as he holds on to my arm.

"You have to go." As the other soldiers head through, I send Kraven and Cairo flying through the stargate, closing it as the castle rumbles into silence. I stood there alone, forgetting that an enemy lurked near. As I turned, he stood before me. Face to face. I could smell his primal form. Like that of a sick, wet animal. He looked demonic, like an angel cast out of heaven, singed in fur and hellfire after the uprising. Is this what people saw when the angels were cast out of heaven?

"You made a grave mistake."

"If you say so," I reply, sending him flying with a gust of wind. He flies around the eaves of the ballroom so quickly I couldn't see him.

"You aren't going to make it out of here alive."

"If I don't, at least you won't receive the true blood."

"Even if I get a taste of your blood, I will be far too powerful for the Sons of Oannes to kill."

He grabbed me, sinking his fangs into my neck as he pulled me through the ceiling, bursting through multiple floors of the castle. I could feel the poison seeping in as he pulled what little blood he could. He flew through the stone like it was paper. He dragged me to the top of the containment spell where he could fly no more.

"I am going to enjoy draining you completely dry."

As I struggled with my breath, I laughed through my bloody mouth. "You wanna know the funny part about being outside of the castle?" He leaned in, holding my face only feet away from his. "You are now in my element."

Thunder crackles overhead as a bolt of lightning shoots directly down into him. He loses his grip on me as I fall back down through the floors he just took me up through. As I landed on the ballroom floor, my side and leg were pierced by the chandelier, which sent me careening into the wall before I hit the floor. The chandelier caught fire to the silk curtain and quickly spread.

Fire roars like a medieval dragon all around me. Blood runs from my neck, leg, and side as I lay on the marbled floor. As the smoke fills my lungs, I watch the fire dance overhead. I looked up at the night sky. It was the most beautiful thing that I had ever seen. It took me back to the accident. Hyperventilating, as my lungs filled with smoke, my head began to spin, until I heard a guttural growl come toward me. Ciprian wasn't dead. Badly burned, but not dead. As I pulled myself into a seated position, I watched as he walked doggedly over to me, growling with his teeth on full display. Suddenly a dark shadow rushes him, sending a wall crumbling onto them. My body slumped over in a puddle of my own blood, and everything went black.

CHAPTER 44: NARRATOR

As Marcus lies there motionless, Poseidon lifts him and shoots up through the opened roof. As he holds the Trident of the Seven Seas in one hand and Marcus in the other, he sends a blast of energy down on the castle that shatters it. The wave of energy destroys the containment spell, and he flies Marcus off.

While flying over the trees, Marcus momentarily opens his eyes, noticing Poseidon holding him.

"You came for me."

"I'll always come for you."

In that moment, Marcus remembers the person who pulled him from the car accident. It wasn't a neighbor. It was Poseidon. He pulled him and Luke from the wreckage and left them there for the ambulance.

"You have been," Marcus replies as his eyes slowly close again.

Poseidon descends over the gypsy encampment. Kraven runs

towards him, grabbing Marcus from his arms.

"Why is he so beaten up?"

"He has not yet come into his full power. He is still mostly human. It will take him time to heal. Right now, you need to get him to the medicine woman so that she can help his body."

Kraven takes Marcus into Curara's home and places him on the table. Blood is still slowly leaking from his leg and side. He has scratches about his face and neck. Kraven can't tell if he's been bitten as he examines his body. Curara pushes Kraven out of the house.

"It's time to let me work."

As Curara mixed leaves and blood from Oannes, she placed the mixture on Marcus's body. He begins to glow again, and then his light dims. She walks outside and looks into Kraven's eyes. He tries to rush her, but Poseidon holds him back.

"You have to let the magic run its course. He is strong. Stronger than you know."

Kraven screams and takes off running towards the lake, jumping in. Cairo watches his brother with tears in his eyes.

"Can I sit with him?"

"Go. But don't do anything. Just hold his hand."

Cairo nods as he slowly walks into the house. There is blood everywhere. Marcus's breathing is faint, and Cairo can see his chest moving ever so slowly up and down. He takes him by the hand and holds it. He sits there with him and waits as the gypsies pray to Oannes to bring Marcus back.

As the sun rises over the treetops, Kraven emerges from the water. As he transforms, walking back onshore with his bare feet hitting the grass, he looks over at Poseidon and Luca, who are talking by a smoldering fire.

Inside the house, Cairo's head slides into the blood. It opens his third eye, and he sees Marcus and Kraven getting married. He is Kraven's best man as he watches Marcus walk down the aisle in a deeply lush wooded area. He picks his head up, gasping in unison with Marcus. The blood slowly seeps into his head without him knowing. As he looks over at Marcus, he turns his head towards him and smiles. Marcus takes his hand through his hair.

"Hey, you."

Tears fill Cairo's eyes as he jumps up, hugging Marcus tightly, causing him to wince in pain.

"Help the old man up," Marcus says, chuckling again and wincing in pain.

He slowly moves from the table, and Cairo places his arm around Marcus's neck, guiding him toward the door. The sun hits his face, causing him to lift his hand. Kraven looks up and notices him standing there. He slowly jogs, which turns into a sprint. Cairo holds his hand up.

"He's still sore. Be careful."

Kraven slows down until they are standing face to face.

"I thought I lost you," he says, taking his thumb over a scrape on his face.

"You couldn't have thought you lost me," Marcus says, pulling at a strand of wet hair.

"Is he?"

"I don't even know. Poseidon would know better than me."

"What happened?"

"He turned into his bat form, and all hell broke loose. I just remember falling backwards through the ceiling, hitting something sharp, and then hitting the floor like a basketball."

Poseidon walked up to the two of them.

"He is dead. I destroyed the castle and the containment spell."

Marcus rests his head on Kraven, and he embraces him.

7 Months Later

CHAPTER 45: MARCUS

W ho would have thought seven months after my life nearly came to an end that I would be preparing to leave this place that I now call home? We've been cleared of any wrongdoing surrounding the destruction of the castle. In addition, we've donated time and resources toward the restoration project. At that time, when everything was happening, I wasn't thinking about the castle as a landmark. I was thinking about the young man who was about to lose his life and destroying the man who had taken so much from so many. Following being cleared, Kraven and I decided that we would have to apply for a K-1 fiancé visa. In order to make it look real, he and I got engaged in a small ceremony surrounded by no more than 400 mythical creatures. Upon the approval of his request, we made our final plans to head back to Maine to visit my parents, followed by our final destination, Victoria, British Columbia. Yes, we are moving into that mansion that was left to me by my late husband.

"Hey, are you ready?" Kraven asks as I close my laptop.

"Yeah, off to the airport."

Luca also found someone to take over Kraven's business in his absence. Cairo graduated high school and intends on attending a local college in BC. Things are turning around. No one ever found the remains of Ciprian, so his death was ruled suspicious. In addition, no one found any remains of the vampire royalty that graced the hallowed halls of that white castle. I knew that many of them incinerated as soon as they were stabbed through the heart or decapitated. I haven't called Chaos in some time. However, I often want to speak to him via our mirror interaction.

Cairo came to my door, grabbed my bag, and looked at me. "If you are going to speak to him, you better say something before Kraven finds out."

I smile at him and turn to the mirror quickly.

"Chaos, come to me." I turned, and when I returned, he wasn't my doppelganger—he appeared as himself.

"It's been some time, and your body has healed nicely. The fact that you were poisoned by the bite of a vampire, impaled by a chandelier, and hit the ground like a ton of bricks, I am shocked by your speedy recovery."

"Well, I am happy that I can still surprise you, seeing as you are a part of me."

"Did you have something that you wanted to ask me?"

"When will I come into my full power?"

"Marcus that is a question that I can't answer for you. You need to continue to practice and become more familiar with the powers that you currently have. The moment your body feels like you can handle more, you will feel it. It feels like nothing you've ever experienced."

"And you will be there the entire way?"

"You ingested me through your tears. I am lodged in your heart. You will never get rid of me."

"But he will stop calling on you," Kraven says, walking into the room looking at Chaos.

"As you wish… fiancé."

As I turn to Kraven, Chaos disappears.

"Don't."

"I will not fight with you, Marcus. We have a long flight ahead of us, and I need your head clear. Are you ready to go?"

"I don't know. This feels so surreal. I've spent so much time here that I've grown to love this small village."

"It loves you back," Kraven replies as he ushers me over to the window. There, standing below, were my students.

It filled my heart with joy to see that they wanted to wish us off as we departed. I grabbed my laptop bag and began to walk toward the door. Kraven looked up toward the castle, which was currently under reconstruction.

"What if he isn't gone?"

"We will be ready," I said as I walked over to him, placing my hand upon his face, making him look into my eyes. "We will be ready."

He leans in, passionately kissing me on the lips, gripping my side. He inhaled as our mouths touched, as if he were trying to record this moment in his mind. I placed my hand upon his chest. The touch of me still made his heart beat out of control. As did mine.

CHAPTER 46: KRAVEN

I didn't know how to feel leaving my homeland. Leaving my business with the brothers. I didn't know about leaving my father, but I knew one thing to be certain. I couldn't live my life without him. So, meeting his family today was just another added stressor. He hadn't really spoken about them since getting to Romania, other than the few times that I saw him speak with his sister. Now we are in an airport in Maine waiting on them. He wanted us to visit before we made our final departure to Victoria. I could tell the moment that he saw his mother. She took off running toward him, and he walked slowly toward her, smiling the biggest smile I've ever seen him muster.

"Mom, I want to introduce you to Kraven and Cairo."

"It's so wonderful to meet you both. Your father is waiting at the house. We got a Tesla, and there isn't a lot of room. I wanted to make sure that you boys felt comfortable."

"Is Marissa there?"

"She is. I'm glad to see that the both of you are on good terms still."

"I mean, I've been gone some time now."

"You look good, but like you are in need of a good meal. All of you look like you are in need of some food."

We made it back to the house, and I met his father. He was a very nice man. He smiled a lot. More than the average man. He asked a lot of questions about me and Cairo. For the purposes of the trip, I just told him that Cairo was my son. So, it's a good thing that the two of us resemble our father. Marissa came into the house like a wild phoenix, and I could tell why he felt that he needed to get away.

"Sooooo, you never told me that the kid was his son."

"Marissa, he is sitting right here, and we are eating dinner. Can you find something else to talk about?"

"What do you want us to talk about?"

"Marissa, anything but that."

"Why haven't we heard from you in like seven months?"

"Marissa, can you please stop."

"Marcus, it's been all over social media. They said that you were a suspect in the disappearance of Prince Ciprian."

"Marissa, we have been cleared of any wrongdoing. They realized that we were just in the wrong place at the wrong time."

"Marcus..."

"Marissa, stop talking. Let everyone eat in peace," says Earl, looking around the table at the tense expressions on everyone's face. You can tell by his tone and demeanor that he doesn't often raise his voice.

Later that night, we all sat around the firepit and watched the embers float up into the night sky. For the first time in a long time, I just looked at Marcus. His beauty was illuminated by the fire's light. I watched as he looked around at his mother, father, and sister. He looked at them like he was looking at strangers. Somehow, I felt that his growing abilities made him feel slightly more distant from them than he had in the past.

As we laid in bed that night, I felt him struggling to sleep. He then just stared up at the ceiling, and the hours of the night slowly ticked away.

"Is everything okay, Marcus?"

"Yeah, something just doesn't feel the same."

"Is it Ciprian?"

"I don't know. If it was him, how did he get here?"

"People with money will find a way to do things. Mythical creatures with money can go undetected for days, months, years, even millennia."

"That's good to know."

"If you want to leave, we can leave."

"Actually, I think I would like to leave. I just don't feel safe here, and I don't want to bring any unnecessary drama to my parents' home."

"Well, are you going to have the conversation with them? They have been expecting us, and I am sure they want to spend some time with you."

"It's fine. We can stay."

After those four days, we headed back to the airport and were on our next flight to Victoria.

CHAPTER 47: NARRATOR

M arissa made her way back to her house. As she approached the door, she noticed that it was slightly ajar. She walked in, and the lights didn't come on.

"I know I paid the bill," she said to herself as she proceeded into the kitchen, placing her keys and purse on the marble countertop.

As she proceeded into the living room, she saw a figure sitting with their back facing her.

"Don't think about running. I will catch you before you can make it to the door," the male voice said in the dark.

Marissa wanted so badly to respond, but it felt like her vocal cords were constricted.

"Come and sit."

She slowly moved closer and sat on an ottoman.

"You will not make it out of this house the same tonight. I will not kill you, but you will not be the same."

The door slams shut, and Marissa's screams are drowned out in the night.

CHAPTER 48: MARCUS

V ictoria is the most beautiful place I've seen outside of Romania. Full of nature, and it just feels private. The house is nestled in a tree line that walks out into a beautiful crystal blue lake. Kraven, Cairo, and I look out at it before we walk into the house. As we walk in, we are greeted by a beautiful semi-spiral staircase that leads to the second floor.

"This is all ours?" Cairo says, looking up and spinning around.

I smile, looking at the pure pleasure on his face. "Yes, this is all ours."

"Are we rich?"

"Cairo, go find a room and stop asking silly questions. For an eighteen-year-old, you are silly."

"Kraven, stop," I say, smiling and placing my hand upon his chest. "He's excited, and so am I. We finally all get to live under the same roof without looking over our shoulder…"

I stopped midsentence as I felt someone approaching from behind. The wind began to pick up, and my hair began to rise from my shoulders. Kraven took a defensive stance. There, standing at our front door, was a beautiful Native Indian male.

"Are you Marcus the tri-bred?"

"I am."

"I need your help."

"How can I help you?"

"My people are being ravaged by a creature that we haven't been able to identify."

I looked at Kraven. Cairo stood behind us.

"Marcus, we have to help them."

I looked up at Kraven and back at Cairo. "Is this going to become our lives?"

"You are here to save our people."

I looked back at the young man. "Come in. Tell us how we can help."

To be continued...

ABOUT THE AUTHOR

Wryter Kiselev-Rolling, the Author of In the Blood. A former federal paralegal for most of his military career, Wryter decided to step out on faith and pursue his passion for writing with an A.S. in Paralegal Studies, a B.A in English, and an MFA in Creative Writing with a Certificate in Online Writing under his belt, Wryter is not only able to give his all to his profession, but he is also able to teach future writers, which is another passion.